I0552970

Table of Content

Dedication

This book is dedicated first to our family. Their support is what allowed us to write this book. Hunter offered a lot of ideas that turned out to be awesome. Theresa was always there to encourage us and support us. Nana has so much faith in us and was always there to support us as well.

We would also like to thank all our TikTok fans who show us love every day. Their support is what made us believe this was even possible. We have so many awesome fans that it is impossible to name them all here. However, you all know who you are, so thank you, from the bottom of our hearts.

This book was not easy. There were many times when we just didn't know if we were going to be able to make it work. With the support from our family and fans, we were able to persevere and finish our very first novel.

We hope you enjoy our work and definitely look out for more books in this series.

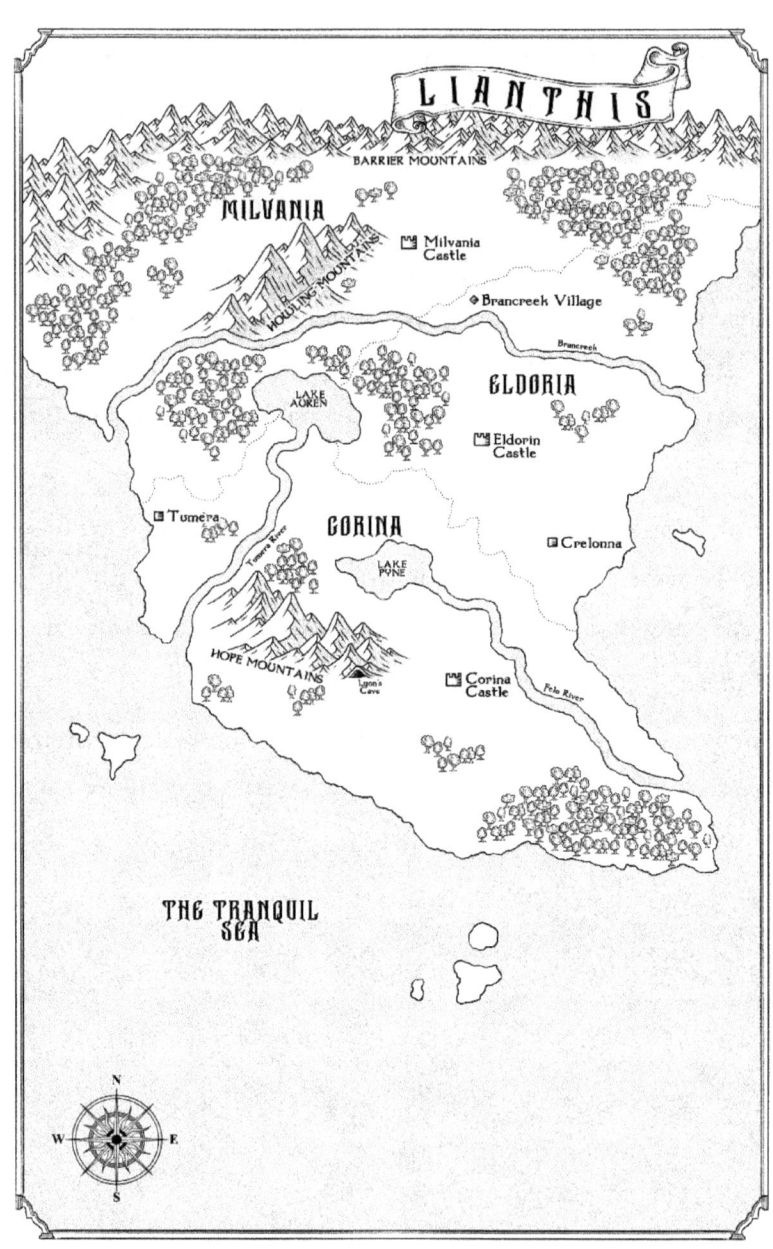

LIANTHIS

BARRIER MOUNTAINS

MILVANIA

Milvania Castle

Brancreek Village

HOLDING MOUNTAINS

ELDORIA

LAKE AUREN

Eldorin Castle

Tumera

CORINA

Crelonna

LAKE PYNE

Tumera River

HOPE MOUNTAINS

Lion's Cave

Corina Castle

Pelo River

THE TRANQUIL SEA

N
W E
S

Chapter 1:

The Forbidden Bond

The light from the sun was just peeking over the hills behind the massive castle, bathing the walls in warm golden light. The two giant towers seemed to reach for the clouds. The outside of the stone walls was dotted with vines and flowers, catching the warm golden light. Inside the walls were many houses and shops just coming alive for the morning. On this delightful spring morning, Jaylen, Princess of Eldoria, took her relaxing stroll around the castle walls, as she usually did every morning right at sunrise ever since she was fourteen. Now about to turn eighteen in a couple of months, she still enjoyed them.

She gazed out over the landscape, feeling refreshed in the cool morning air. The scent of flowers in the field carried on the breeze, mixed with the smells from the various kitchens around the castle and the town inside the walls. Even the sound of birds mixed with the sounds of villagers getting ready for the day made her feel a sense of peace and continuity of life.

Jaylen absolutely loved her morning walks. They helped her get ready for the day, knowing that life was progressing in the kingdom and that her people, for the most part, were happy and healthy, gave her comfort. The morning sun illuminated her flowing blonde hair and her bright blue eyes, revealing a gentle but tough spirit. Her loose brown pants and light blue tunic were moving gently in the breeze, the sunlight reflecting off her sword belted around her waist. As she walked further, her eyes caught sight of something unusual in the moist ground near the gravel road leading to the castle gates. It looked like holes in the ground, but she couldn't tell from this far away.

She decided to get a closer look. She had always loved exploring and investigating new and unusual things. Her father had always joked that she was as curious as a newborn, seeing everything for the first time. Jaylen laughed inwardly at the thought. Her father was always teasing her and joking around; they were very close. Her father had taught her everything. He wanted to prepare her to rule the kingdom one day. He always said that she needed to be beautiful and sweet while being strong and capable.

She arrived at the gate to find one of her own men from the elite guard on duty this morning. "Good morning, Eylon," she said as she walked up to the huge iron gates that separated the castle and the main town from the rest of the kingdom.

"Good morning, Your Highness," he replied with a quick salute. "Where are you off to today? Gathering more herbs for the healers?"

"Not today. I brought enough yesterday to keep them busy. I saw something from the wall that I wanted to check out." She was on easy terms with most of the men under her command. When it came to training and keeping the kingdom safe, however, they obeyed her without question and maintained full discipline.

"Anything I should worry about?" Eylon asked, assuming his 'duty voice', as she liked to call it. "I can send for the others."

"That won't be necessary; it is simply a curiosity. I have my sword." She replied, patting the hilt of the longsword belted to her waist; the jewels on the hilt caught the light of the morning sun, enhancing their brilliant shine. "If I need help, I will sound my signal horn, I promise."

"Very well, milady," said Eylon. With no more argument, he gave the signal to the two men standing by the large wheel that raised the gate. She walked outside as soon as they were raised enough to accommodate her average height. As she approached the place she had seen the unusual markings, she noticed they were footprints—very unusual ones. The footprints were larger than anything she had ever seen, and they had deep indentations in the front that looked like long claws. It was no wonder the guards dismissed it, since from the walls it just looked like a bunch of holes.

Okay, now she had to find out what made those footprints. She couldn't turn back until she knew. Whatever it was, had to be huge. She considered blowing her horn and summoning help, then she reconsidered. If this turned out to be nothing, she would never hear the end of it. It would also be just like Jamore, her second-in-command, to pull a prank like this. Her tracking skills told her the footprints were semi-fresh; whatever it was, it probably walked by in the night. She continued following the footprints until she came upon a large cave opening, one she had explored many times. If there was something that large inside, it must have come recently.

The trail led inside, so Jaylen followed it. She kept her hand on the hilt of her sword. A warrior should always be ready for battle. Ever since her sixteenth birthday last year, she had been placed in charge of the elite guard. It was an honor to command an elite battalion so young, and she always made sure to stay in shape and prove herself worthy of it.

The cave was one of the largest around and had many cracks that allowed natural light in. When it rained, the cracks allowed water through, creating many small waterfalls. Jaylen remembered being in here during the last storm. It had come up suddenly a few days ago when she was collecting mushrooms. She had waited it out in here and enjoyed watching the tiny waterfalls flow into the ruts by the cave walls and then out of the cave. She walked further in until she came close to the back of the cave.

She heard something, so she stopped to listen. Was that moaning? She could also hear what sounded like heavy breathing. It sounded like something was in pain. Moving cautiously, she rounded the corner that led to the back of the cave. To her astonishment, the back wall, which was a kind of softer dirt and clay, had been dug out to make a kind of entrance. There was a large cavern behind the wall. Jaylen was surprised she didn't even know that was there.

But what she saw inside that cavern surprised her even more. Sitting in the middle of the cavern was the most beautiful creature she had ever seen: a dragon. She had heard stories, but never had she imagined seeing one up close. The dragon was huge, larger than the catapult her father was so proud of. Even in the semi-darkness of the cave, its bright red scales glistened and shined like jewels. Its eyes, now looking directly at Jaylen, were a deep forest green. Jaylen could feel her heart pounding in her chest and she wasn't sure if she should run away in terror or help the poor creature.

Looking towards its thick, powerful legs, she saw blood gently seeping from a wound currently hidden from view, and dripping onto the dirt floor, making a small puddle. This confirmed her suspicions that this dragon was injured. At that moment, she made her decision. Despite the stories of dragons being ferocious creatures, she couldn't leave anything injured. Cautiously, Jaylen walked toward the dragon. The dragon moved to a defensive position, growling at the princess.

"It's all right. I will not harm you," Jaylen spoke calmly, showing no fear. She hoped the dragon would understand. She continued toward the dragon with her hands out, trying to calm it. She walked around the massive body to see the wound better. Kneeling beside the dragon, she examined its leg and found the source of its pain: a large wooden arrow lodged in its knee, blood dripping from the wound.

"That must be painful. If you'll let me, I can take that out for you and relieve your pain," said Jaylen in a gentle voice, hoping the dragon could understand her tone if not her words. The dragon hesitated briefly before carefully nodding. Jaylen slowly gripped the arrow. "This is going to hurt a bit, but I promise I'll be as gentle as I can."

Jaylen pulled the arrow out in one swift motion and the dragon let out a ferocious roar, letting the kingdom know of its pain. Jaylen stepped back, wondering if the stories were true after all. Was this dragon about to devour her? A tense moment passed as the dragon bellowed. After a few seconds, the dragon ceased its roar and looked at Jaylen. It seemed to be studying her. Finally, it relaxed and made a slight bow of its head. She assumed that was how it showed gratitude.

She tore off a piece of her tunic. Luckily, the knee where the wound was located wasn't too big around. She tied the makeshift bandage around the knee. "I am not sure if you can speak, but it sure would help if I knew your name," Jaylen said, even though she wasn't sure if the dragon could understand her. "Do dragons even have names?"

The dragon raised its claw and began drawing in the sand. Jaylen watched with curiosity as the dragon appeared to draw a flower she knew well. She had seen it many times around Eldoria. Looking back up at the dragon, she said, "Aurelia?" Why would a dragon be named after a flower? That particular flower had a deep red hue on its petals, so she could understand. If dragons were like humans, then flowers were more of a female thing, so that must mean this dragon was a girl. "Hello, Aurelia. I am Jaylen, Princess of Eldoria."

Aurelia bowed her head. Jaylen swore she saw a smile. Who knew dragons could smile? She just had to tell her father about this. But how would he react? The stories of dragons that were told around the three kingdoms were horrible. It was said that dragons and humans once lived in peace. One day, though, dragons started attacking people. No one knew why, but they had fought back and the dragons eventually flew away to some faraway place.

Aurelia seemed nice, though. She wasn't like other injured animals, which got defensive when they were hurt. She seemed intelligent and even had a name. Jaylen stayed for a while, trying to talk to Aurelia. She swore Aurelia could understand her. Jaylen was no longer afraid at all. She trusted Aurelia; she couldn't understand why, but she just felt like Aurelia and her were destined to be friends.

Aurelia tried to stand, but then roared in pain again. The arrow must have damaged her bone as well. Her injury must be too severe to put weight on right now. Jaylen knew she had to help her fully recover. Her father and mother could help if she could convince them. "Okay, you stay here. I am going to get my father. We will bring medical supplies to help treat your wound better. I will come back for you," Jaylen smiled at her new friend and ran out of the cave.

She arrived back at the castle and ran down the long stone corridors to the chamber her mother and father shared. Her mother was sitting at her vanity dresser, tying her hair up. Her father was signing paperwork at his large oak desk. There were several portraits of family members for generations past, giving a sense of continuity. In the corner was a fireplace, the dancing flames making the entire room seem warm and inviting.

"Father! Mother! I have something important to tell you!" said Jaylen, catching her breath. Given the stories about dragons, she would be surprised if they weren't scared at first. Jaylen was confident she could change their minds. But she had to be careful how she told them.

"What is it, darling?" asked Queen Lyren, her brown hair not quite up yet. King Thadis turned his attention toward his daughter, who was beaming with excitement. She could see they were interested. Her father had always listened to her stories with interest. She knew he was a curious boy himself once. Her grandmother had told him that many times. Her mother always encouraged her to explore and learn as much as she could.

"I have made a new friend. Her name is Aurelia. And she's a dragon." Jaylen blurted out all at once. She probably should have been a bit calmer, but her heart was pounding from her experience, and she was so eager to share it with the two people she loved the most. "She is hurt. I found her in a cave with an arrow in her leg."

Both Lyren and Thadis looked at each other; she knew that they must be stunned that there was a dragon in their kingdom. The last reported sighting was years ago, and nobody really believed the old man that saw it. This was a different look. They looked terrified. Her face went from excited to worried in an instant. "Why do you both look so scared? Is there something wrong?" asked Jaylen.

"Jaylen, you will have no contact with this dragon. They are foul, dangerous creatures. You will not go near this so-called friend again. Do you understand?" said King Thadis. His voice was sterner than she had ever heard it. She had expected resistance, but there was a finality to his voice that she knew she couldn't change.

She had to try, though. She didn't want to go against her father. She wanted him to meet Aurelia. Jaylen couldn't explain it, but she felt

11

connected to Aurelia, like no matter how hard she tried, she couldn't stay away. In that moment, she knew she had to help Aurelia, no matter what her father said. "But, Father, she is injured."

"No, Jaylen! My word is final." His voice was full of authority and an expectation to be obeyed. He was the king, after all. Lyren looked hesitant but didn't want to contradict her husband in front of their daughter. So she nodded in agreement. Jaylen stared at them both in disbelief. She only wanted to help the dragon.

"Fine," said Jaylen, storming out of the room and down the corridor. She would help Aurelia no matter what. Even if it meant disobeying her father's wishes. She walked back to her room and closed the door.

After she was out of hearing range, Lyren spoke up. "We have to tell her someday, Thadis. We can't keep this from her forever." She knew his reasons for keeping it from her. After he had to send Lyon away, he vowed he would not tell his next child about their family history. She, too, had vowed never to reveal her secret.

"She's too young. She wouldn't understand," said Thadis.

Lyren could see the worry on his face. She knew he would not change his mind. She couldn't tell Jaylen the whole truth, but if it really was Aurelia, then she knew Jaylen had to help her.

Lyren sighed and made her way out of the room and down the corridor. It was her duty to help, and unfortunately, it was Jaylen's duty now, too. She arrived outside Jaylen's room and knocked.

"Sweetheart, it is me. Can we talk?"

Jaylen sat on her bed. Why had her parents reacted that way? She knew they would be hesitant, but her father wouldn't even listen. That was not like him. He always trusted her judgment. He always listened to her arguments and even followed a few of her suggestions for improving the kingdom. Why was he taking such a hard stance on this?

She stood up and began pacing. How could she get the supplies she needed without an explanation? How could she leave the castle with them without being seen? This was going to be difficult, but Aurelia needed herbs to stop the wound from getting infected. Her makeshift bandage had just stopped the bleeding. She had to do more.

She sat back down on the bed when she heard her mother knock on the door. "I don't want to hear it, Mother," said Jaylen, sitting on her bed, arms crossed.

"I want to help." Her mother's voice was urgent, and she sounded a little scared to Jaylen. "You have to help this dragon. I can't tell you everything yet, but it is important."

What was going on here? Now her mother wanted to help? Was this a trick? No, it couldn't be. Her mother would never act like that. She had seen the hesitation when her mother had reluctantly agreed with her father. She must not have wanted to disagree with him outwardly.

Jaylen opened the door and looked at her mother, shocked she'd want to help. "She's injured. We need medical supplies, food, and water," said Jaylen, hoping her mother could get what she needed.

"I'll get it. Meet me in the training field by the castle gate tonight at sundown," said Lyren. She began to walk away, but Jaylen stopped her, thanking her. Lyren smiled and continued down the corridor. Jaylen smiled and laid back on her bed.

She lay there, wondering how she would keep this from her father. How would she be able to see Aurelia? How would she tend to her friend's wound? But, in the end, it didn't matter.. Because she knew she'd find a way. Somehow…

Chapter 2:

Healing a Friend

S undown couldn't come fast enough. Jaylen stayed in her room; she wasn't surprised by her father's reaction. She was a bit upset he wasn't even willing to hear her out. No matter, she was going to prove him wrong. She filled her time by reading and drawing. She drew Aurelia and the cave. Thinking about Aurelia made her consider all the stories she had heard growing up. Now that she thought about it, many of those stories contradicted themselves.

Some believed dragons to be mindless predators, killing for food or dominance. Others said that dragons were as intelligent as humans and that they felt superior and wanted to rule over mankind. Still, others believed somewhere in between. She heard one story that the dragons lived in their own city and came down only to spread fear so no human would ever disturb their peace.

After meeting Aurelia, Jaylen doubted any of them were true. She hoped that her leg was doing okay with the makeshift bandage she had applied. The sun was dipping below the horizon now, so Jaylen got up and left her room, heading toward the training grounds. Jaylen often trained in the evening, so her walking to the training grounds would not seem odd to anyone.

She soon saw her mother with a sack over her shoulder. When Lyren spotted Jaylen, she waved her over. "Okay, sweetie, here are all the medical supplies I could get. Remember, dragons may have a high tolerance for pain, but you still need to be careful." She looked like she was about to say more, but didn't.

"Thanks, Mother," said Jaylen gratefully. "Why are you helping me, anyway?"

"Because, sweetheart, I know how important this is. I can't tell you right now, but there are things you will learn about our family soon. For right now, just trust me and go help your friend," Lyren said, hoping Jaylen would not ask any more. She looked nervous and even a little afraid.

"Okay, Mother." Jaylen knew better than to press her mother. If she was keeping secrets, then it must be for a good reason. Jaylen and her mother were very close, and she trusted her without question. She left the castle behind and walked down the path and through the woods to the cave where Aurelia was waiting. At least she hoped Aurelia was waiting.

As Jaylen made it to the shelter in the back of the cave, she saw the bright red form and relaxed. Aurelia was awake, but resting comfortably. The dragon lifted her head and stared at her.

"Jaylen…" Aurelia's voice was deep but still somehow feminine.

Jaylen almost fell over in surprise. She didn't know dragons could talk. "You can talk?" she asked in surprise. Well, that settled the question of whether dragons were sentient or merely animals.

Aurelia said something in a language that was completely foreign to Jaylen. The sounds were very hoarse and hard to understand. But if this was the language her new friend spoke, then Jaylen knew she had to learn it if she was ever going to communicate with her. She took her cue from Aurelia's earlier method. She drew things in the sand; then she would say the name and wait for Aurelia to tell her the name in dragon tongue.

She took a minute to check Aurelia's wound and dress it using the medical supplies her mother had brought. First, she cleaned the wound, then she dressed it with healing herbs and bandages. They enjoyed each other's company, Aurelia laughing at Jaylen's first attempts to pronounce her language. It was now full dark, and Jaylen knew she had to get home before her father realized she wasn't there.

As they parted for the night, Jaylen vowed to herself that she would learn to speak Aurelia's language and prove to her father and the entire kingdom that dragons are friends. She had no idea how she was going to accomplish this feat, but she knew she had to.

The sun was just beginning to rise when Jaylen awoke. She opened her eyes and jumped out of bed. She couldn't wait to see Aurelia, but she knew she had to have breakfast with her parents first. After that, she was free until the evening when she and her parents would have dinner with guests from neighboring kingdoms.

"Good morning, sweetheart," said Thadis, hugging her as she entered the dining hall. "I am sorry I was so firm with you yesterday. I only want to protect you."

"I know that, Father," said Jaylen. She really loved her father. It is true she didn't always agree with him. But he was a great father, always taking time to spend with her, and he was a just and good king. He always did his best to help his subjects, no matter what.

"Do you have any plans today, dear?" said Lyren in a conversational tone. Jaylen knew what her mother meant by that and she had already come up with a plan. Last night before bed, she had thought about how she was going to make time to see Aurelia, and she had come up with a plan.

"Yes, actually. I was planning on spending the day gathering mushrooms and herbs in the forest," she said. "I am hoping to find more dramura mushrooms for the healers to make their numbing salve with."

"Just be careful, Jaylen, honey," Thadis said. "The woods can be dangerous. Take your bow and sword, just in case." Her father was always reminding her of the dangers, even though he knew she could handle pretty much anything. Jaylen knew it was because he was her father and fathers always tried to protect their daughters.

"Of course, Father. I always do." Jaylen smiled. "You know no one in the kingdom would dare challenge my sword skills."

Her parents laughed. Everyone in the kingdom knew that Jaylen, despite being a princess, was probably one of the most skilled swordsmen in the kingdom.

"Of course not," Thadis said with a grin. "I was your teacher, after all."

"Well… That is true." Jaylen couldn't help but tease her father. "Even if the student has surpassed the teacher." The last few times they had sparred, she had come so close to finally beating him. Their bouts always ended in a draw, with neither being able to get the advantage.

"We may have to test that before dinner. If you get back in time." The grin on Thadis's face told Jaylen he was confident that she would not be able to best him. Well, they would find out this evening for sure.

"It's a deal." Jaylen got up and headed for the door. "I love you both. I'll see you tonight." With that, she left them, first heading to the kitchen for some meat and cheese for her lunch and extra meat for Aurelia. Her pack was full and quite heavy, but years of training had toned her muscles, so it wasn't a burden.

After she left the kitchen, she headed straight for her room to get her sword and bow, as she promised her father. She planned on going to her favorite gathering points and getting all the mushrooms and herbs she would need for her story to check out. She frequently spent all day away from the castle, and it only took her a couple of hours to gather what she needed because she knew the best places to go. Then she would spend the rest of the day with Aurelia.

She headed toward the gate. The guard greeted her, then motioned for the gatekeepers to open the gate. Jaylen headed toward the first spot on her gathering tour, a small clearing in the woods to the west of the castle. She noted the flowers in the field that were beginning to bloom.

She saw the familiar red petals of the aurelia flower, which made her think of her new friend. She was anxious to learn more about her, and dragons in general, but she knew she needed to gather some mushrooms first to have a solid alibi.

She scoured the edge of the clearing in the shade by the massive trunks of the jolen trees. That is where dramura mushrooms grew the most. She found enough to fill a small bag. It didn't seem like much, but when boiled and added to other herbs, it would make enough salve to last the healers a month. As long as too many people didn't get hurt.

Next, she needed to gather some wild tralinquis herbs. These would serve as the base for the salve. She knew she could get them right behind the cave where Aurelia was. She walked the short distance through the woods and saw a few deer and rabbits. She loved walking through the woods. She loved nature, the beauty and the complexity always impressed her.

She arrived at the spot behind the cave and began harvesting the tralinquis herbs. When she had a sufficient amount, she walked around the hill to the cave entrance. She could hear laughing. She swore under her breath; how could she forget this was a popular place for kids from the castle and surrounding villages to explore? She had to think of a way to get them to never want to come here again. She could declare it off limits, but word might get back to her father, and he would question it.

She had to think fast because they were approaching quickly. She quickly hid in the entrance, then when they were closer, she ran out screaming for her life. The three boys stopped and looked at her, eyes wide with surprise. "Your Highness," they all said at once, bowing.

She stopped and looked at the boys. "You must stay away from this cave at all costs. It is dangerous. I barely escaped a collapsing ceiling," she said, trying to sound exhausted. "Let everyone else know as well, please. I would not want anyone to get hurt."

"Right away, milady," said the tallest boy. He appeared to be the oldest. He was probably thirteen or so and appeared to have the demeanor of a leader.

"Thank you. Now go and remember to stay away from this cave." Jaylen was pleased with her acting. These boys knew her reputation. So, if she was afraid, then it must be dangerous. That settled, she waited for them to move out of sight, pretending to be doubled over, catching her breath. Once they were gone, she stood straight and headed back.

When she arrived back at the cave, she went in and greeted Aurelia. She checked her wound and changed the dressing. Then she offered the meat she had brought. Aurelia was grateful for something to eat, and while she ate, Jaylen went to a nearby stream with a bowl she had brought and got some water. Aurelia drank the water in what seemed like a single gulp.

They spent the rest of the day doing their picture game, trying to learn each other's language. Jaylen wasn't sure why she felt such a connection with Aurelia, but she was glad they had met. Jaylen didn't have many real friends. Most people were nice to her because she was the princess. Aurelia was different; she listened to Jaylen intently, and they seemed to share so much in common already.

The day went by too quickly, and Jaylen knew her father would expect her on the training grounds before dinner. So, she said goodbye to Aurelia and assured her she would be back in the morning. She was hopeful that Aurelia would be able to go for a short walk tomorrow. It would do her good. She knew the wound would take at least a week to heal properly because the arrow had hit the bone, but putting a little weight on it in short bursts would keep the muscles in shape.

Chapter 3:

A New Friend

As Jaylen made her way back through the castle gates, she felt a little conflicted. She wanted to tell her father about Aurelia, but at the same time, she knew if she did, he would make her stay away. She couldn't do that; Aurelia needed her, especially now, while she was injured. So she chose to keep Aurelia a secret.

She plastered a smile on her face and ran toward the training grounds. She always enjoyed training with her father. They were two of the best swordsmen in the kingdom. As she approached, she saw her mother and father waiting for her. Her father was wearing his sword, ready to fight, while her mother went up into the stands to watch the training.

Jaylen drew her sword and stood, battle-ready. "Are you ready to get beaten not only by a girl but also by your daughter?" she asked playfully.

Thadis laughed. "I haven't lost yet, my dear girl," he said as he drew his sword.

And with that, they began, swords clashing as they fought, sand being thrown up as they moved about the training area. Lyren watched in awe, but was also worried. They were using real swords. Even though she knew neither of them would intentionally hurt the other, accidents could happen. She just hoped they were careful.

Sometimes, it looked as though Jaylen had the advantage; other times, it was Thadis who was pushing back. Their swords clanged together, making a rhythmic metallic music in the crisp evening air. They kept moving together, their feet and bodies moving more like a dance than a fight. The two were so evenly matched that neither of them could gain an advantage.

The match got more and more intense as both tried to secure an advantage. Jaylen swung her sword with such speed and precision that Lyren was surprised that she didn't hit Thadis at all. She knew, of course, since they were using real blades, that Jaylen would stop before ever hitting her father, but how could she stop when she was going that fast? Jaylen had amazing control. Lyren had seen her fight a new recruit once who had questioned her fitness as a leader. Jaylen could have easily defeated him, but she never hit him once; she always stopped mere inches from the fatal blow.

They went on for almost an hour, obviously taking breaks in between matches. They had flasks of water and plates of fruit on the benches beside the training area to keep their strength up during the training. Lyren knew their arms must be tired. The sun had already begun to set. Lyren called to them from the stands, "You two need to get cleaned up for dinner. We have guests."

She pointed to the road leading into the castle. Jaylen and Thadis looked and saw two carriages headed toward the castle. How could they have forgotten that King Balian and Queen Alaria were coming to dinner tonight? They both sheathed their swords and ran into the castle to get changed.

Jaylen decided on a simple, flowing purple velvet dress with flared sleeves. Her choice of accessories was an amethyst necklace her mother had given her for her birthday, a pair of blue earrings, and her favorite tiara. She rarely wore tiaras, but it was a special night, so she chose to wear one. She tied her blonde hair up in a bun, with the tiara resting in front of it. She made her way into the dining hall, greeting the guests.

"King Balian, Queen Alaria, this is my daughter, Princess Jaylen," said Thadis, as she entered and stood next to her parents.

"It's a pleasure to meet you, Your Majesties," said Jaylen, showing respect by curtsying.

The king and queen bowed to Jaylen, a tradition which Jaylen hated, but she returned in kind. She knew the importance of courtesy; she just didn't like it when people bowed to her. Jaylen was no more important than anyone else. Her father felt the same way, but he had always told her it was important to maintain traditions, especially when it came to respect and courtesy.

King Balian and Queen Alaria were not alone. Standing next to them was a young woman. She looked to be about Jaylen's age. She had shoulder-length brown hair and brown eyes. The dress she wore was fancier than Jaylen's. It was light blue with puffy sleeves and was a bit shorter than Jaylen's. She wore a tiara as well, with beautiful green emeralds all around it.

This must be their daughter, Princess Elia, thought Jaylen.

King Balian confirmed her assumptions. "This is our daughter, Princess Elia," he said. Elia curtsied, and Jaylen returned the respect. Jaylen sat next to her mother across from Elia. They made small talk and ate dinner. Elia seemed reserved. Jaylen assumed she was nervous around new people so she didn't address it.

After dinner was over, Thadis asked Jaylen to show Elia around the castle, so she did. She took her through the long stone hallways, then led her to the courtyard. In the middle of the courtyard was a tall baroca tree, which had been there since the castle was built over a thousand years ago. Jaylen touched the tree. "My father says this tree represents the kingdom. Strong and immovable, but beautiful and always growing. The branches are as important as the trunk and roots."

Elia smiled. "Your father sounds like a wise king. He understands the importance of growth and change. My father always told me if you stop growing, then soon you will die."

"He sounds like a wise king as well," said Jaylen, and they both laughed. Jaylen then led her to the training grounds. They walked past some houses just finishing their dinner. They saw a few shops just closing up for the night. When they arrived at the training grounds, Elia looked amazed.

"What is that?" she asked, awe clearly evident in her voice.

Jaylen turned to look where she was looking and laughed. "That is my father's pride and joy. It is a giant catapult."

Elia was just staring. "It's *huge*."

Most catapults in the three kingdoms were just large enough to fit a stone about two feet in diameter, but this one was so large it could launch a stone twice that size up to five hundred feet from the castle walls. Unlike most catapults, though, this one wasn't mobile and had a limited arc right on the road to the gates.

"Yeah, it took our engineers about a year to finish it. I remember coming down when I was ten just to watch them." Looking at the catapult made her think of Aurelia. She was about the same size. She turned her attention away from the catapult and showed Elia the training grounds. "This is where my men and I come to train. As you can see, the ground is pretty beat up from all of our trampling."

"Your men?" Elia sounded quite perplexed. Jaylen had forgotten for a moment that most princesses don't command soldiers.

"Because of my proficiency with a blade, my father made me the commander of the elite guard," Jaylen explained. "It is an honor I don't take lightly. Some of the men questioned my leadership at first, but they came around after a while."

Elia was just standing there, staring at Jaylen. "I have never met a woman who could fight." She smiled. "I think it's great that your father trained you."

"Yeah, he really didn't have much choice. I was always beating the boys in play sword fights growing up," said Jaylen, laughing. She guided Elia to continue toward the gate.

Eylon was on duty again. She saw him straighten up as they approached. "Good evening, Your Highness," he said and bowed. "Who is this lovely young lady who accompanies you?"

Jaylen almost laughed at the tone in his voice but she kept her composure. "This is Princess Elia of Corina," she said, noticing the slight disappointment that flashed across his face. She would tease him about that later.

Eylon's whole demeanor changed instantly, and he bowed once again. "Pleased to meet you, Your Highness."

Elia returned the bow with a curtsy. "Pleased to meet you as well, Eylon."

They continued their walk and ended up at the stables. Jaylen brought Elia in to see her horse, Nado. It was short for tornado because he was fast as the wind but sometimes unpredictable. Jaylen was the only one he would listen to.

"Nado has been my horse since he was very young. You could say we grew up together. He is a good horse, even if he is a bit touchy sometimes."

Elia laughed. "Sounds like my Baenar back home."

They stayed in the stables for a short time. Since it was getting late, Jaylen decided to end the tour by showing Elia her room. They walked back into the castle and down the hall to her room. As she opened the door and walked in, she gestured around the room. "And this is my room. You're welcome to look around. It's not much, but I like it," said Jaylen.

"It's beautiful," said Elia.

Elia sat on Jaylen's bed and stared at the ground. Jaylen noticed and sat down next to her. "Is something wrong, Elia?" asked Jaylen calmly. "You seem a little sad. Didn't you like our castle?"

"It isn't that," said Elia. "I just don't get out much. I don't make many friends."

Jaylen smiled sympathetically. She could relate. Right now, her only friend was a dragon. Granted, a very smart and beautiful dragon, but a dragon nonetheless. Suddenly, Jaylen had an idea. It would be dangerous, though.

"Elia, can I show you something? You have to promise not to tell anyone, though," said Jaylen. She was hoping this would give Elia not one, but two friends.

Elia nodded, a little surprised by Jaylen's sudden outburst. "I promise."

Jaylen quickly changed into a tunic and slacks and belted on her sword. She grabbed her bow and quiver, then grabbed Elia's hand and ran through the corridors. Elia's parents were talking with Jaylen's parents outside. They saw the girls running and stopped them. "Where are you girls off to?" asked Thadis.

Jaylen turned to face her father. "I want to show Elia where I go for walks. Is that all right?" she asked.

"It's all right with me, but you'll have to ask Elia's father," said Thadis.

Elia turned to her father with a pleading look in her eyes. King Balian smiled. "Go. But don't be too long. It's going to be dark soon."

The girls hugged their parents and ran off through the gates and down the path. Jaylen and Elia ran some way until they reached a cave. Yes, the very cave where Jaylen was keeping Aurelia hidden. Elia made a move to enter the cave, but Jaylen stopped her.

"Be careful. She won't recognize you, so you have to let me calm her down. Stay behind me," said Jaylen cryptically. She wanted Elia to like Aurelia, but she also wanted her to feel the awe that Jaylen herself had felt upon seeing the huge red dragon for the first time.

Elia was confused but did what Jaylen said. They walked through the cave until they reached Aurelia's shelter. Aurelia looked up and smiled at Jaylen, but when she saw Elia, she moved back.

"It's all right, Aurelia. This is my friend, Elia. She won't hurt you," said Jaylen.

Aurelia trusted Jaylen, so she calmed down and let Elia near her. Elia cautiously approached Aurelia. She reached up her hand to touch Aurelia's face. Jaylen swore she heard Aurelia purr. Elia smiled while petting this so-called 'dangerous creature'. She was harmless. No sign of malice at all. In fact, she was purring while being petted, just like a cat.

"She's beautiful," said Elia, who looked to be completely at ease.

Jaylen smiled. "She is. She's also injured. I've been taking care of her."

Aurelia lifted her leg to show Elia the wound. Elia looked at it and then at her own hand. She looked back up at Jaylen and said, "I might be able to help. But now you must promise not to tell anyone."

Jaylen looked confused but agreed. Elia raised her hand to hover above Aurelia's leg. Her hand glowed a bright green. Slowly, Aurelia's wound disappeared. That was magic! Elia just used magic.

"How? How did you do that?" asked Jaylen.

"My family is descended from an ancient order known as dragoneers. Many of them developed abilities that aided them in their mission to protect dragons. We know they developed abilities, but it's never clear what they were. That was before the uprising. Only I have the power right now. But my parents don't allow me to use it often," she said.

Jaylen just stared at her, astonished. She knew her family, too, was descended from dragoneers. She did not know they had magic.

"I wasn't able to heal it all. The bone is still quite fragile, but she should be able to walk a little. I wouldn't take her on long walks though," said Elia.

"Thank you," said Jaylen, hugging Elia.

They sat with Aurelia, Jaylen learning more of dragon tongue, and Elia watching with a smile. The first dragon she's ever met, and she helped heal it. She had found a new friend. Not only in Jaylen, but also in Aurelia.

Chapter 4:

A Minor Inconvenience

J aylen and Elia spent a little more time with Aurelia, then headed back to the castle. They began walking down the path when they heard a voice close by. "I know I hit it." The voice was raspy and sounded like one of those bounty hunters that was always after dragons.

Jaylen turned in the direction of the voice. "I want to find out what he is talking about," she whispered to Elia. "Stay here." Jaylen was glad she had brought her sword and bow, but Elia still wore her formal wear and didn't appear to be armed. She crept closer and saw a fire and tents nearby. Crouching at the edge of a small clearing out of sight, she listened.

"That red beast is injured somewhere," said the first man. He was wearing leather armor, and beside him was a rough bow with a quiver of larger-than-normal arrows, just like the one she had pulled out of Aurelia. It took all her strength not to rush in and kill the man where he sat for injuring her beloved friend.

She needed a solid reason to tell her father. She surveyed the camp closely. There were four men in total. The first one was the one she knew had shot Aurelia. Two of the others almost looked like twins. They also wore leather armor, and each carried a short sword on their hip. The fourth was a larger man with a broadsword and chain mail armor. It was clear he was accustomed to fighting, so she would have to be cautious when confronting him.

"We need to find it," said the large man. "Remember that King Adrin pays extra for the red ones on account of they are more valuable." He spoke with a thick accent, like some barbarian from the north.

"We know it came this way because my brother followed its trail, but it ends a few miles back," said one of the twins. "It probably found just enough strength for a short flight. We will find its trail around here somewhere in the morning."

"When we find it, I get the kill. It was me who first hit it," said the first man. Jaylen had heard enough. She crept back to where Elia was waiting to try to find an excuse to attack these men. She knew nobody else was around, so she could tell her father they attacked her and that would be that, but she couldn't live with a lie like that.

If they were from King Adrin's kingdom, then she knew they were doing other things that were illegal in her kingdom; she just had to prove it. She decided to wait till they fell asleep, then check their camp for evidence. She explained to Elia what was going on.

"There're men from King Adrin's kingdom over there. They claim to have been the ones that shot Aurelia," Jaylen whispered.

"Then we have to stop them," said Elia

"I agree. But if I just go in there and attack them for seemingly no reason, my father will question it. I cannot tell him about Aurelia. I have to search their camp and find something I can tell my father," said Jaylen.

"I want to come too. I may not be proficient with a sword like you, but I am quite good at sneaking around. I'm always avoiding royal business by sneaking through secret passages in my castle." Elia laughed.

Jaylen stared at her, smiling. "I knew there was a reason I liked you."

Jaylen and Elia moved close enough to see the camp and then waited. Soon, the men started staggering into their tents. When the last man was asleep, Jaylen put her plan into action. As a member of the royal family and a warrior of Eldoria, she had the authority to make arrests. She knew the men would attack her if she was alone, but she also knew she could beat them all without breaking a sweat.

"Elia, do me a favor," she whispered. "Go back to the castle and tell my father I found a group of smugglers. Tell him I am going to make an arrest before they have a chance to get away, but I could use backup. Tell him to send out the elite guard because they will listen to me without question." She was praying she would find something in their camp else she would have a lot of explaining to do.

"Are you sure about this, Jaylen?" Elia asked in an equally quiet voice. "What if they attack you?"

Jaylen could tell she was worried. She had to reassure her. "That is what I have this for," she replied, patting the scabbard that held her long sword. "I am known as one of Eldoria's finest warriors, so don't worry. They won't be alive to tell anyone about Aurelia."

Elia looked hesitant, but she left anyway, choosing to trust her new friend. She walked quietly until she was sure she was out of earshot, then ran the rest of the way. Jaylen watched her leave then, hand on the hilt of her sword, silently walked into the camp. She carefully opened chest after chest one by one. Just when she thought she might be out of luck, she found what she had been hoping for.

In a chest by the tent that the large barbarian man occupied, she found a large supply of gerona leaves. They were illegal in her kingdom, and fields were burned as soon as they were found. The leaves had mind-altering effects and were very dangerous. This was it. She now had a legal reason to arrest these men. If they resisted, she could defend herself with deadly force if necessary.

She walked over to the edge of the camp and shouted in an authoritative and loud voice, "You, in the tents. By order of the royal family of Eldoria, you are under arrest for smuggling." She paused. "Come out and lay down your weapons; any resistance will be met with deadly force." She could hear the men scrambling to get out of their sleeping furs and grab their swords. It was the barbarian who made it out first.

"Young lady, I see nobody to support you, and there are four of us," he said with a malicious grin on his face. "Why should we surrender to you?"

"I am Jaylen, commander of the elite guard, and Princess of Eldoria," she replied. "Even scum like you should have heard of me." She noted the pause on the faces of the other three, but the large man looked unfazed. Obviously, he was confident in his skills. She was glad. The others might have given up. However, since their companion was confident, it gave them confidence.

"Well, pleased to meet you, Your Highness." He spat the title like a curse and bowed weakly and insultingly. He grabbed the hilt of his broadsword and pulled it from its sheath. Raising the sword with a single hand, he lunged forward and arced the sword through the air toward Jaylen's right shoulder.

Jaylen was ready, however, and had her sword up to meet his without much effort. She nimbly danced aside, keeping the others in her peripheral vision the whole time. The man seemed slightly surprised by her quick response, but he recovered quickly. Their swords crossed several times. He was an aggressive fighter, swinging his sword at every part of her, trying to get an opening. Jaylen was too skilled for that to work and she blocked each swing. A few of them were so fierce that it shook her arm as their swords met.

She watched his movements closely, waiting for an opening. She found one and kicked the man in the stomach, sending him reeling. She didn't have the opportunity to capitalize on it, however, because she noticed the first man knocking an arrow in his bow. She reacted instantly, grabbing her own bow and, in one swift motion, dodged his arrow and let one of her own fly. The arrow found its mark dead square in the middle of his chest. The man's lifeless body hit the ground with a thud, completing her revenge for his attack on Aurelia.

She whirled around and saw the first man getting up. She closed the distance, grabbing her sword from the ground and settling in to fight him once more. The other two looked shocked at what was happening.

"Get her, you idiots," growled the barbarian, still trying to get up. "She can't take us all on." They snapped out of it and drew their short swords, running to attack her.

Wow, they really were idiots, thought Jaylen as she turned away from the barbarian and turned her attention to the two men racing toward her. One of the first things her father had taught her was to never run in a fight. You put yourself off balance and your opponent, if he was any kind of fighter, would easily take advantage of that. Which is exactly what she did. She stepped easily to the side and sliced across the first man's stomach, then turned just in time to block the second man's strike. Twirling her blade with his, she quickly disarmed him and plunged her blade through his chest.

Only the barbarian remained. She could hear the sound of hooves in the distance and knew her backup would be there shortly. She almost made a fatal mistake by being distracted as the barbarian swung

35

his sword downward. She barely dodged the attack and his sword sliced the arm of her tunic, barely missing her shoulder.

"Damn it," she swore. "That was one of my best tunics. I will have to make you pay for that."

She stabilized herself and, out of the corner of her eye, she saw her men burst into the camp, swords drawn and ready. "We're here, Your Highness," Lieutenant Jamore, her second-in-command, said.

"Stay back," she commanded. "This one is mine." The barbarian had recovered from his last attack and was determined to at least kill her before he was taken out by her companions. Of course, this made him much easier to defeat because he was too angry. Lesson two from her father: 'battling is about being calm and thinking rationally. Those who get emotional always make a fatal mistake'. She almost heard her father's voice.

Sure enough, he made a fatal mistake. In his desire for revenge, he over-committed to his attack. Being the practiced fighter she was, Jaylen stepped to the side and as soon as his back was open to her, she swung, slicing diagonally down his back. As he fell to his knees, dropping his sword, she finished him by grabbing him around the chest and plunging her blade through his back and out through his chest. As she pulled her sword free, his lifeless body crumpled to the ground.

Jamore walked over to her, sheathing his sword. "For a second there, I thought we were going to have to help you." He smiled.

"Oh, come on, you know me better than that," she replied with an innocent expression.

He laughed. "What do you require of us?"

"I found Gerona Leaves in that trunk over there," she said, taking on a commanding voice. "Search the rest of the camp. Burn any leaves you find and then we will head back to the palace. I am sure my father is going to have words for me."

"No doubt," Jamore replied, then assumed his command voice. "You heard the commander. Let's get it done."

"Yes, sir!" The chorus of voices said in unison. They all split up and searched the whole camp.

Before long, all the leaves were found and destroyed. They packed up the rest of the camp and loaded it on their horses. Jamore had even brought her horse. Within minutes, they were all on their horses and returning to the palace.

Jaylen rode through the palace gates. Her father and mother were there to greet her. She climbed off her horse and was immediately hugged by her mother. Her father hugged her as well, then grabbed her shoulders and held her. She could see the anger in his eyes.

"Jaylen, what were you thinking? You could've been hurt, or worse," said King Thadis. She could tell he was angry, but also proud of how well she handled herself. "And what were you doing in the woods at this time of night, anyway?"

"I'm sorry, Father. I wanted to show Elia where I gather herbs. I heard the men talking about the gerona leaves. I didn't want them to get away," said Jaylen. "Those leaves could have been dangerous for our people. They were definitely brought in from Milvania. They were too dull colored to have grown here. The soil in Milvania isn't as rich, so they can't produce the lush green leaves we could here."

Thadis hugged Jaylen, obviously relieved his daughter was alive. Her men bowed to the royal family and rode off to the stables. Jaylen told Jamore to take her horse and feed him before putting him back in his stable.

"Did Elia make it back okay?" asked Jaylen. Her men had found her so obviously Elia delivered the message, but she was still concerned that she may have been hurt.

"She did. She's waiting for you in your room," said Queen Lyren. Jaylen could tell her mother was dying to hear what really happened. Since she knew about Aurelia, she would have figured that Jaylen and Elia were visiting the cave.

Jaylen made her way to her room, stopping for hugs from all the castle staff who thanked her for stopping the smugglers. She opened the door to her room and Elia saw her and ran to give her a hug. "Are you all right?" asked Elia.

Jaylen laughed. "Elia, I'm the best swordsman in my kingdom. Of course, I'm all right. Those smugglers didn't stand a chance. I wish they had surrendered, though. I didn't want to have to kill them all."

"And what about Aurelia? Is she okay?" asked Elia.

Jaylen's heart dropped. She couldn't have really made an excuse to go back to the cave since her men were there. However, it was still a little worrying. "I couldn't check on her, not with my men with me. After that fight, they never would have let me go alone," said Jaylen.

"I'm sure she's fine. The smugglers didn't know she was there, right?" asked Elia. She was also worried, but knew Jaylen would check on her tomorrow.

Jaylen nodded. She had to go out as fast as possible tomorrow morning to check on Aurelia.

Chapter 5:

Friends for Life

J aylen and Elia spent the rest of the evening talking, mostly about Aurelia and their kingdoms. Neither of them had ever felt this comfortable talking to another person. Being princesses, they had not really gotten out much beyond their castles. Sure, Thadis had taken Jaylen to some of the villages, and she had met many young people her own age, but they all treated her like the princess. Since Elia was a princess herself, she treated Jaylen like just another person.

They laughed and joked and talked until late, then settled in and went to sleep. As Jaylen lay there drifting off to sleep, she thought of Aurelia and how she wanted so desperately to convince her kingdom that dragons weren't their enemy.

The next day, Elia and her parents left early to return to their kingdom. Jaylen said goodbye to them and immediately left for the cave. She made sure Aurelia was ok then spent the rest of the day trying to learn more dragon tongue. Jaylen was a fast learner and picked up on a lot of it quickly. For the next week, this was their routine. Jaylen would visit Aurelia every day. Unless she had duties for the kingdom. They would spend the day talking and when Aurelia said something Jaylen didn't recognize, she would draw it in the sand and Jaylen would repeat it back.

By the end of the week, Jaylen had become fluent in understanding dragon tongue. Something bothered her though that she had to ask about. Aurelia seemed to always understand everything that

Jaylen said in the human tongue. How did Aurelia already know her language?

The next morning, she headed back to the cave to ask Aurelia just that. Jaylen arrived at the entrance to the cave and noted everything looked the same. Nobody else had been there since they left last night. She walked inside and all the way to the back to find Aurelia still sleeping soundly. Jaylen sighed in relief.

Aurelia slowly opened her eyes and looked at Jaylen. "Good morning, Jaylen," she said, speaking in dragon tongue.

"Hello, Aurelia," Jaylen replied. "How is it that you can understand my language perfectly?"

Aurelia laughed. "Humans and dragons were once very close. We have a lot of your books in our library. We always teach our children to understand your language, patiently waiting for the day humans and dragons can once again come together."

"Then why don't you just speak to me in my language?" Jaylen asked, feeling a little frustrated that she went through all that learning for nothing.

Aurelia looked a little sad. "Our voices are so different. We have a hard time speaking your language and being understood." She said, "Just like you have a hard time pronouncing our language. So it is better to just understand each other and speak our own languages."

"Oh," said Jaylen. "By the way, last week I found the man who shot you, dear Aurelia. He and his friends were also smugglers, so I confronted them. They are all dead now. You are avenged," Jaylen spoke calmly, but she was not feeling at ease with what she had done. She should have waited for backup. Then maybe those men would have stood trial and gone to prison.

"I did not ask for revenge, Jaylen," said Aurelia in a kind of sad tone. "There has been too much violence on both sides of this conflict already." She seemed so sad.

Jaylen looked down. Aurelia was right. She had heard of dragons being killed before and reports of dragons fighting back and killing humans. Calling this a conflict was accurate since humans had banned dragons from the kingdoms and any spotted were usually killed on sight. Jaylen also knew that taking revenge like that was wrong. She just couldn't help herself. Anyone who would want to harm such a beautiful and intelligent creature was evil, and she hated evil. "I'm sorry, dear friend. I just got so angry when I realized he hurt you."

"Thanks, but I don't need you to fight my battles for me," said Aurelia, relenting and grinning. "Do I look fragile to you?" She lifted her head and stood up, stretching her full form.

"Oh no, definitely not," Jaylen replied, seeming more like herself. "Why, you are the picture of strength, my dear dragon. Shall we go out for your first short walk?" Even though it had been over a week now, they had to take it easy so they didn't overdo it, but a walk should help strengthen the muscles.

"Of course, milady." Aurelia was almost laughing now. Her smile made her look like a grinning cat Jaylen thought "After you." With that, she bowed and followed Jaylen out of the cave.

When they emerged from the cave, Jaylen was in awe. Aurelia's scales glistened brilliantly in the sun. She almost seemed to be glowing. Her whole body was like a light. Jaylen could not believe how beautiful Aurelia truly was. No wonder Milvania was paying extra for red dragons.

Thinking of Milvania brought Jaylen back to the moment. That King Adrin was some piece of work. She had only met him once. He had come to their kingdom for supplies and had actually asked her father if he could marry her. Thadis politely refused, giving the excuse that he needed Jaylen to lead the army. He had told Adrin that he might consider his offer at a later time. He was ever so polite, but afterwards, he had told Jaylen not to worry; she would decide who to marry. Also, he would not even consider letting that evil bastard anywhere near her, anyway.

Jaylen and Aurelia walked slowly together. Aurelia had a slight limp, but nothing too bad. Jaylen once again admired the blooming flowers, including a few Aurelias which her friend shared a name with. The sun rose higher in the sky, and they could hear birds singing in the trees. The forest was alive and busy, but peaceful at the same time.

"All right, my friend, that is enough for day one," Jaylen said, motioning for Aurelia to head back to the cave. They turned around and started walking back side by side like they had been friends forever.

Jaylen left Aurelia and went home. She knew Aurelia would be safe. However, she would visit every day just to be sure. She arrived back at the castle and went straight to the stables. She had to check on her horse. After the run last night to get to her, Nado must have been exhausted.

When she arrived at the stables, Nado was eating. Jaylen opened the stall and patted the horse's neck, then gently checked his legs and feet. Two of Nado's shoes were cracked. He must have hit some rocks while running. Jaylen closed the stall and walked the short distance to the blacksmith.

Talin was a shorter man and well-built from shaping steel every day. He looked up from his anvil as Jaylen approached. "Good morning, Your Highness," he said, bowing courteously.

"Good morning, Talin," replied Jaylen. "Nado has a couple of cracked shoes. Can you fit him with a new set? Go ahead and make four new ones so they all match up."

"Of course, milady." Talin smiled. "Running him a bit rough last night?" Jaylen wasn't surprised; news of the evening's events had already been told throughout the castle and town. If there was one thing her kingdom was good at, it was telling stories. She just hoped it was the facts, not a lot of embellishment.

Jaylen had been in a small battle once, but the way the kingdom described it, you would have thought that Jaylen single-handedly took out a hundred men. She didn't like hearing the stories told because she didn't want people to think she was some great hero. She was confident in her abilities, but she also knew there could always be someone better.

Jaylen expressed concern once that the stories were way too exaggerated. Thadis had just laughed and told her, "Stories like that also get back to those who would be our enemy and make them think twice before attacking. Besides, it comforts the villagers to think of us as great heroes. They feel protected, and that helps them live happily."

The days went by pretty fast. Days turned into a week. Aurelia had regained her strength enough to go on more short walks. One day, Jaylen was out gathering fulna mushrooms; she had to maintain her cover after all. When she received the shock of her life.

She was behind the cave amongst the trees. She bent down to pick some mushrooms and heard a noise behind her, a tree branch breaking. She whirled around, instinctively grabbing her sword hilt. Just as she turned to face the sound, she came face to face with a massive red nose. Jaylen staggered back, tripping over a root and landing on her butt in the mossy grass.

"I thought you were supposed to be the bravest swordsman in the kingdom," said Aurelia, for it was her nose and head.

Jaylen just stared at Aurelia. "You are positively annoying. Did you know that?" said Jaylen, trying not to laugh at herself.

"Oh, come now…Your Highness," said Aurelia, extending her giant paw to help Jaylen up.

Jaylen accepted the help and walked with Aurelia back to the cave. Aurelia immediately laid down when they arrived back at the shelter. She winced when she put too much pressure on her leg. Jaylen sat next to Aurelia and helped her extend her leg and set it on Jaylen's lap.

"Wow. I thought a dragon's leg would be heavier than this," she said.

Aurelia laughed. "Are you saying you thought I was fat?" She loved teasing Jaylen. She knew Jaylen was quite the sarcastic young lady herself, so they got along well.

Jaylen smiled. "Oh no, my dear dragon, you are quite lean. Although you have been lounging in this cave too much recently. Are you sure you didn't put on a few pounds?" She was glad that they were communicating better.

"I have not!" Aurelia feigned surprise. Then neither of them could hold it in anymore. They burst out laughing.

Aurelia brought her head down and rested it on Jaylen's shoulder. Jaylen put her arms around Aurelia's neck, as far as they would go, seeing as Aurelia was so big. Jaylen could hear Aurelia purring as she was hugging her. A big cat is all she was.

"If this is dangerous, then my life is a lie," said Jaylen. She could feel the neck tense up at her words, and she immediately regretted them. Of course, Aurelia would be sensitive about such things.

Jaylen released the hug and Aurelia looked at her, getting serious for the first time since they had known each other. "There are so many misconceptions about my kind. That we're dangerous. That we eat people. That we're naturally aggressive. It's just not true."

Jaylen looked sad for Aurelia. She knew the misconceptions. She knew they were not true. And that's what she would prove. She would make everyone see that dragons were smart, gentle, and kind creatures who they should be friends with, not enemies.

"I'm sorry, dear friend. I wish I could make them understand. I wish I could make them see they're wrong. You are sweet, smart, and beautiful," said Jaylen.

Aurelia smiled. She could feel Jaylen was being truthful. She knew her friend didn't believe everything that people were saying. Aurelia could feel a connection to Jaylen, and she knew that someday that connection would form into something more. "I know, Jaylen, and I love you for that."

"I have to go for now, Aurelia," said Jaylen. "But I'll be back tomorrow."

She hugged Aurelia one last time before leaving the cave. As she walked back toward the castle, she thought about what Aurelia had said. People were so close-minded about dragons. They're beautiful creatures! It angered her how mean people can be towards a creature they know nothing about.

She made it back home just in time for dinner. She and her parents always ate dinner together. Tonight they were having a roast

45

with carrots and beans. Jaylen entered the dining hall and was hit with a glorious smell. She knew what it was.

"Did you bake bread, Mother?" she asked.

"I did, darling. Just for you," said Lyren.

Jaylen sat next to her mother and across from her father. They enjoyed their meal, making small talk, and Jaylen told them about the herbs and mushrooms she had found. The medical team was already creating more healing salves.

After dinner was over, Jaylen went back to her room. She was working on a painting when her mother knocked.

"Come in," said Jaylen, not looking up from her project.

"Just came to bring you some dessert. I made some applesauce," said Lyren.

Jaylen smiled and thanked her mother. Lyren watched Jaylen paint for a while. She knew she was painting a dragon, but she couldn't help but wonder if…

"Sweetheart? Is that Aurelia?" she asked. Jaylen nodded. "She's beautiful. I bet she's more beautiful in person."

Suddenly, Jaylen had an idea. It may take some convincing, but she had to ask. "Why don't you come with me tomorrow and meet her?" said Jaylen.

"Oh honey, I don't know," said Lyren.

"Come on, Mother, she's so gentle. I promise she'll love you," said Jaylen.

"All right. We'll leave tomorrow morning at dawn," said Lyren, getting up to leave.

Jaylen hugged her mother and went back to painting. She slept well that night, knowing Aurelia would have another friend in Eldoria.

Dawn came, and Jaylen was up, dressed, and ready to go in record time. Lyren was already waiting at the palace gates. She was wearing a simple tunic, slacks, and riding boots. She was holding the reins of hers and Jaylen's horses.

"I told your father we're going out for a ride," she said.

"Well then, let's get going."

Jaylen mounted her horse and they rode to the cave. When they arrived, they left the horses at the entrance so as not to scare Aurelia or the horses. Jaylen went in first since she's the one Aurelia trusts.

"Aurelia, I have someone I'd like you to meet. My mother. Don't worry. She's like me. She believes dragons are misunderstood," said Jaylen.

Aurelia hesitated, but nodded. Jaylen signaled for her mother to enter. Lyren came around the corner, and when she saw just how beautiful Aurelia was, she nearly lost her breath. Aurelia's eyes widened a little in recognition. The queen winked at her and smiled.

"Jaylen…she's absolutely beautiful," said Lyren.

Aurelia laid down to let Lyren pet her. And once again, Aurelia purred. Lyren touched her face and smiled. She couldn't believe her daughter was friends with a dragon.

"Say hi to her, Mother," said Jaylen.

"Hello, Aurelia. I am Lyren. Queen of Eldoria and Jaylen's mother."

"Hello, Your Majesty. I am Aurelia," said Aurelia. Jaylen knew her mother could not understand, so she decided to translate for her.

"She said 'hello, Your Majesty'," Jaylen said. She wasn't sure why her mother was smiling like that. It was like she knew something Jaylen didn't.

Jaylen and Lyren spent the rest of the morning admiring Aurelia. Lyren talking to her, Aurelia talking back, and Jaylen translating. Lyren seemed surprised that Jaylen could understand her.

Chapter 6:

A Secret

Lyren woke up the next morning, worried that Aurelia might tell Jaylen the truth. It wasn't time yet. They had to proceed carefully or risk losing Jaylen. She decided to excuse herself from supper tonight, saying she was going to visit some of the outlying towns. This was not unusual for her to do, since it was her job to make sure their subjects were getting everything they needed. Instead, she would send the only other person in the castle that she could trust to cover for her.

Lyren found her handmaiden, in the kitchen. She was helping the kitchen staff prepare for lunch. She walked over to the table where she was cutting up some ham. "Minaren, dear, could you attend to me in my bedroom directly, please?"

"Of course, milady," Minaren replied. She put down her knife, signaling for another servant to take her place, and followed Lyren to her bedroom. Luckily, King Thadis was out with the palace guard doing routine training, so Minaren and Lyren were alone.

"Minaren," Lyren began, "I need your help, dear. You know Jaylen found a wounded dragon?"

"Yes, milady," Minaren replied. That was common knowledge now, but everyone thought she had not seen the dragon again. Rumors always circulated fast around the castle and the town within the walls. Some of those stories said that Jaylen found a dragon, and it tried to eat her. Others said Jaylen was now under its spell and was being a spy for the dragons. This is how hate and mistrust were spread.

"She is helping it," continued Lyren. "The dragon was wounded. I encouraged her to keep helping it, even against the king's wishes. I could not let a wounded dragon wander the kingdom, especially since it is Aurelia."

"Aurelia!" exclaimed Minaren. Lyren quieted her with a quick motion of her hand. Nobody knew who Aurelia was, but she still couldn't risk that name being heard too much, just in case someone had heard of her.

"Yes, Aurelia. Jaylen must help her get back to the other dragons." Lyren looked worried. "However, I don't want Jaylen finding out the whole truth yet. We must proceed cautiously because you know what Thadis's reaction will be if he finds out."

"How can I help?" asked Minaren, ready to do whatever was necessary. She knew everything about the dragons. Lyren had made sure she found a handmaiden that she could trust with this secret. Trying to hide her excursions to go to the dragon city was hard. She had asked Minaren to cover for her a lot.

"I need to talk to Aurelia alone. I told Thadis and Jaylen I was going to the outlying villages this evening. I need you to go, in my place, and gather petitions for me, so it looks like I actually went."

"Very well, milady." Minaren had done this several times to give her mistress a break here and there to take care of business even King Thadis knew nothing about. Minaren had been Lyren's handmaiden for many years and was the only one outside of her family whom Lyren trusted without question.

Lyren knew she had to wait until evening when Jaylen left Aurelia to come home for dinner. It wasn't even one o'clock yet. So she decided to go out to the market square and get some food for the people on the lower side of town. She had done this as much as she could since she had become queen.

When she arrived at the market, she saw a woman in torn clothes running from the food merchant. He had his sword drawn, ready to attack her. The woman looked like she was starving and her hair was all knotted. Lyren could see the woman carrying something in her arms. It must be food, thought Lyren. The poor woman must have been desperate.

Without a second thought, she stopped the woman and when the merchant caught up, holding his sword up to strike, she commanded, "Stop at once!"

The merchant stopped and lowered his sword. "Your Majesty, this woman stole from me," he said. "She must be punished."

"So, what, you're going to kill a woman for a loaf of bread?" Lyren was almost angry enough to shout. "I don't think so. Both of you are to report to the castle tomorrow morning. Princess Jaylen will resolve this and determine the woman's punishment."

"What if she runs away before then? At least arrest her," pleaded the merchant.

"I'll not throw this woman in the dungeon with real criminals when her only crime is being desperate. If either of you don't show up tomorrow, then you will be punished for disobeying your queen," said Lyren, staring at each in turn before taking the merchant's arm and leading him back toward his shop. "Come now, I need to buy food for my people."

The merchant hesitated, then turned and walked beside the queen back to his shop. She purchased many loaves of bread and some cheese. Then filled a basket with apples. She couldn't carry all of it, so she stopped a couple guardsmen on patrol and asked them to give her a hand.

She then proceeded down the streets to the lower town. This is where those who barely made enough to survive lived. She distributed the food to as many as she could, then headed back to the castle.

Soon it was time. Lyren knew Jaylen would be returning from spending the day with Aurelia. She grabbed her horse from the stables and headed out of the castle. It didn't take long to reach the cave on horseback. Lyren waited patiently. Sure enough, Jaylen emerged from the cave on her way back to have dinner.

As soon as she was out of earshot, Lyren approached the cave. She tied the horse outside, then walked into the cave. It was getting dark, so she had brought a lantern with her. The soft glow from the lantern did little to light the dark cave, but Lyren was used to walking around in the dark. She always walked the corridors of the castle late at night to unwind before bed. She continued walking to the room at the back of the cave where Aurelia was.

"I wondered when you would show up, Your Majesty," Aurelia's e deep voice cut through the air like a hot knife through butter. Lyren should have known Aurelia would be expecting her.

"Aurelia, dear sweet Aurelia," said Lyren. "I hope your wound has healed."

"Thanks to your sweet daughter," the dragon's head peeked around the corner.

"That is what I am here to talk to you about." Lyren moved closer. "Did you know Jaylen was my daughter?" she asked in an almost accusing tone.

"No, of course not," replied Aurelia, her scales glistening in the moonlight. "I knew she was a princess, of course, but I thought she might have been visiting. Honestly, I should have put it together sooner, but she was so nice I didn't care who her family was."

"We have to proceed very carefully." Lyren was not sure how, but she needed to get Aurelia to understand. "She is at a delicate age. She might not be able to handle the whole truth all at once."

"Agreed," said Aurelia. "That is the one thing I have not told her is of my true identity. I believe she would be overjoyed to learn more about me, but she may ask to visit the city and I would prefer to keep her away for the moment."

"As much as we both want to, we can't tell Jaylen the truth yet." Lyren sounded really worried. "When she told me she found you injured, I knew this was our opportunity. I went to see the others, so they didn't send out search parties. However, they won't stay back forever. You are too important to them."

"I don't like lying to my best friend," Aurelia replied, holding up her front foot when Lyren started to protest. "However, I know you are right. Jaylen killed the man who shot me."

"He must have been one of the smugglers?" Lyren knew what that meant. Jaylen was going to protect Aurelia at all costs.

"Exactly, this is a fragile time for her and we must proceed carefully." Aurelia sounded worried as well. "I can already feel the bond forming. It is okay. I believe we are meant to be bonded."

"I know, I see it too." Lyren paused. "I must ask you to hold the truth a little longer. There is only one man who can help her come to the truth without throwing her into a spiral that could lead us to war."

"You mean Lyon?" Aurelia's tone was matter-of-fact and although it was a question, she already knew the answer.

"Yes, he is the only one." Lyren looked up at Aurelia pleadingly. "I need you to take her to him." Her voice broke a bit, as though she didn't want to say the next part. "I will arrange for her to get caught coming to see you. I know my husband; he will confront her, and she will want to run away. Tell her you met someone before coming to this kingdom and you think he will help."

"Then, when they meet, he will tell her the truth," concluded Aurelia. "Since she will be so far from home, she should be able to take her time learning and eventually break through the king's stubbornness."

"Exactly!" Lyren knew what she had to do. Unfortunately, she had to wait another couple of weeks before doing anything. Jaylen would need to master riding Aurelia and then they can take the long trip.

"I will do as you ask, Your Majesty." Aurelia was still uncomfortable with the idea, but she knew it was the best option.

"Thank you, Aurelia," Lyren said, bowing slightly to the dragon. "Please promise me you will protect Jaylen and take care of her for me. I know she can take care of herself, but I am a mother. I still worry. I am sure you can relate."

"Of course, Your Majesty." Aurelia missed her own children. One day they would be reunited, and her children would never have to live in fear of humans again. Aurelia would make sure that Jaylen could finally break down the walls between humans and dragons and there would be peace.

Lyren bowed again. "Goodbye, Aurelia. May the wind always lift you up, and your flight be easy." She recited the traditional dragon farewell, then turned and left the cave. She was sure that Minaren was back by now, so she would go collect the petitions at the usual meeting place, then head back into the castle and give them to Thadis before they settled in for the night.

When she arrived at the meeting spot, there was nobody there. That was odd; Minaren should have been there waiting for her. She started to turn towards the road to the village where Minaren went, and she saw a horse galloping in her direction. It was Minaren's; the young woman was slumped over in the saddle. Lyren was horrified to think Minaren may have been hurt or worse.

As Lyren watched, a second form came up over the crest of the hill. There was someone chasing Minaren. It looked like he would catch her before she reached safety. Lyren had no choice, but if she showed her power in the kingdom and someone saw her, she would lose everything.

She couldn't let Minaren get hurt, so she had to risk it. Lyren dismounted. She couldn't do this on her horse, or she may be thrown. She raised her arm, calling up the power that would knock the man from his horse. She caught a red flash out of the corner of her eye. The man's horse reared, knocking him to the ground and giving Minaren time to get to Lyren. Lyren didn't even look back, but jumped into her saddle and ran alongside Minaren.

"Thank you, Aurelia," she said under her breath. She knew it was her, and that she had scared the man's horse, hopefully without being seen.

They made it to the castle gates, where the guard immediately opened it for them. Lyren called her steed to a halt, and Minaren did the same. "Lieutenant, there is a man on the road back a ways. Send men to capture him if he is still alive. He is charged with attempted murder of a member of the court."

"Yes, milady," the guard said, and immediately complied. Lyren was not sure if the man was dead or alive; she hoped he was dead.

However, if he was alive, he might be able to tell her why he was chasing Minaren. Lyren guided the horses toward the stables, and when they arrived, checked to see if anyone was there.

They were alone, so she laid Minaren on some hay bales and put her hands on the wound that she found on Minaren's chest. It was obviously made with a long blade. Gold light illuminated the wound as the power surged through Lyren. The wound disappeared, and Minaren opened her eyes.

"Thank you, milady," she said in a weak voice. "The petitions are in my saddlebag. Hurry and bring them to the king. He must know what is happening."

"What do you mean?" asked Lyren. "What is happening?"

"There are rumors of more smugglers all across Eldoria." Minaren's voice was getting stronger. "It seems that they are not only searching for herbs. They are searching for Aurelia."

"What?" Lyren looked around nervously. "How do they even know she is here?"

"It seems we have a spy in the castle," Minaren said. "That is not all. There are reports of a black dragon in Milvania."

"We need to move fast." Lyren looked almost panicked. "Tell the king nothing of this. I will handle it, change your torn clothes, and I will take the normal petitions to the king."

Minaren complied with no questions. Lyren headed for the castle, noticing that the guards had found the body. Good, the man was dead and couldn't reveal what was going on. Lyren put on her biggest smile and walked up the stairs to her bedroom. She was going to have to move up her timeframe and get Jaylen to leave with Aurelia as soon as possible. If HE was here, then she knew they didn't have much time.

***

Lyren awoke at dawn, as she always did. She dressed, then headed out to the market to buy the ingredients she would need to make bread for dinner. She had to keep herself busy. After the events of yesterday, Lyren was on edge. Knowing that people were searching for Aurelia made her nervous whenever Jaylen went out to see her. If they found Aurelia while Jaylen was with her, then she knew Jaylen would protect Aurelia with her life if necessary. If someone found Aurelia at night and killed her, Jaylen would feel responsible. Either way could be bad for Jaylen.

She knew she needed to move up her timetable and get Jaylen and Aurelia to Lyon as quickly as possible. Of course, she could always tell Jaylen the truth and convince her to go see Lyon. No, that wouldn't work. Jaylen might decide that it was better for her to learn from her mother than someone she didn't know, even if it was her brother. She had to make Jaylen run away. That meant setting it up so that Thadis drove her away.

Lyren knew how to make it happen, but it could be dangerous. What if Thadis actually heard Jaylen out and was convinced? She could use her influence behind the scenes to press on him with magic and make him angry. She had acquired the ability to influence others' emotions. It was not common even among the dragoneers, but occasionally a person gained this ability. It was thought that it had to do with certain traits, like leadership ability. Lyren suspected it had something to do with the fact that Feora was a former queen.

Well, this line of thought was just making her more anxious, so she decided to go visit her friend Carasa and spend the day just doing things she enjoyed. She could worry about the rest tomorrow. Carasa's house was not far; she made her way down the streets until she arrived at a small cottage near the wall. It was a comfy-looking home, and smoke billowed out of the chimney, indicating a fire was burning inside.

Lyren knocked on the door. Inside, she heard the voice of her friend. "I'm coming; just be patient. I don't move as fast as I used to, you know." Lyren could also hear things falling as her friend made her way through the house to open the door. The door suddenly swung open, revealing an older lady with dark skin and gray hair. Her clothes were covered in stains. She wore a long dark green dress and an apron. She had a serious look on her face until she saw Lyren. "Oh my dear, I didn't expect to see you today, Lyren. Please come in."

Lyren smiled; she could not remember the last time Carasa used her title. To her, Lyren was just a friend. She was too old to stand on ceremony or mince words. The last time she was at the castle, Thadis had burped, and Carasa flat out told him, "You could say excuse me, you know. Being king doesn't mean you don't have to use proper manners." Thadis had laughed and apologized.

She entered the home and went into the kitchen, Carasa a short distance behind. "I needed to spend some time with a friend today," Lyren said, sitting at the table where she had spent so much time talking to Carasa.

"Ah, I see. In other words, you are questioning whether to use your power to influence Thadis to drive Jaylen to run away with Aurelia.

59

I assume you asked Aurelia to take her to Lyon as well." Carasa put a pot of water on the hearth to heat up for tea.

It always amazed Lyren how much Carasa knew. "Why am I not surprised you actually know all that?" She laughed. "But I actually wanted to take my mind off that today so I could enjoy the day."

"Well then, we will speak of other things. Just know that you are doing the right thing. Lyon must be the one to teach Jaylen. It is only right since he is bonded to Tauren, and I believe Tauren needs to see Aurelia again anyway." Carasa poured them some tea, then sat at the table. "I can see trouble coming soon, Lyren. I do hope that you are prepared for it."

"With you around, how can I not be?" said Lyren, taking a sip of her tea. They continued to talk for hours about various things, but as she stood up to head home for the evening, she felt confident in her choice and much less stressed.

Chapter 7:

Duties Call

Jaylen sat at her desk just finishing up a letter to Elia. They had become good friends since they met. They tried to stay in contact as much as possible. She made sure not to mention Aurelia in the letters in case someone got curious and read them, but she mentioned their 'mutual friend,' and in this way, was able to reassure Elia that Aurelia was doing well. As she stamped the royal seal on the letter, she heard a knock at the door.

"Enter," she said, standing up and facing the door.

A young woman with long red hair came into the room. She had a fading red dress on and was carrying a basket of fruit. She was smiling and looked happy. "This was just delivered for you, milady. I believe it's from Elia," said Aliysa, Jaylen's handmaiden.

"Thank you, Aliysa. Just set it on the bed," replied Jaylen. Aliysa had been her handmaiden for only a short time, but they had become fast friends. She was fiercely loyal and always upbeat. She enjoyed her work and was always telling Jaylen how beautiful she was.

"I was also told to have you meet your parents in the throne room," Aliysa said, picking up Jaylen's dirty laundry. "I will get these washed as soon as possible, Your Highness," with that she turned and left the room.

Jaylen laughed. That girl was completely devoted to doing the best job possible. She never slowed down for even a minute. Jaylen had to force her to take breaks and slow down now and then. She was afraid Aliysa would burn herself out if she kept at that pace all the time.

Jaylen knew her parents would be waiting for her and she also knew what they wanted her for. She left her room and handed the letter to one of the messengers. "Please have this delivered to Princess Elia in Corina as soon as possible," she told the young man, who just bowed and ran off to do as she asked.

She then made her way to the throne room, as her parents had asked. When she got there, she saw her parents, Lieutenant Jamore, and two villagers. One of the villagers, a woman in tattered clothing, had a small child with her.

She walked over to her place on her small throne between her parents. This was royal business. As soon as she had turned 16, her parents gave her the task of resolving any conflict between the villagers. It was their way of helping her learn what it meant to be a leader. She didn't really hate it, but sometimes it got tedious.

It appeared only one conflict needed resolution today, so she was thankful for that, at least. Sometimes these took all day.

Jaylen turned to Jamore and assumed her 'princess voice' as he liked to refer to it. "Lieutenant, you may proceed."

"Thank you, milady," said Jamore. "This merchant has a grievance against this woman."

Jaylen looked at the merchant. He had a clean-shaven face and nicely groomed brown hair. "What is your grievance, sir?" she asked.

"Your Highness, this woman stole from me," said the merchant. "She must be punished!"

"What did she steal?" asked Jaylen, looking at the woman briefly.

"A loaf of bread and some apples," said the merchant. He was a taller man, but not very muscular. He spoke well and seemed to be doing all right for himself. He was wearing a green silk tunic and leather slacks and had a large money pack on his belt.

Jaylen looked at the woman. She looked like she hadn't eaten in days. She was dirty and looked very weak. The child looked a bit better, indicating to Jaylen that the woman put her child first. This observation told Jaylen what she needed to know, but she had to ask, anyway.

"Is this true?" asked Jaylen, turning her full attention to the woman.

"It is, Your Highness," the woman said, hanging her head in shame. "I am sorry. It is no excuse, but my son needed food, and I had no other way to get it."

"What's your name?" Jaylen asked in a gentle tone.

The woman looked surprised. The royal family didn't usually ask for names during hearings. "Kilana, Your Highness," she said.

Jaylen looked at the child, who was also dirty. She felt conflicted. She knew she had to punish the woman for stealing, but she couldn't let them suffer. It was her duty as the princess of Eldoria to make sure her subjects didn't suffer.

"Kilana, I understand your situation. However, I cannot allow theft to go unpunished. You should know you have the right to petition us if you are in need, and we will do our best to help. I know you want to provide for your son. That much is obvious, as you put his needs before your own." Jaylen paused, allowing her words to sink in for a minute. "That being said, I don't think it will do you or your son any good if I throw you in the dungeon. So I am hereby ordering you to work off your debt to this merchant by assisting him around his shop until such time as he is satisfied that the cost of the items you stole has been met."

The merchant wasn't happy with Jaylen's decision. He protested. "Milady, this is unacceptable. She must be punished. She must…"

Jaylen held up her hand. "Good sir, I understand your anger. Please understand, though, I will not let a woman and her child suffer because she stole food to survive." She looked at Kilana. "What she did was wrong, so she must work to pay it back; that should be sufficient punishment," she said.

"With all due respect, Your Majesty, theft is a crime," said the man.

"Yes. And she is paying for her crime. What would you have me do, throw her in the dungeon and make her son an orphan? We are a just kingdom, sir. I must serve justice but also be kind. I will not let anyone in my kingdom suffer; compassion is also needed at times to help those who need it," said Jaylen.

The man apologized and left. Jaylen turned to the woman, who stared at her with a bleak expression. "I am sorry, Your Highness."

Jaylen stepped down from the throne and walked to the woman, putting her hand gently on her shoulder. "Why is it you need to steal food? Do you not have a means to earn a living?"

The woman started to cry. "No, milady, my husband died of fever a few weeks ago." Jaylen could barely understand her through the sobs. "I have not been able to find anywhere to work, and our reserves ran out days ago. I had to feed my son." She was crying uncontrollably now.

Jaylen was almost crying herself. "That is horrible." She held the woman for a few minutes while she calmed down. "I know of someone in the village to the south who needs help to tend their farm. There is a small house there that you and your son could use, and their daughter is about the same age. As soon as you have worked off your debt to the merchant, I will take you there myself."

The woman's face beamed with gratitude. "Oh, thank you, Your Highness. I promise I will work hard."

"I have no doubt you will." Jaylen stepped back to her throne. "In the meantime, we can't have you starving or showing up to work filthy. Jamore, take Kilana to the bathing room that the servants use and allow her and her child to bathe. In the meantime, send for clean clothes and at least a week's worth of food for her and the child."

Kilana's eyes widened in surprise. "Milady, that is too much. I cannot ask…"

Jaylen cut her off with a raise of her hand. "You did not ask. I am doing what I must to help you and your child. We have more than enough to spare. I will not allow my subjects to starve if I can help it. That is final."

Kilana bowed. "Thank you, Your Highness." Jamore escorted them out, and Thadis and Lyren both turned to Jaylen, smiling.

"What?" Jaylen asked when she noticed them smiling at her.

"I'm so proud of you Jaylen," said Thadis. "You did a fine job resolving that."

"Yes. You showed authority by punishing that woman, but also compassion by helping her. That is exactly how a princess, and future queen, should treat her subjects," said Lyren.

Jaylen smiled. "I learned from the best," she said. Remembering all the times her parents had dealt with conflicts with similar compassion, as she sat and watched when she was younger. "Time for me to go. I am losing daylight, and I still want to gather a few herbs before I run out of daylight."

She hugged both her parents and left to go back to her room. She changed into her riding clothes and grabbed her sword so she could go see Aurelia. Jaylen hadn't seen her at all today because she was busy. She finally had a free moment, so she decided to spend it with her best friend.

She left the castle and walked straight to the cave. She had some herbs stored inside that she had stockpiled to give her more time to spend with Aurelia. Jaylen entered the cave and walked back to Aurelia's 'little home,' as she called it.

Aurelia saw Jaylen approaching and grinned. "I was beginning to think you weren't coming today."

"Oh, come on. I've been here every day since I found you. You really think I'm going to miss a day with my favorite dragon?" said Jaylen, returning the tease.

Aurelia laughed. Even though she was keeping a secret from Jaylen, she still felt at ease with her friend. Like nothing in the world could break their friendship. "Favorite? Have you seen another dragon that I don't know about?" Aurelia teased.

Jaylen laughed. "You're the only dragon I have ever seen, dear friend." She had brought an apple and a good portion of meat for Aurelia. She threw the apple up into the air, and Aurelia caught it with ease, eating it, core and all. Jaylen placed the meat on a flat rock next to Aurelia. She knew Aurelia would prefer to hunt for her own food, but she also knew that sometimes she enjoyed cooked and seasoned meat.

She sprinkled some salt and a few other herbs on the meat, then stepped back. "All right, go ahead," she said.

"What do you expect me to do?" said Aurelia, smiling at her friend. This was a common game they played. Aurelia knew what Jaylen wanted. Ever since she had first seen dragon fire, Jaylen had been fascinated by the intensity and bright color.

Jaylen looked at her, confused. "Cook it with your fire, obviously." Jaylen could never figure out how Aurelia knew just exactly how much fire would cook the meat just perfectly. The talents of her friend fascinated her.

"Oh, right," said Aurelia, acting like she just remembered.

She pulled her head back, took a deep breath in, then aimed her mouth at the meat on the rock and released a jet of the brightest orange fire. The flames licked the meat for a few seconds, then Aurelia cut them off. Jaylen stared in amazement, eyes wide.

"That was hot," she said, stepping up to retrieve some of the meat. "It was amazing, as always."

Aurelia laughed and took a piece of meat. "It is perfectly cooked too."

Jaylen ate her piece, too. "Best friend, smart, and an amazing cook. I think I'll keep you around." They ate their food and talked. Aurelia told her about the things she had seen in the cave, and Jaylen told Aurelia about the hearing earlier that morning. They could talk for hours. About anything.

"Well, it's just about time for dinner, so I better head back to the palace. I'll see you tomorrow, Aurelia," said Jaylen.

She hugged Aurelia and left the cave. Climbing on her horse, she headed toward the castle. She got home and settled her horse back into the stables, and headed to the dining hall to meet her parents. They ate dinner and chatted for a while. Jaylen was tired, so she went back to her room to settle into bed. Tomorrow, she was going to bring some of her paintings to show Aurelia. Jaylen had drawn a lot of the area around the castle, sometimes even drawing animals that she saw in the woods. Maybe Aurelia would like the painting that Jaylen had made of her. Whatever ones she liked; Jaylen would give to her.

Chapter 8:

A Parting of Ways

Queen Lyren stood at the window, looking out from the hallway towards the cave where she knew Aurelia was. "I know I told you a couple of weeks, but we can't wait that long," she muttered under her breath. "Please forgive me, dear Aurelia, and take care of Jaylen as you promised." With that, she headed to her bedroom to set things in motion.

King Thadis was sitting at his desk when Lyren walked in. "Hello, my love," he said as she entered. His expression changed when he saw how worried she looked. "What's wrong, Lyren?"

"I am worried about Jaylen," Lyren put a note of fear in her voice. "I noticed in her room the other day that she had painted a picture of a dragon. I know it could be from her memory of the dragon she saw, but that brief encounter would not leave such a lasting impression.

"You think she is still going to see this dragon?" asked Thadis, hoping that she was wrong. He didn't really hate dragons, but he didn't trust them. Too many stories of dragon attacks seen by too many people to discount. He knew there was a time when dragons and humans were friends, but according to the tales he heard, the dragons broke that trust.

"I hope not," Lyren said in hushed tones. "But you know how stubborn she is." She hoped he would do what she wanted, send someone to follow Jaylen and report back.

"If it will make you feel better, I will have one of the guards follow her in secret and see where she goes," Thadis said. He didn't believe Jaylen would disobey him. However, if it set Lyren's mind at ease, he would check. "Grelan!" he called, raising his voice to be heard.

A man with a well-trimmed beard wearing chain mail burst into the room. "What is wrong, Your Majesty?" His face was well-tanned, and he looked around the room, hand on his sword.

"We are fine," said the king, motioning for the man to relax. "I need you to do me a favor. In the morning, when Jaylen leaves to gather herbs, follow her. *Do not* be seen. Stay with her until she returns to the castle in the evening, then report back to me and *only* me where she goes and what she does."

"Yes, sir!" replied Grelan, not entirely sure what was going on but his king gave him an order and he intended to follow it.

The next morning, he sat by the main gate in a thicket of bushes, waiting for Jaylen to come out. Sure enough, right at dawn, she exited the gate and walked towards the woods. He was surprised she didn't have her horse; then he remembered she never rides when going to pick herbs. She had a rather large bag with her. Grelan wondered what was inside.

He followed close behind her, but not too close. He knew if he made any sound, she would hear it, so he had left his armor and weapons in his room. Jaylen went around behind a natural cave and began picking mushrooms and plants. Grelan didn't know what they were, only that they helped the healers.

After an hour or so of this, she headed back around the cave to its entrance. She disappeared into its wide mouth. Grelan followed. He nearly jumped out of his skin when he saw Aurelia. He knew he was supposed to wait until evening, but the king and queen needed to know how much danger their daughter was in.

***

Jaylen and Aurelia talked back and forth. Jaylen took out the rolled-up paintings she had brought with her and showed them to Aurelia. "These are some of my paintings. If you like any, they are yours," said Jaylen.

Aurelia looked at the paintings one by one till she came to the one of her. Her eyes studied it, and she looked at Jaylen. "I want this one," she said. "I think it is beautiful. No one has ever painted me before."

"It is yours then, dear friend." Jaylen rolled up the others and put them back in her pack. "I had to draw you because you are so beautiful. I hope I did you justice."

"It is absolutely stunning." Aurelia looked as though she may cry. "You are very talented. I love it. I am glad we are friends."

"So am I," Jaylen said and hugged Aurelia.

"Tomorrow we should try to fly together for a short time," Aurelia said, changing the subject. "I want you to see what it is like to fly."

"I am not sure about that," said Jaylen. Flying on a dragon? She thought. High up in the air where if she fell, she would be dead for sure. "Maybe we should wait a while longer to be safe."

"You're not scared, are you?" teased Aurelia.

"Of course not, I am a warrior," said Jaylen, hoping she sounded confident. "I fear nothing."

"Good, then it is settled. Tomorrow we fly."

"Very well, but as for now I must get back and have dinner with my parents. I will see you in the morning," Jaylen hoped it wouldn't be as scary as she thought. She patted Aurelia's side, then left the cave and went straight home.

When Jaylen walked in, she instantly knew something was wrong. "What is it?" she asked, not sure she wanted to know.

"Sit down, dear," Lyren said calmly.

"Ok...?" Jaylen was confused.

Her father looked absolutely livid. "How... *dare... you?*" he shouted, jumping to his feet and knocking over his chair in the process. Jaylen was taken aback. She had never seen her father so angry. That it was apparently directed at her made it worse. "All this time, you have been going to see that dragon! You have also apparently kept it close by putting your whole kingdom in danger as well."

That was the last straw. She could have weathered his anger if he had not said *that*. "*My* kingdom was *never* in danger. Aurelia would never hurt anyone. If you weren't such a stubborn bull, you would see that dragons aren't dangerous. It is us humans that are dangerous with our unfounded prejudice." She wasn't pulling any punches this time.

"That's it; this dragon has poisoned your mind long enough." He said, then completely shocked her with his next words, "Guards, take the princess to the dungeon while I deal with this threat to the kingdom." As soon as the words were out of his mouth, he instantly regretted them.

"Would you really have your own daughter arrested for disagreeing with you?" asked Jaylen. She could feel her whole body getting hotter. She gripped the table tighter. How could her own father do this to her?

"It is for your protection and the protection of the kingdom. You are associating with an enemy of Eldoria," said Thadis. He couldn't take back his words now. He must see this through, and he was still extremely angry, even though he didn't know why.

He looked into Jaylen's eyes and his heart sank. It was too late, though he saw it in her eyes. He had driven his daughter away. Where had all that anger come from? He wanted to stop this; he wanted to take it back and reason with Jaylen, but for some reason he couldn't move or speak.

Two guards entered the dining hall. They looked confused but were too used to taking orders to disobey. They started toward Jaylen, who was shocked that her father was going to not only have her arrested but kill her friend. "Boys, you may want to think about this." She forced herself to focus on the task at hand; saving Aurelia. "I don't want to hurt you, but I will if I have to."

The two men hesitated briefly, but then continued toward Jaylen. She didn't wait for them. Closing the distance between herself and the guards quickly, she blocked the first one's attempt to grab her and punched him in the gut, then swiftly threw him to the ground with a thud. The other man grabbed her from behind. Jaylen didn't even hesitate, bringing her head back and smashing it into his nose, then grabbing his arm and throwing him to the ground as well. He tried to get up, but she kicked him in the head, knocking him out.

"Jaylen, stop this," shouted her mother, tears in her eyes.

Jaylen turned briefly and said, "Sorry, Mother, I have to prove that dragons are not dangerous and I have to protect Aurelia. I will be back when I have done that." She had to stop herself from crying. Now was not the time for that. "I love you both." and she looked once more at her father, who had slumped in another chair at the table.

Jaylen grabbed her bag and ran out of the hall and headed to her bedroom. She had to be quick before more guards showed up. She knew what she had to do. She had to leave the kingdom with Aurelia and learn everything she could about dragons. Then she could prove to everyone that they were not dangerous. She belted on her sword and grabbed her bow and quiver. Then filled her bag with clothes. Last, she grabbed her money pouch. She would need that for sure.

As she came out of her bedroom, she almost ran straight into Jamore. He was faster than her. He grabbed her and restrained her. "I am sorry, Your Highness. I must obey my king. You are under arrest. I am sure this will be resolved soon. For now, please come quietly. I don't want to see you get hurt," he said. She could hear the hesitation in his voice.

She knew she could probably break free, but would the other guards be as gentle? No, she had to find a way out that didn't involve taking out all her men and the others who protected her kingdom. She relented and let him bring her to the dungeon. She could escape before her father had a chance to get to Aurelia. She knew he would wait till morning, at least.

Jamore took her weapons and her bag and handed it to another guardsman. He guided her down the hall, then downstairs to the dungeon area. She continued to look around, trying to figure out how to get out of this.

They were finally at the cell and Jamore left her inside and left, locking the door behind her. Jaylen sat on the bed in the corner. "I forgive you, Jamore." She said, wanting him to know she would not hold this against him. He was doing his duty and following the orders of the king. That was his job.

Jamore paused, then continued up the stairs. Jaylen sat there looking around, trying to plan her escape. Suddenly, she heard a female voice. "I want to see her now, Lieutenant." It was her mother's voice. "She is my daughter."

"I am sorry, Your Majesty," replied Jamore. "The king told me no visitors." He sounded to Jaylen like he was completely against all of this, but he knew he had to follow orders. She had known him a long time, and she thought of him as a friend. She didn't hold any of this against him.

"Do you think that includes me?" Jaylen could hear the business in her mother's voice. Jamore must be trembling by now. No one could stand up to her mother when she was in business mode. Not even her father. "I am, after all, the chief magistrate of this kingdom, responsible for scheduling all hearings. Therefore, it is essential that I speak with her."

"Yes, Your Majesty," Jamore relented. "Please go right in."

Jaylen saw her mother come down the stairs from the guardroom. She really was all business. Jaylen was sure her mother was about to give her a very long lecture. There was something about her mother's demeanor, though that made Jaylen wonder. Her mother looked tired. Nobody else would have even noticed. Jaylen only knew because she was close to her mother and knew every tiny expression she made.

"Jaylen, why did you let yourself get caught?" She was whispering, "You need to get out of here. Aurelia needs to be protected, and you are the only one who can do it."

"Why did you let Father throw me in here?" Jaylen countered, a little upset that her mother kept telling her to protect Aurelia but never explaining why.

"I can't openly disagree with him. You know that. He is the king. His authority must remain intact and there were guards nearby. We have to show a unified front." Her mom sounded desperate. Jaylen wasn't sure what was going on but for her mother to show so much emotion, there were high stakes indeed.

"I need to get out of here. I am already planning my escape. I let myself get caught, so I didn't hurt anyone else. Also, it made them let their guard down. They think I am trapped in here, so they aren't guarding the whole castle as diligently anymore," Jaylen explained. She already had a plan, but wasn't sure if it would work.

"I will help you. Be ready in an hour." Her mother just turned and left before Jaylen could say anymore. Jaylen was left with so many questions. She filed them away for later. She had to be ready, and she had to protect Aurelia.

***

It had been almost an hour since her mother left. Jaylen was ready for whatever her mother was planning. She heard a commotion coming from the guard room upstairs. The guards were screaming.

"There is a gold dragon sighted above the castle! We have to take it down. Everyone to your positions!" That was Jamore, taking command like she knew he could.

A few minutes passed, and Jaylen's mom appeared, coming down the stairs. She walked over to Jaylen's cell and unlocked the door. She gave her a quick hug, then said, "Your Armor and weapons are in the guardroom. I also packed more clothes in your bag and some meat and cheese. Now go!”

“Next time I see you, you have to tell me everything. Especially how you got a dragon to cause a distraction,” said Jaylen, wanting the answers now but knowing she didn’t have time for them. She ran up the stairs and grabbed her gear. She ran out the door and turned toward the stairs to the courtyard.

Jaylen leaped down the stairs and out into the courtyard. She saw an opportunity and leaped onto the horse that was pulling a cart full of fruit. Drawing her sword, she cut the harness that tied the animal to the cart and signaled it to move.

The horse took off at a gallop, and she steered it toward the gate. To her horror, the gate was closing. Obviously, the guard had seen her. She ducked low, urging the horse to go faster. The gate slammed shut behind her, barely missing her by an inch. She didn’t stop until she reached the cave, where she pulled the horse to a stop and jumped off.

Jaylen ran into the cave, yelling for Aurelia. “Get up, we have to go!” she shouted. “My father is coming to kill you.”

Aurelia rose to her feet and met Jaylen halfway. She hesitated a little and looked around, but crouched low anyway. “Get on. I know someone who can help us, but we will have to fly.”

“But we have never flown together,” said Jaylen. She was nervous enough about a short flight for practice, but having to fly for an extended period of time scared her.

"Just hold on tight." Aurelia knelt to allow Jaylen to mount her neck. "I will do the rest." Jaylen didn't hesitate; she leaped into place on Aurelia's powerful neck. Aurelia ran to the entrance and as soon as she was out in the open, she unfurled her powerful wings bent down slightly and with a huge downstroke of her wings and a leap, they were airborne.

Jaylen held tightly to Aurelia's neck. Being a practiced horse rider helped a little, but a dragon was much different. As Aurelia gained altitude, Jaylen watched as her kingdom fell away. She was more terrified than she had ever been, but she was determined not to let Aurelia know that.

Soon they were above the clouds and flying forward at an incredible speed. Soon Jaylen relaxed and stopped being nervous about flying. She thought about all that had happened. Tears streamed down her face. Why had her dad reacted like that? She had never seen him get so angry. Jaylen was outright crying now, thinking she might never see her dad again. She wanted to apologize, tell him that no matter what, she still loved him.

Aurelia turned toward Corina. Now why would she be taking them there? Jaylen trusted Aurelia, so she just enjoyed the flight and soon she felt tired. Before she knew it, she was asleep.

Lyren could hear the commotion, and she knew Jaylen had gotten away. Thadis was hunched over the table sobbing. She may have taken it too far, influencing his anger with magic. He was too calm when she told him, and he may not have been able to drive Jaylen off. It was crucial for Jaylen to leave because *he* would be looking for her here and Lyren needed Jaylen to be bonded with Aurelia before *he* found her.

She hoped that Thadis would be all right. Until he was, she would keep the kingdom running. Jaylen would return and save their kingdom from hate and mistrust. Lyren had seen it in her vision.

Chapter 9:

Who is Lyon?

Lyren sat alone in her bed, thinking about how she had now lost both of her children. She remembered the day she lost her son, Lyon.

Twenty Years Ago

On that bright, beautiful morning, the sun was shining through the curtains. Lyren, Queen of Eldoria, was getting ready to take her only son, Lyon, up to see the dragons. She had to be careful not to let her husband know; he was totally against any contact with dragons. It wasn't his fault, really. He knew dragons weren't vicious creatures, but the rest of the kingdom didn't. He had to keep the kingdom together, so he needed to maintain no contact with dragons.

He had no idea that his wife was bonded to a dragon. If he had known that, he would have had to send her away. She kept up the illusion so that she could remain in a position to be of some help.

She found Lyon playing in his room. "Are you ready, my son?" she asked, smiling down at him.

"Are we going to see the dragons, Mother?" asked Lyon, jumping up immediately and running to her. His mother had told him of the dragons, that they were beautiful creatures—strong, powerful, but also gentle. They came in all colors: blue, red, green, silver, and even gold. They were also highly intelligent and lived a long time. She had told him so many stories of how they built their great city and how they kept it hidden from everyone.

"I told you I'd take you to meet them one day," said Lyren, almost laughing at Lyon's reaction. She wasn't sure if this was wise, but she wanted him to know the dragons the way she did. Lyren was hoping one day that dragons could once again visit the three kingdoms.

Lyren held Lyon's hand as they walked from his room to the stables. Once there, she saddled her horse and climbed up. Lyren reached her hand down and picked her son up into the saddle behind her, then they were off. The only way to get to the dragon's home was to fly. The dragon kingdom is a city in the sky, kept afloat by a magic spell. The only way to get there was on the back of a dragon.

They rode for about twenty minutes, then reached a huge clearing. Lyren stopped the horse and dismounted. She lifted Lyon down and tied the horse to a tree. Then they walked further out into the clearing.

"Where are the dragons?" asked Lyon, looking around expectantly.

"Look up, son," said Lyren, pointing to the sky.

Lyon looked up and still couldn't see anything. "Where are they, Mother?" Lyren could hear the frustration in his voice.

"They are hidden. Let me call our ride," Lyren said, then raised her voice. "Feora, please descend from your place in the clouds."

Lyon continued looking, then his eyes got big, and his mouth hung open as he saw a beautiful gold dragon descending from the sky. Its golden scales glistened in the sunlight, bright green eyes reflecting the light. Strong, powerful wings created a wind so strong it almost knocked Lyon over.

"Wow..." was all he could say.

"Thank you for coming, dear friend," said Lyren, reaching up and petting the huge nose.

"My pleasure, Your Majesty," the dragon replied in a rough but gentle voice.

"I want you to meet my son, Lyon," said Lyren then continued "Lyon, this is my best friend, Feora, we have been bonded for many years."

"Pleased to meet you, young one," said Feora, bowing her head.

Lyon just stood there. Lyren almost forgot he couldn't understand Feora. She dutifully translated what the dragon had said.

Lyon waved. Then quickly bowed. Feora extended one of her massive paws in a wave back to Lyon, which made him laugh. Lyren was amazed at how well her Lyon was getting along with Feora already. She hoped he would get along with the rest of them as well.

"We had better get going. Thadis is expecting us for dinner," said Lyren, still smiling.

"As you wish, milady," said Feora, bowing her head to give Lyren and Lyon room to climb onto her neck. Lyren lifted Lyon onto Feora's neck and climbed up behind him. Lyon seemed to be a little tense. Of course, he would be a little scared at the prospect of flying.

"Hold on to her horns, sweetheart." Lyren went into mother mode. "There is nothing to fear. Trust me, you will be safe." When Lyon hesitated, she added, "Oh, don't worry, they are strong enough and it won't hurt her a bit."

Lyon did as he was told and held on. Lyren held onto one of Feora's horns as well and wrapped her free hand around Lyon, holding onto him tightly.

"Feora, take wing!" Lyren called out, and with one giant leap and a downstroke of her massive wings, Feora was in the air, climbing quickly with every beat of her powerful wings.

They flew high into the sky. So high that within minutes, the kingdom below became almost invisible. Lyon watched as they passed through a layer of clouds and emerged into a beautiful city.

The city was adorned with sculpted mountains, with caves carved into them; Lyon assumed those were the dragons' homes; beautiful valleys separating the mountains, trees lining every corner, and right in the center of the city was a huge clearing, and in the middle of the clearing stood a huge flame.

"What's that flame for?" asked Lyon.

"That is what keeps them hidden. Every month, they must gather around the flame and recite an ancient spell to keep their city from being detected by humans," explained Lyren, translating for Feora.

Obviously not all humans. Lyren and Lyon were pretty understanding, but most people had the worst misconceptions about dragons. There was a time when dragons and humans could live together in harmony. But that time was no more.

"Mother? Why can't the dragons come visit us?" asked Lyon.

"Because, honey, not everyone feels the way we do. They think dragons are mean and dangerous," explained Lyren.

Feora landed in what appeared to be a throne room. Not like their throne room. In this one there was a giant throne made from polished stone, and sitting on the throne was a bright blue dragon. Next to him was a smaller red dragon. The red dragon wasn't small, just smaller than the blue one. There was a roof and walls, but the doorways were massive so that a dragon could pass through easily. The rook was very high and colored to look like the sky.

"Welcome back, Queen Lyren," said the blue dragon, voice reverberating off the walls. He was smiling at them. Lyon couldn't understand what he said, but he imagined that the big blue dragon was greeting them. Their language sounded so different.

"Thank you, Your Majesty," said Lyren, bowing deeply.

"Is he a king? Like Father?" asked Lyon. He was elated that he got to meet the king of all dragons.

"Sweetheart, this is Tauren, king of the dragons," said Lyren, grinning at Lyon's reaction.

"And who might this be?" asked Tauren, looking over the small boy.

"This is my son, Prince Lyon of Eldoria," said Lyren. Lyon straightened and tried to look like a prince.

Tauren laughed, seeing Lyon try to be proper. "Feora, bring him to me," said Tauren.

Feora gently nudged Lyon forward with her head. Lyon hesitated.

"It's all right, Lyon. He just wants to say hello," said Lyren, also gently pushing him forward.

Lyon walked over to the king and stood at his feet. Tauren was so big that Lyon had to look all the way up to see his face. He couldn't believe he was standing in front of the king of dragons. Tauren was huge, but his face was so gentle. His eyes were a deep green. The many horns on his head looked like a crown to Lyon.

Lyon was so happy to meet the king that he couldn't help himself. He ran forward.

"No, Lyon!" Lyren called out, but it was too late. Lyon wrapped his arms around the leg of the king, since that was the closest part. All he wanted to do was hug a dragon. The wind picked up. A powerful gust blew through the throne room, and blue sparks of magic flowed from Lyon's fingers.

"Lyon… what have you done?" said Lyren, worried. She should have stopped him. She should have warned him.

"Did I do something wrong, Mother?" asked Lyon, stepping back and looking worried and scared. He didn't mean to do something wrong. Lyon started to cry.

"No. You did nothing wrong, dear child," said Tauren. He knew exactly what had happened, and so did Lyren. The same thing happened the first time she touched Feora. Lyon had just accidentally bonded with Tauren. This was not common in their world, but it happened sometimes. It was thought that when an innocent child touched a dragon that matched his or her personality, because of the magic in the kingdom of dragons, they would be bonded. Usually, it took time and much training to form the bond with a dragon.

Lyon looked up and stared at Tauren. "I-I can understand you," he said, confused.

"Well, of course you can, child. We're bonded now. You can understand all dragons. Because you've bonded with the dragon king, you don't need to learn our language," said Tauren. What he failed to mention was just how much Lyon would change because of the bond. He was worried for the child living with humans who were terrified of magic because it came from dragons. But now that they were bonded, he had a duty to protect this child.

"Wow. Who knew I could speak to dragons?" said Lyon. He was feeling better. This was fun.

"Now I can say a proper hello," said Feora, reaching her nose down to touch Lyon on the forehead.

"Hello, Feora," said Lyon, a little hesitant to be touched after what had just happened.

Feora sensed his hesitation. "It's all right, young Lyon, that will never happen again. You are bonded to Tauren. You can't bond with other dragons, so you can touch and hug them all you want."

So Lyon did. He hugged Feora's nose and even kissed her. She purred loudly and pulled her head away, smiling. Lyren regained her composure and turned to Tauren. "As much as I would love to stay, unfortunately, we must get back home. Thadis is expecting us," she said.

She and Lyon said their goodbyes and climbed aboard Feora once more to head back down to their kingdom. Once on the ground, Feora said goodbye to Lyon and Lyren and flew off once again.

"Come now, my son, we must be getting home," said Lyren.

They climbed on Lyren's horse and headed back home. The whole twenty minutes Lyren kept thinking about Thadis. Over the next few weeks, Lyon would show signs of the bond in the form of strength and reflexes as well as healing. She had to keep Thadis from noticing. But how?

***

Over the next few days, Lyren tried to hide Lyon from his father. She hoped she could teach him to control his power so Thadis would never find out. Unfortunately, she couldn't. One evening, while she was baking cookies for Lyon, she accidentally burned herself on a pan. Before she could hide it from Lyon, he ran over to her, concerned for his mother. As he reached out his hand in sympathy, a blue light passed from his hand to hers, and the burn disappeared.

"What was that?" said Thadis, walking in at just that moment. "It must have been a trick of the light." He shrugged it off and didn't say any more about it. Lyren knew, however, that he had recognized what happened from the stories of his ancestors and hers. He knew about the healing power of the dragoneers.

A few days later, though, something happened that changed everything. Thadis was willing to overlook the healing power because it had to be called up by compassion for someone who was injured, and that was rare. But what happened that day he could not overlook. He and Lyon were playing with wooden swords. It was training, but a bit more relaxed, getting Lyon used to the weight of a sword.

Lyon was very competitive, and he got frustrated that he could not seem to get past his father's defense. Frustration built to anger, then when his father tapped him on the back playfully and said, "Keep practicing, Son. You will have to be much better if you expect to beat me."

Lyon had a bit of a temper, and this made him angry. Normally, he would stomp off at this point and let out his frustration somewhere, and everything would be fine. It was Thadis' way of teaching his son. However, today Lyon got too angry. Suddenly, a blast of blue light burst from Lyon in all directions. Luckily, it was only his father close enough to get hit or see what happened. The blue light hit Thadis, knocking him back, and then dissipated.

Lyren immediately stood up and rushed to Lyon's side. She wished he hadn't got so mad. That was the one power that might tip the balance and make Thadis send Lyon away. Although Lyren knew where Lyon had gotten these powers, she could not tell Thadis. He would expel them from the kingdom, and she would lose her chance to help bring dragons and humans back together. She knew that Thadis assumed it was a fluke left over from their family history as dragoneers.

So, she convinced Thadis to send their son to Corina. Corina was a neighboring kingdom ruled by distant relatives of Lyren. King Balian and Queen Alaria were sympathetic to dragons and had secretly helped them on occasion. Lyon would be safe there and free to develop his gifts without the danger of undermining his parents' rule.

That night, the king and queen sat Lyon down and gave him the worst news they'd ever had to give. "Son… this has been happening for a while; you just haven't realized it. You're developing powers. I can't tell you where they come from, but I'm afraid I have to send you away," explained the king.

"No! Father, I don't want to leave!" screamed Lyon.

Lyren wanted to cry. "I know, sweetheart, but it's for your own good," she said.

Lyon continued crying, but reluctantly agreed. After what had happened earlier, he knew it was probably best. He packed his clothes, toys, and his art supplies and headed out of the castle where a carriage was waiting.

Balian and Alaria had come personally to get Lyon. Alaria stepped out of the carriage, seeing the distress on Lyren's face. "Don't you worry about a thing, Lyren. Balian and I will make sure Lyon is safe," she reassured. Lyren nodded her thanks; she didn't trust herself to speak.

Lyon hugged his mother and father one last time before climbing into the carriage. As the carriage was pulled out of sight, Lyren cried in her husband's arms. Her only son had just been taken away. She knew it was for his own good and the good of the kingdom, but it still hurt.

The next day, she called for Feora and went to see Tauren. She was a little angry, but not at the king of dragons, but at herself for bringing Lyon to the dragons. She vowed she would never bring another of her children to the dragon kingdom or even tell them about dragons.

When she arrived, she saw the look on Tauren's face, and she knew he had seen what had happened. "I am so sorry, dear lady," Tauren's voice showed real remorse. "I wish I had not allowed the boy to get closer. I never imagined he would just hug me like that."

"It's not your fault, Tauren," said Lyren, forgetting formality as they had been friends for a while. "I should never have brought him here; I knew the risks."

"Be that as it may, I am still responsible for him. I have decided to join him in Corina. My daughter shall assume the throne here. I will protect him and train him to help when the day comes that we can be reunited with humans in peace."

Gratitude lit up Lyren's face as she bowed deeply to him. "Thank you, dear friend."

Present day

Lyren stared out her window, crying at the thought of her long-lost son and her recently lost daughter.

"Protect her, Lyon. Please," she said to nothing.

Wherever Jaylen was, she knew she'd find her way to Lyon.

Chapter 10:

Corina

King Balian surveyed the path ahead. Lyon had been living at the foot of Hope Mountain for a long time. Ever since he had been brought to their kingdom, Tauren had come down to raise and protect Lyon. Balian and his wife, Alaria, had made regular trips to see them and make sure they had everything they needed. It was hard to keep a dragon like Tauren a secret, but they had managed it for the last twenty years.

Balian looked up and saw Tauren just above the tree line descending toward the home where he and Lyon had lived for many years. It was a natural cave system, but inside, Tauren had built a room for Lyon, a spare bedroom that he had insisted be fit for a young woman, and two dragon-size rooms for Tauren and another dragon that Lyon insisted would be coming soon.

Balian rode up to the entrance, which they had disguised with bushes and a door made of stone that only Lyon, with his increased strength, and of course, Tauren, could open. "Good morning, Lyon," he said. "Greetings to you as well, mighty Tauren."

"We are honored by your greeting, Your Majesty," said Tauren. "Please join us for some tea." He grabbed the hidden handle of the large stone door and opened it enough to admit himself and the two humans. On the outside, the door looked like a normal rock. On the side of it, there was what looked like a simple dip in the face of the rock where either Tauren or Lyon could get a grip to open it.

The inside, however, was much different. The rock was mostly smooth, with a large rope bolted to one side, which, as they entered the cave, Lyon grabbed and pulled the door shut once more. This effectively hid them from anyone who might happen by. Nobody really came to this part of the kingdom, however, as it was thought to be haunted. A belief that had been fostered by all the makeshift wind chimes that they had set up throughout the forest.

To further deter any would-be visitors, Tauren made regular visits to the woods. If someone was trying to brave the woods, he would growl. Just a soft growl that sounded like a ghost or demon. Lyon, too, liked to have fun now and then by cracking branches nearby or rustling bushes. They were both adept at not being seen.

The inside of their cave was a sight to behold. The rock had been carved out to make several rooms. The first, of course, was the stables for the king and queen to put their horses. This time it was just Balian. Alaria was home with their daughter, Elia. Further in, there was a kitchen. Lyon's room, the spare room, and the two dragon rooms were off the main hall, which was large enough to fit four dragons and many guests.

Balian surveyed the workmanship of the caves. Tauren had dug all this out himself, which was impressive. Lyon broke the silence. "How is Elia?" He always liked to inquire after her, as she had become like a sister to him. She came to visit sometimes and was always fun to have around.

"She is fine," said the king, sitting at the table in the middle of the room. "I came today because I needed to let you know that there have been a growing number of dragon hunters wandering the lands, so please be extra careful. I am not sure why, but it seems Adrin is stepping up his campaign to rid the kingdoms of dragons."

Balian never was one for much small talk, thought Lyon, smiling slightly. "Thanks for the warning, Your Majesty. Tauren is always careful when he goes out. No one should find us here." He said, "Plus, it would be hard for anyone to notice us here, as the cave itself is well hidden."

"The men who hunt my kind are cowards," Tauren said. He didn't need Lyon to translate for him since Balian had taken the time to learn dragon language. "They would be scared away by the 'ghosts' that haunt this forest."

"Nonetheless, please be careful," Balian sounded worried. Lyon had gone to the stove and now brought back two cups and a teapot. He poured tea into the two cups, and already knowing how Balian liked it, he added one small lump of sugar to both.

"Hey, where's mine?" said Tauren, acting hurt.

"Where it always is," said Lyon, smiling broadly. Over by the entrance to the kitchen was a bowl carved out of stone. Written on the bowl in dragon language was 'Doggy Bowl.' Lyon had made it for his friend as a joke. Everyone thought of dragons as nothing more than dumb beasts. They had no idea how intelligent dragons really were. So, Lyon had always said if dragons were stupid beasts, that would make Tauren his giant puppy dog.

"One of these days, Lyon, I am going to melt that bowl into something I can use to knock some sense into you." Tauren had been like a father to Lyon since he was ten years old. They always teased back and forth. It was natural. Tauren remembered his own daughter. He hoped she was doing well. He had, of course, visited her on occasion, and she had visited him. Not recently, though; perhaps he would go see her soon.

"I eagerly await that day, oh mighty dragon." Lyon laughed. Balian watched the exchange in wonder. He had known the two of them for twenty years, and it always amazed him how close they were. He wondered again how humans could possibly believe that dragons were dangerous. Then he remembered the large black dragon that had terrorized the land not that long ago. He was the exception, and Balian wished fervently that he could have found him and disposed of him. Maybe if he had, people would not be so terrified of dragons.

"You two sure do like to tease each other," said Balian, smiling. "It is almost like you really are a father and son." He only had Elia, but he still teased her occasionally, and she teased him. It was always in good fun and deepened the bond between them.

"We may as well be," said Tauren. "We are as close as family. Maybe even closer. The bond we share is stronger than any friendship I have ever had."

"This is totally true. I have no secrets from Tauren," said Lyon. "I really can't keep anything from him. We are in this together, so secrets would not be a good idea."

Finishing his tea, he arose from the table and looked straight at Lyon. "See that you be careful as well. If anyone finds out about your gifts, they will deem you a sympathizer, and you know what that means."

Lyon definitely did. It had been drilled into him by both Balian and Tauren since he was a boy. If they deemed you a 'sympathizer,' you were thrown in prison at best and disposed of at worst. "Do not worry, Your Majesty, I have the mighty Tauren to protect me," he said with a snarky grin. "Not to mention my own capable sword arm. We will be fine."

"Very well then, since I have seen that you were warned, I must get back." He smiled at his friends. "The job of a king is quite demanding on my time."

"Don't I know it," said Tauren, remembering his own time as king of the dragons and all the tedious duties he had to perform. Together, he and Lyon escorted Balian out and watched him ride off. Once he was out of sight, Tauren looked down at his best friend. "I need some food. I think I will go catch a couple of deer for dinner." He unfurled his wings and, with a quick leap, was airborne, kicking up dirt onto Lyon. A couple of deer? Lyon was always amazed at how much Tauren ate sometimes.

"Don't be gone long; remember, I need my meat cooked." Lyon shouted after him, then turned to look at the sky in the direction of his former home. He wondered how his mother and father were doing. One day he would return home with Tauren, and they would both be welcomed. He saw a single cloud in the sky. It was fluffy and white and kind of looked like a bowl with a spoon... A bowl with a spoon! That cloud looked exactly like the one from his vision. That meant today was the day. He recalled the vision and what it meant.

Seventeen Years Ago

Young Lyon was sitting on the bed in the room Tauren had made for him. It had only been three years since his father sent him away. He hoped that someday he could return home. He loved Tauren. King Balian and Queen Alaria were very nice and visited often. Lyon just missed home.

Today was a very special day in Eldoria, although he did not know it then; it was the birthday of his sister. As he sat on the bed thinking of home, a vision came to him: a bright red dragon flying directly toward him. On its back was a young woman. Her hair was flowing behind her as they flew. She had blonde hair and wore a bow and a longsword. Lyon wished Tauren was there; he had no idea what this pair was after. Then he recognized Aurelia. What was she doing here? Who was the girl?

Aurelia dropped to the ground, backwinging mightily before touching down gracefully. The woman slid down off of her neck and turned to Lyon. "I am Jaylen, Princess of Eldoria. This is my friend Aurelia. I apologize if we scared you. She is not dangerous, I assure you."

Present Day

Well, thought Lyon, *no mistaking that cloud*.

Today was the day he would finally meet his sister. The cloud was in the exact position it was supposed to be so they would be visible soon, so he decided to wait.

He needed something for them to eat and drink after their long trip, so he made a small fire and put a couple of rabbits on a spit. But what would he feed Aurelia? He recalled she was partial to wild boar, so he found a pig in the kitchen that he was going to turn into hams and a couple of roasts. He dragged it out with him.

Lyon wasn't sure what was going on. Why was his sister coming to him now? How was Aurelia involved? So many questions that would hopefully be answered when they arrived. He also wondered if Jaylen knew who Aurelia really was. He knew he couldn't say anything, just in case.

Well, he had food and drink for them. All he could do now was wait. He settled on a nearby rock and watched the direction from which Aurelia would come.

Chapter 11:

Meeting For the First Time

J aylen awoke to a breeze on her face. The sky was clear with a singular cloud. Jaylen thought it looked like a bowl with a spoon. She looked up and realized she was still flying with Aurelia. She remembered what had happened with her father and sighed. Why did he blow up like that? That wasn't like him. Sure, he got angry at times, but he had *never* yelled like that.

"Ah. You're awake," said Aurelia, the rhythmic beating of her wings a calming sound amidst the relative silence. Jaylen imagined that was why she fell asleep in the first place.

"Where are we?" asked Jaylen, looking around but not recognizing anything. Not that she had ever seen her kingdom from the air, but she knew her kingdom well enough to know this wasn't it.

Aurelia turned her attention back to the sky ahead. "Just on the outskirts of Corina. Our friend Elia's kingdom," she said. Jaylen looked down and saw a castle, and just on the other side of the castle walls was a village. She wondered why they were passing the castle.

"Why are we not going to the castle?" asked Jaylen.

Aurelia smiled. "I know of someone who can help more than the king and queen. Someone I met years ago," she said.

They continued flying for a while until they reached what looked like a mountain cliff. In front of the mountain stood a man. The man was of medium height with a muscular build. He had a longsword belted to his waist and long, dark hair waving in the wind. Aurelia descended. As she neared the ground, she back-winged powerfully. She landed with absolute grace, and Jaylen slid off Aurelia's neck, landing gracefully herself.

She turned to the man. "I am Jaylen, Princess of Eldoria. This is my friend Aurelia. I apologize if we scared you. She is not dangerous, I assure you."

"Oh, I know that," said Lyon, smiling at her. Who was this man? He seemed really at ease considering a dragon had just landed in front of him. Most people would be terrified and draw their swords or run away. How did Aurelia know him? So many questions raced through Jaylen's mind.

"Greetings, Aurelia. It's been a long time," said Lyon.

"Too long, my friend," said Aurelia.

Jaylen looked from Lyon back to Aurelia. "Okay, first of all, how do you know Aurelia? Secondly, you can speak dragon tongue?" said Jaylen, absolutely confused.

Lyon laughed. "I have known Aurelia since I was ten. She was a very young dragon. Not as young as you think, as dragons live a very long time, but in her kingdom, she was very young."

"Was? Are you calling me old?" said Aurelia.

"Definitely not, oh great Aurelia," said Lyon teasingly. Jaylen was still utterly confused. She couldn't understand why Aurelia would bring them here. To this strange man. This whole couple of days had been strange. First, her father acted completely out of character, threatened Aurelia, and even tried to arrest her. Now she had flown god knows how far on a dragon to a strange man, who apparently was good friends with a dragon since he was ten years old. This all made no sense.

"No offense, Aurelia, but why are we here?" asked Jaylen.

Aurelia smiled. "Why don't you introduce yourself?" she said to Lyon.

"Oh, I apologize, dear lady," said Lyon, bowing. "How rude of me. I am Lyon... Prince of Eldoria."

"What?" Jaylen couldn't believe it. She stumbled backwards and sat down on a nearby rock. How could this be? When she turned sixteen and her father had deemed her old enough, he had told her about her brother Lyon. He had said that he loved Lyon, but for his own safety, he had to send him away. He never told her more, but he seemed sad, so she didn't press him.

It was starting to make sense, though. If Lyon had indeed met Aurelia, then contact with a dragon could be the reason. Maybe Lyon was like Elia since their family was descended from dragoneers as well. Maybe Lyon had the same power. It didn't matter anymore. She had a brother now. She was still with family. Together, they would prove dragons were not a danger to humans. She couldn't help herself; she was just so happy she ran the short distance to Lyon and wrapped her arms around him.

"I have a brother!" she said, almost crying. "I didn't think I'd ever be able to meet you."

Lyon smiled. As they were talking, Jaylen heard the familiar thunder of wings and looked up. To her surprise, she saw a gorgeous, bright blue dragon. Its translucent blue wings were shining even brighter in the sunlight. He was massive, easily twice the size of Aurelia. He wheeled toward them and descended.

Jaylen turned to Lyon. "Who is that?" she asked.

"Oh, him?" said Lyon, laughing. "Don't worry about him."

"Don't worry about me?" said Tauren, settling to the ground as gracefully as Aurelia had done just a few moments before. "Oh, come now Lyon. I thought we were friends."

Jaylen just started laughing. She couldn't help it. His tone and his manner were so much like Aurelia when she was teasing Jaylen. "Yup, He's a dragon," she said, settling down a bit. She turned to Aurelia. "Are all dragons as snarky as you two?"

"Snarky? Me?" Aurelia laughed. "Well, maybe a little."

"Hello, Aurelia," Tauren said, a strange note in his voice that Jaylen couldn't quite identify.

"Hello… Tauren," said Aurelia, almost hesitating to say his name. Jaylen resigned to ask Aurelia about that later.

They all walked the short distance to the cave. Lyon opened the door of the cave and invited Jaylen and Aurelia inside. Once inside, Jaylen admired how beautiful this home was. A kitchen, two bedrooms; one she assumed was Lyon's room, as it didn't look big enough for a dragon. The other was decorated like a girl slept there, and two giant rooms in the back of the absolutely huge main hall.

"Why are there two huge rooms back there? Is there another dragon I should know about? Also, do you have a lady friend?" asked Jaylen.

"Nope, these are the only two dragons around," said Lyon, pointing to Aurelia and Tauren. "That other room you saw is for you." Jaylen looked confused so Lyon explained. "You see, I've known you were coming for a while. I had Tauren build these rooms years ago in preparation for your arrival," said Lyon.

"So you knew I'd be coming?" asked Jaylen.

"I had a vision one night about seventeen years ago," explained Lyon. "I saw the exact scene of you and Aurelia landing in the field and you introducing yourself. I didn't think much of it then, but recently Balian told me about you when they got back from visiting Eldoria. I can't believe I didn't put it together sooner. You introduced yourself as Princess of Eldoria, so you would have to be my sister. In my defense, I was only thirteen at the time."

"Wait, how does a dragon build a room?" Jaylen asked.

Lyon laughed. "Well, he has huge claws and the clay here is easily manipulated and his fire hardened it and make it stable."

Jaylen just stared at him. She was amazed by all of this. Her brother had a vision ability. Where did it come from? "I am seventeen," said Jaylen. "Do you remember the day you had the vision?"

"I believe it was the fifth day of the tenth month," said Lyon. Jaylen's eyes went wide in surprise. "Why?"

"You had a vision of me coming here today... on the day I was born," Jaylen explained. "How were you able to get this vision?"

Lyon smiled and looked up at Tauren. "My bond with this one. We've been bonded for so long that my abilities just kept growing stronger and stronger. My abilities are more heightened senses: hearing, strength, sight. But I do have the healing ability and I have visions, but that's really the only magic I have," he said.

Jaylen enjoyed listening to him. His voice was so smooth, and he was very well-spoken for a man isolated from the world. She was interested in this bond her brother spoke of. She felt like asking about it, but they had only just met, so she decided to wait.

Jaylen watched Aurelia and Tauren. They seemed to be good friends. She loved that Aurelia had a friend of her own kind. She needed that. Even though Jaylen tried to be the best friend she could, she knew Aurelia missed the contact with her own kind. There was a sort of hesitation between them that Jaylen couldn't figure out. They were talking like they'd known each other forever, but she had the feeling they were holding something back.

"I think it's time we had some dinner," said Tauren.

"Yes, of course. You two must be hungry after your long trip." Lyon pulled open the pantry and retrieved a bag of deer meat. He led Aurelia and Jaylen to the fire pit outside behind the cave. "Aurelia, would you like to do the honors?" asked Lyon.

Aurelia smiled and lit the wood on fire with her flames. Jaylen was always amazed by the sheer heat her best friend could produce with a single breath. They cooked the meat and ate. Jaylen and Lyon shared stories of their own lives while Aurelia and Tauren listened. By the time the sun went down, Jaylen was yawning, so Lyon figured they should get some sleep. Aurelia and Tauren curled up in their rooms, Lyon in his bedroom, and Jaylen went to the bedroom that Lyon had apparently prepared just for her.

Dreams took Jaylen, Aurelia, and Tauren, but Lyon couldn't sleep. He stayed awake, wondering how Aurelia ended up with his sister. That was tomorrow's task. To figure out how his sister met Aurelia.

Chapter 12:

A King in Distress

King Thadis awoke the next morning, praying that the previous evening was nothing but a nightmare. He dressed and went down to the dining hall, hoping he would see Jaylen there waiting for him. No such luck. Instead, Jamore was talking to Lyren. "Your Majesty," Jamore said as he saw Thadis enter, "I regret to report that Jaylen slipped by us. The last report I got was that she flew away on a large red dragon."

"Thank you, Jamore," the king said in a weak voice. "Please leave us and take the men out to train. Until further notice, you are the commander of the elite guard." None of this made any sense. Why would Jaylen have continued to visit the dragon? What was a dragon doing in his kingdom to begin with? They all knew how much humans distrusted them, and some even hated them. Why couldn't they just stay in their own kingdom?

"Yes, sir!" Jamore replied and turned away. "I will only assume the role until Jaylen returns."

Jamore was a very loyal man, and Thadis knew he considered Jaylen his friend. However, he had to take a firm stance on this or lose the kingdom. "As of this moment, Jamore, Jaylen is to be considered a fugitive and an enemy of Eldoria," said Thadis, barely able to say the words. "She is not to be harmed if it can be helped, but she is to be arrested on sight. She is a dragon sympathizer and needs help."

"But sir…" began Jamore.

"Those are my orders, Commander," said Thadis, using the new title for emphasis. "If you cannot carry them out, I will appoint someone else." He stopped, looking at Jamore, so he understood that someone else may not be sympathetic to Jaylen and she may get hurt in the struggle.

"Very well, Your Majesty." Jamore got the message. He had to be the one to find Jaylen and bring her in peacefully. "I will do as you command." With that, he turned and left the room.

As soon as he was out of the room, Thadis slumped into a chair at the table. "What have I done, Lyren?" He began to sob uncontrollably. "I… lost her," he continued between sobs.

Lyren ran to her husband and comforted him. "You must keep it together, my love," she said in her sweetest voice. "We will bring her home somehow. Lyon too. We will get both of our children back. You will see." She continued to hug him and waited until he cried himself out.

The sun was at its highest now. Lyren had sent Thadis back to their room. She told him to rest, and she would handle whatever duties he had today. Lyren surveyed the man in front of her closely. "Please deliver this letter to Queen Alaria as quickly as possible," she told him. "Do not open it. If you break the royal seal or fail to deliver the letter, you will be guilty of treason." She didn't have to say more. Everyone in the kingdom knew that the only crime in Eldoria besides murder that was punishable by death was treason.

"Understood, milady," the man responded and left on his errand. The letter contained instructions to make sure Jaylen remained safe. When the time was right, she was to inform Jaylen of what her mother had done so that Jaylen would understand that she could return to Eldoria one day.

Now that she had sent that off, she needed to inspect the guardsmen. Usually, it was Thadis who did that, but in rare times when he had been sick, she had done it, so she knew she could handle it. The men sometimes tried to press her, but she had the backing of Jamore and the other leaders. Plus, she wasn't exactly a meek woman.

She arrived at the training grounds where the men had lined up for inspection. Her job was to make sure their armor and weapons were in top condition, and they observed all military protocols. "Attention!" she called out, and the men snapped to attention. They knew if they disobeyed her, King Thadis would have their heads.

Lyren walked the line, inspecting everyone until she got to a young man on the end of the fourth battalion. He looked not ready for battle, but kind of ready to take a nap. He slouched. She hated that, so she stood in front of him and said, "What is your name, young man?" she asked.

"I am Pawlna," he replied.

"Pawlna, you are in no shape to fight. So perhaps you should spend the day polishing your armor and weapons," she paused to give that a moment to sink in, "as well as everyone else's."

"You don't need to be so hard on him," said another voice from the line. Lyren had heard that voice before. "He is green and doesn't know any better." It was Ricalda, one of the older guards. He spoke with contempt and no respect.

Lyren closed the distance quickly and stood in front of him. "Excuse me, Captain," Lyren put all her authority into that single line. "I will hand out punishment as I see fit," she was staring him down now.

"Why don't you leave this to us? You are not suited to be in charge of everything," the disgust in the man's voice was clearly evident. If she didn't establish her authority now, then she would lose control of the army, and Eldoria would be vulnerable to attack until the king was back on his feet.

"Really..." she said, shifting the tone of her voice to sound threatening, "I would suggest that you alter your tone. I am your queen. I demand an apology and to be shown the proper respect. Or else..." She let the threat hang in the air, hoping he would disobey. This was the opportunity for her to make everyone show her respect.

"Or else what, Your Majesty?" The tone in his voice was so disrespectful that she was amazed he had the audacity to speak that way in front of Jamore. "You are not Jaylen; you have no skills with a blade. Why should we listen to you?" Jamore took a step, but Lyren was faster. With one swift motion, she drew his own sword, and with a strength that surprised everyone, she threw him to the ground, pointing his own sword at his throat.

"Don't ever judge a book by its cover... Lieutenant," she said, emphasizing the fact that she had just demoted him. "I may not flaunt it, but I am a skilled warrior as well." She flipped the sword around, handing it back to him and indicating that he should take his place in line. Then she raised her voice so all could hear her. "We are Eldoria; we have one of the finest armies in the land. Until such time as the king is able to return to his duties, I am in charge. Does anyone have a problem with that?"

"No, Your Majesty!" everyone said in unison. Including Ricalda.

The rest of the inspection went easily enough. After which, she headed to the throne room. For the rest of the day, she was in a whirlwind of duties, from signing papers to sentencing criminals and everything in between.

After all was done, she went to bed. Tomorrow was another day, and she knew she had to be on her game.

Chapter 13:

A Truth Revealed

Lyon and Tauren had both woken up early the next morning. The sun was rising, peeking over the mountain, casting an orange glow over the landscape. Lyon was collecting wood for the fire while Tauren went hunting for breakfast.

He had just picked up the last piece of firewood when Tauren came back with a wild boar.

"And how long did it take for you to catch that?" asked Lyon, smiling.

Boars were always hard for Tauren to catch. They were always so sneaky and fast. They could get into a lot of places that he couldn't because of his size.

"Too long. The little bugger kept running from me. Pissed me off, so I fried it," said Tauren, showing Lyon the already cooked meat.

Lyon stared at the boar and then looked at Tauren. "Wow. Okay. Remind me not to make you angry," he said, laughing.

Just then, Lyon saw Jaylen come out of the cave. She was working on tying her blonde hair up into a ponytail. She had a crimson red tunic on and simple black pants. She was thankful her mom had packed clothes for her.

"Good morning, Jaylen," said Lyon with a smile.

"Good morning, Lyon," said Jaylen, smiling back.

Soon after Jaylen, Aurelia came out of the cave. The morning sunrise reflected off her scales, giving them an orange hue. She was a very beautiful dragon.

They all sat around the fire while Lyon prepared the food. Since it had already been cooked, it was much easier to cut. He cut three pieces for Jaylen, three pieces for himself, and then set the rest in between Tauren and Aurelia.

"Have at it," said Lyon.

Both dragons ate with no hesitation. Lyon was always amazed by the appetite of a dragon. Tauren could eat a whole deer and still be hungry. Granted, he had curbed his appetite during the time he spent with Lyon, but he still had a pretty big appetite.

They finished breakfast, and Lyon decided to take Jaylen to the castle to see Elia. They began the long trek into the kingdom on foot, as they didn't have horses.

The sun had risen now. The bright light was warm on Jaylen's and Lyon's faces as they walked. Just before they got to the castle walls, Lyon stopped.

"What is it?" Jaylen asked.

"Elia doesn't know about Tauren. She thinks I'm a man her father rescued when I was a child. We have to be careful what we say around her," said Lyon.

"But she knows Aurelia. She may ask about her," Jaylen said.

"Then I'll just pretend to be oblivious," said Lyon with a laugh.

When they finally made it through the castle gates, they noticed Elia sitting on the stairs that led to the entrance of the castle.

"Elia!" Jaylen called.

She saw Elia look at her and smiled. Elia jumped off the stairs and ran straight for her. She nearly knocked her over with the force of her hug.

"Jaylen! I'm so happy to see you," said Elia, happy to finally see her best friend again.

Noticing Lyon, she said "Hello, Lyon. where did you find my best friend?"

"She just sort of dropped in on me," said Lyon, laughing.

"Well, I am glad she did," said Elia, then turned to Jaylen and whispered, "How's Aurelia?"

"She's great," Jaylen whispered back.

Lyon just stood there, acting oblivious. He, of course, heard everything, but he had to make it seem like he didn't. He knew Elia would eventually find out about him, but it had to be the right time. And now it was not. Ever since Elia was little, she had been attached to Lyon like a big brother. Lyon didn't mind. He loved Elia and would always take her on hikes and fishing trips and even camping once in a while. He had kept her from meeting Tauren. He didn't know how she would react.

"Come. Let's go say hi to my mother and father," said Elia, already making a run for the castle.

Jaylen and Lyon laughed and then followed Elia into the castle. King Balian and Queen Alaria were preparing dinner. Elia hugged her mother and father and then told them that Jaylen was there.

"Jaylen dear. Welcome. It's been too long," said Queen Alaria, giving Jaylen a hug.

"Thank you, Your Majesty," said Jaylen, showing the respect a queen deserves.

"Any friend of Elia's may call me Alaria," said the queen.

Jaylen smiled. "Very well, Alaria," she said.

Elia insisted on giving Jaylen a tour of the castle. Lyon told her to go. He'd stay behind and help with dinner. Elia showed Jaylen all her favorite parts of the castle, ending with her room. It was a beautiful room. Gray stone walls, a wooden arch door, a wooden canopy bed, tons of beautiful paintings, and, of course, a desk. Jaylen assumed all the paintings were Elia's own creation, judging by the paint and paintbrush on her desk.

They spent some time in Elia's room, just talking until Lyon knocked. "Come in," said Elia.

"Sorry to interrupt, but Jaylen, we need to head back to my place," Lyon said. He seemed a bit worried, like something was wrong.

"Why? What's wrong?" asked Jaylen, fearing something might have happened to Aurelia or Tauren.

"There's been an accident. Just come with me," said Lyon.

Jaylen was definitely worried now. Her heart was beating ten times faster than normal. What if Aurelia was hurt? What if Tauren was hurt? What if they both were hurt? All these questions were flowing through Jaylen's head.

"I'll come too. Maybe I can help," said Elia, getting up to help them.

"I'm sorry, Elia, but you must stay here. I can't explain right now, but trust me, it's for your own good," said Lyon, his eyes shining with urgency.

Lyon and Jaylen ran through the halls and out the castle gates. Lyon had two horses in the stables that he had bought prior to Jaylen's arrival. They climbed into the saddles and rode down the path back to the cave.

Lyon and Jaylen made it back to the cave and rushed inside, Elia following close behind but far enough to stay out of sight. Jaylen could hear Aurelia in the back room. She was calming someone down.

When they reached the back wall, they saw Tauren, bleeding. Jaylen asked Aurelia what happened, and she said, "We were flying around the kingdom and an arrow came out of nowhere and pierced his wing."

She sounded concerned, almost sad. But more than a friend would feel for another friend. There was definitely something between these two. But what? Jaylen needed to figure it out.

"It's all right, dear friend. I will help you," said Lyon.

He gripped the arrow and pulled it out in one swift motion, Tauren roaring. Louder than Aurelia had ever roared. Jaylen got flashbacks of the morning she met Aurelia. Lyon brought his hand up to Tauren's wing and blue sparks of magic flowed from the palm of his hand, healing the wound.

"Thank you, my friend," said Tauren.

Elia jumped out from behind the rock she was hiding behind, startling her friends. "You're a dragoneer?" she yelled.

Chapter 14:

Time to Train

Aurelia, Lyon, and Tauren looked at Elia, then at Jaylen. The instant recognition of that title that crossed Jaylen's face made Lyon cringe. He had hoped to have more time before he had to start Jaylen's training.

Jaylen turned to look at her brother. She could feel the rage bubbling to the surface. Why was she always kept in the dark about everything? Did everyone in her life have secrets? She pushed the rage down. Losing her temper now could alienate everyone, and she needed them. She clenched her jaw and chose her words carefully. "So, that is why you were sent away," she said. She could hear the frustration in her voice. She had to get it under control. "Mother and Father lied to me. They knew you were a dragoneer. They told me that the dragoneers were gone."

She had assumed Lyon and Tauren met after he had been sent here, and that he was sent away for some other reason. Now she knew the truth. How had he become a dragoneer? Did their parents know? Too many questions ran through her head. One thing was for sure. She would find out.

Lyon had to come up with an explanation fast, or Jaylen may stay mad at their parents. That would be bad if Eldoria ever needed them. "No, Jaylen. They assumed I got my powers the same way Elia did, through our family line. They did send me away to protect the kingdom and me. They never knew about my bond with Tauren." It was at least half true. "It happened by accident. Normally, one must train a lot with a dragon and form a true friendship in order to form the bond. I am sure you feel it starting to form with Aurelia?"

"Yes, I actually do," Jaylen replied, getting control of herself now.

Lyon continued, "There is a rare occurrence that has been a part of the interactions between dragons and humans for generations. I call it the destiny bond." He smiled at his clever name. The dragons never had a name for it. He thought it should have a special name, though. "It only occurs in young children who happen to touch a dragon who is very much like them."

"But dragons don't come to Eldoria unless necessary," Jaylen said, curious about how Lyon could have met Tauren back then.

"Actually, I stumbled on Tauren while walking in the woods one day," Lyon lied. He didn't want Jaylen to know their mother was a dragoneer, because it might make her resent their mother. "I was scared, of course, but Tauren reassured me with a bow of his head. I slowly walked closer and reached out to touch his tail."

Tauren continued for him, "You see, I have always loved humans. I was hoping I could help build a little trust. When he touched my tail, I instantly realized my mistake." He looked at Lyon, feeling sorry for putting it that way. "Not that meeting you was a mistake, dear friend. I just mean, allowing you to touch me was a mistake. Anyway, I knew the bond had formed. I flew off, but it was too late."

"Shortly after I got home, I started showing signs of the healing power, and Father had me sent away. He knew Balian and Alaria were sympathetic to dragons and those who show signs of power," Lyon smiled. "The rest is history. Tauren heard of my exile and came down to raise and protect me."

"Okay, so now what?" Jaylen had more questions, but for some reason she felt some urgency to form the bond with Aurelia. "How do I form the bond with Aurelia?"

"You train *hard*!" said all three in unison.

Elia had stood there in stunned silence, listening to the whole exchange. She finally found her voice. "Wait a minute. You two are siblings?" She was completely lost.

Jaylen went to her friend's side. "I am sorry, Elia. I just found out myself the other day." She paused, seeing that Elia was still confused. "We will let you visit anytime and stay whenever you like so you can learn everything."

"Well said, Jaylen," Lyon interjected. He smiled at Elia. "I am sorry I could not tell you sooner, Elia. Your parents and I thought it was best to keep you out of it as long as possible."

"Fine, I guess I can forgive you both." Elia relented. "Just don't keep secrets from me anymore."

Lyon and Jaylen nodded. Lyon, however, was a little hesitant. There was one more secret he was keeping from Elia. However, he swore an oath to never tell her about that. Jaylen turned to Lyon and

Tauren. "So, how do I train to bond with this oversized lizard, anyway?" she asked, nodding in Aurelia's direction. She could feel the stare without even looking.

"Not by insulting me, that's for sure," Aurelia grinned. "How many lizards do you know that shine as brightly as me?"

They couldn't hold it in any longer. Tauren and Lyon burst out laughing. "Well, you are definitely friends, no doubt," said Tauren. "So tomorrow really starts the training." They spent the rest of the day laughing, eating, and talking. The dancing flames of the torches lit the walls of the cave.

The next morning, Jaylen woke before dawn. Standing up, she opened her bag and grabbed her training gear. It consisted of a dark blue short-sleeve tunic and black pants. Over the tunic, she put on her leather cuirass. Next, she belted on her longsword, and she was ready. She left the other leather pieces in her bag. She would need them in actual battle, but not for training.

She entered the great hall and saw everyone was already up. "Good morning, everyone," she said, a small pang of nervousness for the upcoming training giving her a moment's pause. "I am ready to learn. I will do my absolute best."

Tauren smiled. "Do you think your best is going to be good enough, young one?"

"It usually is," replied Jaylen, with more confidence than she actually felt.

"Oh, stop teasing her, Tauren," said Lyon. "Jaylen, relax, this is not formal training." He smiled. "We do things a bit differently. Since forming the bond takes real emotion, we try to keep training informal to allow you to find how to connect with the dragon you have chosen."

"That's right," said Tauren, assuming his "teacher" voice, as Lyon called it. "Think of us more like guides. We are here to help you find the connection that already exists between the two of you."

Aurelia moved closer to Jaylen. "Then shall we begin?" she said and started walking toward the door.

Jaylen followed along with Elia, Lyon, and Tauren. Elia turned to Jaylen and asked, "How hard is it to learn the dragon language?"

Jaylen laughed. "It takes lots of practice. I will help you learn in between my training, I promise." She hugged her friend. "For now, I will try to remember to translate for you." She proceeded to tell her everything that had been said that morning in order to catch her up.

Once out in the open field, Jaylen looked at Lyon. "So, the bond forms when we get closer, right?" She was genuinely curious about how they could train to be closer friends.

"Partially." Lyon looked thoughtful. "It is not just about being close, but almost being of one mind. You have to connect on a level deeper than friendship. You have to become one." He hoped he was doing the description justice. It was hard to explain.

"You need to think alike. Learning about each other is one way. To that end, we are going to ask you questions about yourself. You must be honest for this to work. Next, we will have you doing everything together. For the next few days, you two will never be apart." Tauren had helped a few young people form the bond with dragons when he was king.

Lyon began by asking Jaylen, "What is your favorite food?"

"I really like strawberry pie," Jaylen responded without hesitation.

"I love deer," said Aurelia. "Especially the ones on the south plains in Eldoria. That is how I was shot. I was hunting that day, and got distracted."

"I never knew that." Jaylen turned to her friend. "I am sorry humans have become so mean and cold-hearted toward dragons."

"Good," said Tauren. "Learning about each other will help you start to think like each other." He knew these two were meant for each other from the moment he had heard of Jaylen's birth all those years ago. "So, what is your favorite activity?"

"That is easy," said Aurelia, speaking first this time. "I love to fly low over the treetops. I like the feel of the leaves tickling my belly." She smiled at the thought. "Sorry, I know it sounds childish."

"Not at all. One of my favorite things to do is run through fields of flowers." Jaylen could almost feel the flowers on her feet and legs.

Lyon and Tauren nodded at each other. These two were so much alike they would probably have the strongest bond of all. They continued the questions, letting both answer before moving on. The sun slowly began its descent, and evening was almost upon them.

Chapter 15:

A Darkness Looms

The sun had just set behind the mountains of Milvania. King Adrin sat on his golden throne and surveyed the two people in front of him with disgust. A small fire lit the throne room with an eerie light. Solving disputes was so tedious. He knew he must in order to maintain order, but he hated this duty most of all. He waved his hand for the first man to speak.

"Your Majesty, I caught this man grazing his herd on my land," said a tall man with a fine tunic and a jeweled belt. The man bowed as he spoke.

"Your Majesty, I did not know it was his land, sir. No markers existed to show me," said a smaller man with torn clothes. He also bowed, but much less gracefully.

King Adrin could clearly see who was in the right here. A man of such obvious status must have all the land he could to raise the best cattle for the kingdom. "The offending farmer shall give half his herd to the landowner as compensation," he declared.

"But, My Lord, I have only ten. If I give him five, I will not be able to sell enough meat to survive the winter," said the second man. He was barely scraping by in this hideous kingdom as it was.

"Ha, you should have thought about that before invading this man's property." Adrin was in no mood for this man's whining. "Now go before I make you give him everything and toss you in the dungeon."

Both men bowed and left the room. Adrin left too, as this was his last audience for the day. He walked through the dimly lit corridors and looked out over his large castle. It was an old stone castle, vines covering most of it. The walls around the castle were lined with sharp stakes to prevent anyone from climbing over them. There were guards stationed at every entrance and exit point. No one was allowed in unless King Adrin gave his permission.

Milvania was the most northern of the kingdoms. The weather was bad for much of the year, and the ground was rocky, making crops difficult to grow. There was some good land in the southern part of the kingdom, but not nearly as much as the other two kingdoms. Adrin was bitter about that and vowed one day he would take their land and rule over it all.

On this starry, moonlit night, King Adrin decided to bring the news he had just received from his spy to his friend. Then again, calling him a friend was a stretch, more like a business partner. Adrin found his horse at the stables and rode out towards the caves on the northern side of the Howling Mountains. The wind coming over the mountains gave the sound of dark creatures howling in the night. He found the one he was looking for and entered.

Inside, the cave was dull and moist. It was as if this cave was meant to house something sinister. He found the latch for the secret door. It made an awful creak, then a thud as it swung open, revealing a larger cave. Adrin went inside. He walked down a path, through a tunnel. The tunnel opened into a massive cave opening, and sitting on a stone slab was a massive black dragon. Its scales were as black as the night sky, and its claws looked like they could cut through the strongest of metals. Its bright green eyes glowed with the shining of the moonlight seeping in through the cracks in the cave ceiling.

"Who dares to awaken a sleeping dragon?" said the dragon.

"Now, Elvaroth. Is that any way to greet a friend?" said King Adrin, obviously unbothered by the dragon's threat.

"Oh, hello Adrin," said Elvaroth. The way he spoke would send shivers down anyone's spine. It was low, almost to the point of not being able to hear it. Even King Adrin was scared at first, though he'd never admit it.

Elvaroth turned toward Adrin. He wouldn't call him a friend; after all, he was a human. Such a lowly creature with a limited lifespan and barely any intelligence. Humans needed more structure. Dragons should rule over the land and all its inhabitants. If Elvaroth had anything to say about it, they would, very soon.

"We have news," said King Adrin. "Eldoria has lost their princess. King Thadis is beside himself with grief. We may finally get revenge on that ghastly kingdom." He felt so much hate whenever he thought about Eldoria. They were the worst of the three kingdoms. They were all so smug. That was the first kingdom Adrin wanted to capture. Soon they would be ripe for the picking.

"And how did you come upon this information?" asked Elvaroth, suspicion evident in his voice.

"I have a spy among them," said King Adrin. He was clearly proud of this fact. "Someone close to the royal family, actually."

Elvaroth smiled. He had been waiting for this day. He despised Eldoria for they were the ones who had assisted the other dragons in destroying the 'true believers'. After Elvaroth had led them to destroy villages to frame the dragon kingdom and build mistrust. It worked eventually, but not before that blasted spell.

During the battle, the other dragons had needed a way to find those who believed in ruling over humans. So the three elders and the King of Dragons had woven into their blasted spell that gave the dragoneers their power, a way to distinguish those who went against them.

Any dragon who 'betrayed' the oath to protect humans and to live in harmony with them would lose all pigmentation in their scales, leaving them black, like Elvaroth, or gray. So, they found and killed any dragon that didn't agree with them. It was all crazy. Why side with humans over their own kind?

"Oh, how I've waited for this day," said Elvaroth, his deep voice sounding malicious. "Do we have a battle plan?" He hoped that his alliance with this foul human could soon come to an end, and he could subjugate him with the rest of humanity.

"Not yet, old friend. We must wait until their guard is down. Only then will we be able to successfully take their kingdom," said King Adrin. He knew he had the larger army and was fully confident in their abilities, but King Thadis was crafty. True, he had lost his best warrior when his daughter had left, but he could still cause a lot of damage. He may even be able to hold them long enough to get help from his buddy King Balian. No, he must wait till the king's grief made him unable to command the army.

Elvaroth laughed. It was an evil, bone-chilling laugh. King Adrin laughed along with him, but it was a raspy, awkward laugh. "Stop. Just stop. You sound like a wild boar dying of heat stroke," said Elvaroth.

King Adrin looked stunned. "Well, no wonder the kingdoms banned your kind. You're exceptionally rude," he said.

Elvaroth laughed once more. "My friend, you have not seen rude yet," he said, turning around to go back to sleep.

"Foul beast," King Adrin whispered under his breath. He couldn't wait till he could rid himself of this beast. He needed the power Elvaroth had given him, but soon he wouldn't need him anymore. He turned to leave and felt fire singe his coat. He turned back to Elvaroth. "Damn you! You could've killed me!"

"Could've. But I didn't. Believe me, if I wanted you dead, you would be," said Elvaroth.

King Adrin wiped his coat and stormed out of the cave. He would not lose his chance at defeating Eldoria because a dragon wanted to be stubborn. If Elvaroth doesn't agree to his plan, then he would find a dragon that would. He just had to figure out what his plan would be.

***

Jaylen once again fell to the ground after the millionth try to mount a dragon gracefully. The first time she did it, Aurelia lifted her. She had to figure out how to do it herself. But every time she tried, she ended up falling. Lyon and Tauren were having a laugh at her expense.

Jaylen glared at them. "You know, sometimes I think you're making me do this just for a laugh," she said, dusting herself off. She was a little sore but otherwise ready to keep going until she succeeded.

"Who, us? We would never do such a thing," said Tauren, pretending to be innocent. He was immensely enjoying being back in a teacher's role. That had been his favorite part of being king: training the new recruits.

"Why do I find that hard to believe?" asked Jaylen, smiling. She may have been frustrated with constantly failing to mount Aurelia; however, she enjoyed the jokes and the happy moments. She felt at home with Lyon and her dragon friends. Of course, she felt at home in Eldoria, but she felt like this was a second home for her. Her brother, her best friend, and Tauren, whom she liked to call her mentor. He sometimes felt like a second father to her.

Thinking about fathers made her miss hers. And her mother. She wished she could go back, but she couldn't. Not until she could prove that dragons aren't the evil creatures everyone believes them to be.

"How are they?" Lyon asked. At Jaylen's confused face, he clarified, "Mother and Father, I mean."

"Oh, well, last time I saw them, Father screamed at me and mother cried, so..." she said, with sadness in her voice.

Lyon felt bad for Jaylen. "I'm sorry, Jaylen. Father didn't react like that when I left," he said.

"Well, you weren't hiding a dragon in a cave for weeks," she said. She didn't really regret her decision, since it meant finding friendship with Aurelia. She did, however, regret that she couldn't make her father understand. Also, what was up with mother? She had looked so tense, like she was concentrating.

"Very true," Lyon laughed a little, trying to lighten the mood. He couldn't imagine Father blowing up like that. He was always so calm and disciplined. He wondered if mother had influenced him. But why? Why had she sent Jaylen to him?

Aurelia looked sad. She couldn't help but feel like it was her fault. "I am sorry, dear one," she said, feeling regret at having shown up and made Jaylen be at odds with her family. Aurelia missed her own family. She cast a sideways glance at Tauren, then quickly remembered herself.

Jaylen turned to Aurelia. "What are you apologizing for?" she asked.

"If I had not gone into a cave so close to the kingdom, you wouldn't have found me, and you'd still be living happily with your parents," said Aurelia, almost crying.

"Exactly. I never would've found you, and you'd probably be dead. Do not apologize, my friend. It's not your fault. It's my own fault for trying to hide you," said Jaylen.

This made Lyon's blood boil. "You shouldn't have had to hide her in the first place! The stories and misconceptions people have about dragons are ridiculous!" he yelled. This whole situation was ridiculous. A few bad dragons had tried to take over, and all of a sudden *all* dragons were evil. It just wasn't fair.

Jaylen, Aurelia, and Elia stared at him in disbelief. They had never heard him yell like that. Even Tauren was stunned. "Calm down, Lyon. You must remain calm," said Tauren. He knew his friend well. He knew that Lyon hated that dragons and humans didn't get along anymore. He also knew that Lyon missed his family greatly, and that he wanted to see his parents again.

Lyon closed his eyes and breathed deeply. He apologized for losing control like he did. The things people say about dragons just made his heart hurt. He decided to take a flight with Tauren and told Jaylen and Aurelia to take a break.

Jaylen felt sorry for her brother. He had lived in exile from his birthright for so long. He didn't have the chance to grow up and be a part of the kingdom he had been born into. That was it. She vowed she would end both their exile one day and return home to Eldoria.

Chapter 16:

Worsening Depression Advice from a Friend

King Thadis sat upon his throne, hearing petitions from the villagers. Although he was listening, he couldn't stop thinking about Jaylen. Why had she gone so far? He didn't understand why he got so angry. He wanted to apologize to her, but he had no idea where she had gone.

Even if Thadis knew where Jaylen was, he was almost certain that he was the last person she'd want to see. What had gone wrong that day? Sure, he had been mad at her for hiding the dragon. He was scared because of the stories. However, he had been prepared to hear her side of it.

He had not been prepared for the rage he felt. The moment Jaylen entered the room, he just got so angry. What is worse, he tried to have her arrested. What he did was unforgivable. If he ever found Jaylen, she would probably hate him.

"Thadis?" said Lyren, breaking him out of his thoughts.

"Hm? Oh, sorry, my dear. I was distracted," said Thadis, trying to keep his voice even. He felt like he had no emotion left. It was as if someone had ripped all the emotion out of his soul. He knew Lyren was worried about him. He hadn't eaten in days, and he barely came out of his room. The only time he came out was to do these petition hearings, and only because he knew he had to.

Lyren pointed to a man kneeling before them. "Please, sir, tell us why you are here," she said. Thadis turned his attention to the man.

"Your Majesty, my cattle have been dying because I live too close to the mountains. The wolves keep attacking them," said the man. He felt nervous. He knew the king was having a hard time since his daughter left. No one knew why she had left, only that there had been a big commotion, and the guards were trying to arrest her. One man said he saw her fly off on a dragon, but that was ridiculous; there hadn't been a dragon seen in their kingdom in over twenty years.

Thadis sighed. "Jamore, find this man a home in the village with plenty of land for his cattle," he said. Why couldn't he master his own voice? It would not be good for his people to think he was in distress, or they might panic.

Thadis looked away, out the window. He was wondering where Jaylen was and if she was okay. He knew she could protect herself, but that dragon of hers might harm her. He would never forgive himself if it hurt her. He was the one who refused to tell Jaylen about her ancestors. So if that dragon hurt her, it would be his fault.

Lyren looked at Thadis and sighed. "All right, everyone, I am truly sorry, but the rest of you will have to wait until another day. The king needs rest; he has not been feeling well. I promise you will all be heard. Come back later, and I will help you," said Lyren. She could almost see right through him. She knew he was thinking about Jaylen, and that would distract him from the petitioners.

Jamore escorted the villagers out of the castle while Lyren took Thadis back to their room. He immediately slipped off his boots and crawled into bed. Lyren sighed again; why had she pushed him so hard that day? Maybe she had gone too far. Maybe Jaylen was gone for good and she had doomed their kingdom. *No!* She had to stop; she did what was needed. Jaylen would forgive her father. She would not let one outburst destroy a lifetime of kindness and love.

"Thadis. You have to stop this nonsense. Your people need you. Jaylen will come back. We have to trust and move on while we wait," she said, trying to comfort him.

"I can't, Lyren. It's my fault she left. If I had just told her about her ancestors, then we wouldn't be in this situation," said Thadis, almost crying.

Lyren's heart was breaking. He blamed himself. She knew he was upset, but that was to be expected. His only daughter had run away. That would make any father upset. But she didn't know he blamed himself. That made her feel worse that she had caused this pain. True, she had initially courted him because she needed to be in a position of power to help the new dragoneers, but she had genuinely fallen in love with him. He was one of the sweetest and kindest men she knew. He was a fair and just king, and Eldoria thrived under his leadership. She went and sat on the bed next to Thadis.

"Oh, my love. You can't blame yourself. It's not your fault. She left because she's a determined girl. Not because you didn't tell her. Please don't blame yourself," said Lyren. "Even if we had told her, she probably would have done the same thing. You know that she never really believed the stories about dragons."

Thadis began to cry. He was trying not to blame himself, but he couldn't help it. He had never gotten that angry at anyone, let alone his own daughter. He felt Jaylen hated him now. He believed he would never see her again. "She hates me, Lyren. She'll probably never want to see me again," he said.

"Nonsense, my love." Lyren pulled her husband into a hug. "You know how much Jaylen loves you. One outburst isn't going to make her hate you." She comforted him and let him cry. She had tried many times in the past to talk him out of these emotional outbursts, but it never worked. She found it best to let him cry, scream, or laugh it out. In this case, she let him cry it out.

Once Lyren felt he had cried enough, she let him go but held his arms. "We will see our daughter again, my dear. We just have to believe. If we believe we will, then we will," she said.

Thadis nodded. Lyren didn't believe that nod, but she let him go, anyway. No sense in making the situation worse. She left him to sleep, knowing he was tired, and left the room. As she stepped out, she saw Degore, the king's servant.

"Excuse me, milady," Degore said politely. "Is the king all right? Does he need attending?" He was hopeful. He had heard what was said, and he knew it was finally time. He would report this to Adrin and be rewarded. He smiled at the queen. It wouldn't do for him to reveal himself now.

Lyren smiled back. "No, Degore, he just needs his rest." She squeezed his shoulder gently. "Take the rest of the day off." With that, she turned and headed for the stables. Lyren took her horse and rode to a clearing not very far from the castle. The same clearing where she had introduced Lyon to her best friend, and had started the chain of events that led to her losing him.

"Feora! Please descend from your place in the clouds! I need your help!" Lyren yelled. This clearing had been chosen because it was directly under the dragon's city in the clouds. She knew the watch dragon would hear her and recognize the password. He would alert Feora to her presence. All she had to do was wait. Sure enough, after a short time, she could see the form of a big golden dragon descending from the clouds. She was beautiful. Her wings sparkled in the sunlight as they moved up and down. She touched down gracefully right in front of Lyren.

"My dear Feora. It's been so long," said Lyren.

"Too long, dear one," replied Feora. They tried to keep their visits short and infrequent because anyone could come by and see them. "You sound distressed; is everything all right?"

Lyren had known Feora since a child. She had accidentally bonded with her at a very young age. She was only ten when she first touched Feora and bonded with her. The same age Lyon had been when he bonded with Tauren. "The king is overwhelmed with sadness and guilt over our daughter's departure," said Lyren. "I don't know what to do. I feel responsible."

"I am sorry, dear friend," said Feora. She felt so bad for Lyren having to go through this. She wished fervently that there was something she could say or do to ease her friend's pain. Through their bond, she felt it, too, and she was almost ready to cry. "But you know I

133

can't do anything. We agreed this is how it had to be. Nothing short of an outburst would have made Jaylen leave."

"But, Feora..." began Lyren.

"But nothing, my friend; don't second guess yourself. You need to keep the kingdom stable. Aurelia will protect Jaylen. You know who she is. You know how important she is to us," said Feora firmly. "If we can handle the uncertainty of having her in the human kingdoms, you can handle Thadis."

Lyren stared at her friend. She had never heard that particular note in Feora's voice before... Was it fear? Considering who Aurelia was, that would make sense. She straightened up and collected her thoughts. "You are correct, dear Feora. I can handle it. Aurelia will protect Jaylen," she said, then in an attempt to comfort her friend she added, "and, Jaylen will protect Aurelia."

"Aurelia could not have a better protector," said Feora, smiling, her mood getting a bit better. "Now I must return. You know I can't stay long or we risk discovery."

"Farewell, dear friend. May the wind always lift you up, and your flight be easy," she said, reciting the traditional dragon farewell.

Feora took off into the sky, and Lyren mounted her horse and rode back to the castle. She was feeling a little better. She knew things were going to work out. Once she got back to the castle, she went straight back to her room. She was careful not to wake Thadis. Obviously, she couldn't tell him about Feora, Aurelia, or even Lyon and Tauren. She loved him, but she also knew it was going to take extreme measures to change his opinion and that of the kingdoms regarding dragons. She closed her eyes to rest for a while herself.

At that moment, Degore was riding out of the castle swiftly, on his way back to Milvania to reveal what he knows to his real king. Adrin would be so pleased. All the years of playing good servant boy would pay off and he would be a lord. It wasn't as though Degore disliked Thadis or Lyren; they were good people. He would just rather be a lord than a servant. He fervently hoped that Jaylen survived the upcoming battle. He wanted her to be his wife. Of course, him betraying her father might make her not want him, but then again, now that she hated her father, at least according to what he had heard, she might understand.

Chapter 17:

Training; Phase Two

Jaylen awoke early the next morning, ready to begin the next phase of her training. Now that she had somewhat mastered mounting, after much laughter from Lyon and Tauren, it was time to start flying. Granted, she had flown on Aurelia before, but it was a quick flight. Nothing fancy. They were going to be learning fast, semi-long, twisting flights. Of course, with Tauren and Lyon right by their side. She picked a simple black tunic and simple black pants for her outfit today. As she entered the main hall for breakfast, she could hear Aurelia talking.

"I wish we didn't have to wait. I want to go home," she heard Aurelia say.

"I know, dear one." That was definitely Tauren's voice. Not wanting to interrupt them, Jaylen stood on the other side of the wall and listened. She felt bad for eavesdropping, but she was almost certain there was something that Aurelia and Tauren weren't telling her, and she was determined to find out what that was. "However, right now, Jaylen needs you as you needed her back in the cave."

"I know. But I need to see them again," Aurelia said. There was a note of sadness in her voice that Jaylen had never heard before.

Them? Who's them? Jaylen thought.

"Patience, my dear Aurelia. You will see them again. You just have to wait a little longer," said Tauren. Jaylen could hear a hint of something in his voice. Compassion? She couldn't tell. Now she was sure there was something they weren't telling her. She moved and accidentally kicked a rock. She mentally cursed herself.

"Jaylen? Is that you?" asked Aurelia, a hint of panic in her voice.

Jaylen emerged from behind the wall. "Yeah. Sorry. I kicked a rock by accident. Am I interrupting something?" she asked, acting as though she hadn't heard anything. She desperately wanted to ask them about who they were, but she knew if they were keeping it secret, then they must not want to talk about it.

"No. We were just talking. Actually, I'm rather hungry. Why don't we go see if Lyon has breakfast ready yet?" said Aurelia, not waiting for a response.

Jaylen found that strange but followed her out, anyway. Lyon was standing in front of a fire. Two stone slabs had an already cooked deer on each. He was cooking two rabbits; one for him and one for Jaylen.

"Good morning, Lyon," said Jaylen, waving to her brother.

Lyon turned and smiled at his sister. "Good morning, Jaylen," he said, then motioned to a seat at the table.

They ate their breakfast and shared some laughs. Aurelia had seemed to loosen up, and Jaylen was relieved. She didn't like when Aurelia was tense. They all made their way to the clearing behind the mountain. Lyon brought out two thick sets of reins. "Now normally we don't wear these reins. Most of the time, it isn't necessary," said Tauren. "However, when doing longer flights which may require tighter maneuvers, we have to."

"Dragons are not horses," said Lyon, taking over as he often did during these lessons. He and Tauren seemed to be in perfect sync. Was that part of the bond Lyon had mentioned? When would they be ready for that? "We don't control them with these. They are for us to hang onto so we don't fall off. Saddles are not required, of course, because of the soft scales on the neck between the third and fourth ridge."

"We tie these around our outer two horns. Since there are no nerves there, we can make a groove in each to hold the ropes so they don't just pull off." Again, it was a seamless transition from Lyon back to Tauren. Lyon fit the reins to Tauren and Aurelia, then signaled for Jaylen to mount.

Jaylen mounted Aurelia as she had learned yesterday. That had been an interesting day. Lyon and Tauren didn't stop teasing them until they had got it right. Lyon leaped to Tauren's neck with the grace of many years of practice. "Okay, so there are three things to remember when riding a dragon. First, the only time you can ride is if they agree. Don't ever assume. Second, they can't see when you are ready, so you will need to let them know by telling them. It has been a tradition in the dragoneers that the ready signal is saying 'take wing.' Third, let the dragon do the flying. It is their wings that lift us up, so don't try to guide them unless you need them to do a specific maneuver to dodge a bird they didn't see or in battle to dodge an attack."

"I understand," said Jaylen, listening eagerly. She really wanted to learn everything about how to fly with Aurelia. The flight here was fun, but she knew there was more to flying.

Lyon took the lead. He settled himself on Tauren's neck, then raised his arm. "Tauren, take wing." He spoke loudly, so he knew Tauren could hear. With that, Tauren lifted off the ground and soared into the air.

"I guess it is our turn, my friend," Jaylen said as she patted the side of Aurelia's neck. Settling herself and gripping the reins. "Aurelia, take wing." She called out. Immediately, the ground fell away from them as Aurelia leaped into the air and, with a powerful downstroke of her wings, left the ground far behind.

They flew faster and faster. Jaylen's hair was billowing behind her. She could see the ground below them speeding past as if they were in a carriage powered by supercharged horses. It was mind-blowing. The rush of air and emotions was amazing. She felt scared and jubilant all at once. It was incredible.

"Now hold on tight!" Lyon yelled over the wind.

Jaylen gripped the reins even tighter as Lyon called out, "Dive!" Before she could breathe, Jaylen found herself still on her dragon, falling headfirst toward the ground. Just as she thought Aurelia had made a terrible mistake and they would crash, Aurelia spread her wings again and corrected her downward plunge with ease and grace.

"Are you all right back there?" asked Aurelia.

"Yes!" said Jaylen, barely able to catch her breath.

"Carry!" Lyon yelled, and Aurelia flew up again, but at a much slower pace, almost like a floating kite. "Good, now dodge right." Aurelia rolled to the right and swept her wings back, giving them a burst of speed in the proper direction.

"Very good Aurelia," said Tauren. It sounded to Jaylen like he was proud.

"All right now, land," Lyon said. He didn't have to yell anymore, as they weren't going as fast. Both Aurelia and Tauren descended. Their powerful wings blew dust as they slowed their descent just in time to touch down with grace.

Jaylen slowly slid off of Aurelia and held her stomach. "I think I'm going to be sick," she said, trying to master the impulse.

Lyon laughed. "The feeling will pass. It happened to me the first time I flew like that with Tauren," he said.

She sat down on a nearby rock to let her nausea pass. Flying like that was one of the most magical experiences she had ever had. The sharp turns and quick descents, however, made her queasy. She knew she would get used to it in time, however, right now wasn't that time.

She looked out over the horizon and realized they weren't back at the camp. They were actually on top of a very high mountain. The sky was a blue backdrop to the most beautiful sight she had ever seen. The rest of the mountains around them were small in comparison to the one they were perched atop. She could see waterfalls, trees, birds flying, and even rocky cliffs reflecting the sunlight. It nearly took her breath away. "Where are we?" she asked, in complete awe.

"At the peak of Hope Mountain. Tauren and I come up here a lot," Lyon answered, looking out over the horizon as well.

Hope Mountain, Jaylen thought. What a perfect name. She looked in the direction of Eldoria, and she could see the tops of the castle turrets. Eldoria was beautiful during the early morning hours. She often found herself remembering the sight of waking up in her room in the castle. The golden light from the sun reflecting off her mirror on her vanity. The warmth of the sun washing over her. She longed to feel that again. Eventually, she would. She looked toward Aurelia, still confused at how her father could've gotten so angry. It wasn't like him at all. She promised herself she was going to ask him directly when she returned home.

Aurelia came and sat next to her. "I used to wonder what it was like down here. I'd sit on the edge of the city just looking down, wondering when I'd be able to see the human world I'd heard my father talk about. He said it was one of the most beautiful places he'd ever visited. Now that I've seen it… I know that's the truth," she said.

"My mother told me stories of how she used to play in the fields of Crelonna Village as a young girl. She told me there are beautiful flowers, tall thick trees and tons of beautiful animals out there. I've, unfortunately, never been there, but I hope someday I get to go," said Jaylen.

Aurelia smiled at hearing Jaylen speak so highly of her mother. She too loved Lyren. She knew Jaylen loved her more, of course, but somehow Aurelia felt like a part of Jaylen's family. She was sad that King Thadis had not accepted her. One day, that would change.

"What about your father? Did he tell you stories of when he was a boy?" asked Aurelia.

She knew that King Thadis was a touchy subject right now, but she felt that if Jaylen could talk about him, it would make her feel better. Aurelia didn't blame him for his feelings. Unfortunately, the dragons had decided to stay apart until humans could once again accept them. Dragon culture abhorred violence: they preferred to solve their problems through discussion and understanding. Of course, when the need arose, they would fight for what was right, but it was always a last resort.

"He told me stories of how he would go out hunting with my grandfather. But every time he raised the bow, he couldn't release the arrow. He would see the innocence in the animals' eyes and he wouldn't have the heart to kill it. He always told me that he understood the need for us to eat the deer and rabbits and other animals, however, he personally didn't have the heart for killing. I can see why. I have the same feeling. I can't kill an innocent creature. Which is why I can't understand why those men wanted to kill you. You're innocent," said Jaylen, looking up at Aurelia, tears in her eyes.

"Some people just have dark thoughts, dear friend. We can't stop them; we just have to learn to ignore them," said Aurelia. "I hope you don't think less of me because I kill innocent creatures for food."

"Of course not, dear friend. As I said, I eat meat too. I just can't kill unless I have to. It is my choice. I would never judge another for theirs." Jaylen knew she sounded contradictory. She could not understand it herself.

"But you killed those men effortlessly," Aurelia said, trying to understand her friend. "You even bragged about it a bit to me at the cave."

"That is different. I said I could not kill an innocent creature. Those men were not innocent. I gave them the opportunity to come peacefully." She replied, even though they had not been innocent, the truth was Jaylen was not completely unaffected by having to kill them.

They sat in silence, just watching the birds fly past and the deer graze below the mountain. Their world was beautiful. And someday, if it's Jaylen's last act, she would bring humans and dragons together again to live in harmony in this beautiful world. After a brief time in silence, Aurelia could see there was something on Jaylen's mind, so she asked, "What is troubling you, Jaylen?"

"Well, it is about how you ended up in that cave." Jaylen was curious. She knew that Aurelia had been shot, but why was she in their kingdom, anyway. She must have known there may be hunters about.

Aurelia smiled. "I was not paying attention. You see, dragons come to Eldoria and even Corina to hunt or just to enjoy the sights." She said, "I thought I was being careful, but I flew too close to the inner

142

part of the kingdom and next thing I know, I have a thick arrow sticking out of my knee. I had no time to prepare, so I skimmed the tree line till I found a cave."

Jaylen listened intently. She knew Aurelia was embarrassed because she got hit.

Aurelia couldn't tell her everything because it hurt. However, she had to satisfy Jaylen's curiosity. "I landed as close as I could and walked the rest of the way. I was hoping to be alone so I could heal. Then you came along, and I knew you were the one to help me reunite the kingdoms and dragons."

Chapter 18:

Secrets Revealed

Jaylen, Lyon, Aurelia, and Tauren were enjoying the view from Hope Mountain. The breeze gently moved the grass and trees. The bright sunshine made everything feel warm and bright. They didn't want to leave, but they had to return to the cave that had become their home. As they descended to land in front of the hidden door, Elia was waiting with a fruit basket. Aurelia and Tauren touched down gracefully. Lyon jumped off Tauren with ease; Jaylen, on the other hand, was not as graceful. She still had a little trouble with her dismount. She slid off Aurelia easily enough, but stumbled a little. Tauren and Lyon laughed, but at Jaylen's and Aurelia's glares, she quickly covered it with a cough.

Jaylen turned to Elia, greeting her with a hug. "Hello, Elia," she said.

"Hi, Jaylen. My mother made a fruit basket for you and Lyon," said Elia, handing Jaylen the fruit basket. She smiled brightly, and Jaylen knew it was just an excuse to come visit.

"Tell her we said thank you," said Lyon, smiling back at her. Jaylen could tell he, too, knew what Elia's true motivation was.

Jaylen took the fruit basket inside, Aurelia and Tauren following close behind her. Elia sat on a rock and looked at the ground. She looked almost confused. Lyon noticed her confused look and sat down next to her. Gently, he grasped her shoulder. "Now, what's a nice girl like you doing with such a puzzled look on her face?" he asked, trying to lighten the mood a little. He could tell she was worried about something;

having known her all her life, he could always pick up on the changes in her mood.

Elia laughed slightly. "Well... I'm just curious. Your bond with Tauren is what gives you your abilities, right? I'm not bonded with a dragon, but we have the same powers. How is that possible?" she asked, looking at Lyon with a pleading look.

He knew this day would come. He was conflicted. He knew the answer, but he had given his word to her parents to never tell her. They wanted to tell her themselves, because they felt it would be better coming from them. They said they would tell her when they thought she was ready. He must honor that promise. "That's something you have to ask your parents. It's not my place to say," said Lyon, then saw the disappointment in Elia's eyes. "I am sure they will tell you when they think you are ready."

Elia sighed. "I was afraid you'd say that. They told me it's because of my family history. An aftereffect of us being descended from the old dragoneers. I know it's not that. If it were, we would all have them." Elia stood up and began pacing. "Lately, every time I ask them, they just tell me I'm not old enough. I'm seventeen! Almost eighteen! I think I'm old enough to know how I have magical powers! They trust me with the affairs of the kingdom, but not the truth about my gifts?"

Lyon could tell she was getting frustrated. He was the same way at that age. He smiled fondly, remembering his teen years, but then frowned, realizing Elia was right. She was old enough. It was time she knew. He had promised not to tell her, but he had not promised not to convince her parents to tell her. "How about we both go back down to the castle? I'll talk to your parents and see if I can convince them to tell you," said Lyon, smiling at Elia.

Elia's smile grew ten times bigger. She could always count on Lyon to help her. She thought of him as more like a brother than just a friend. He had always taken her to cool places around the kingdom, like the time he had shown her the best fishing spot, tucked away at the bottom of a waterfall in a dense area of the forest.

"Let's go then!" said Elia, already running off down the path to get back to the castle.

Lyon laughed and told her to wait. "Okay, but I need to tell Jaylen and the others where we are going." He went inside. He found Jaylen in the kitchen slicing some of the fruit for a pie, most likely. "I'm going down to the castle with Elia. I'll be back before sundown," he said.

"Okay. Have fun," said Jaylen, hugging her brother goodbye, then turning back to her work.

"You sure you don't want me to come too, Lyon?" asked Tauren. Lyon knew he had been listening through their bond and was offering his support.

"It's okay, old friend. I just need to talk to Balian and Alaria." He replied, hoping Tauren would understand that he didn't want Elia to know everything just yet. It was hard keeping this secret from Jaylen, too. He knew if Elia knew, then she would want to tell Jaylen, and it would just make it that much harder for Jaylen and Aurelia to bond.

Lyon left. When he got outside, he smiled at Elia and motioned for her to lead the way. The two of them walked together in silence the whole way. They arrived at the gates, and Elia signaled for the guards to lift the gate. After there was enough room for them to pass, they made their way up the stairs and into the castle.

Elia's home was beautiful. Gray stone walls, tapestries, and pictures adorned every corner, big wooden doors for every room. Approaching the throne room, Lyon could see the three golden thrones, Elia's in the middle and Alaria and Balian's on either side. Going past the throne room, they came to a large wooden door with a guard outside. Elia nodded to the guard, and he opened the door, announcing as he did, "Her Highness, Elia and Lord Lyon to see you, Your Majesties."

"Mother, Father, Lyon's here to see you," said Elia, walking past the guard and into her parents' chambers. There was, of course, a fire in the fireplace. In the center of the room was a table and a well-groomed bearskin rug. At the table, having a mid-afternoon snack and some tea, were King Balian and Queen Alaria.

Lyon bowed, showing the proper decorum in the presence of the royal family was something he always did. "Your Majesties," he said.

"Lyon. How many times are we going to have to tell you? Quit with the bowing. We're family," said Alaria, smiling at him and motioning for him to have a seat and join them.

"Force of habit," said Lyon. "You know how my family is with tradition. Even spending just ten years with them was enough to ingrain those traditions into me." He smiled, though, and moved to the table. Alaria and Balian stood to greet him. Alaria hugged Lyon, and Balian shook his hand, giving his shoulder a squeeze. That was his show of affection. Lyon had observed that Balian was not great at showing his emotions. He was a good and just king. He was friendly and loved to joke and tease, but he was also very stern and gruff when speaking.

"Elia, why don't you wait outside? I need to speak to your parents alone," Lyon said. He winked at her, as if to say, "play along," because she obviously already knew what he was talking to them about.

147

Apparently, she got the hint because she smiled and left the room, closing the door behind her. Once she had left the room, he turned to her parents. "She's getting suspicious. She outright asked me why I have the same powers as her today."

Alaria and Balian exchanged looks, and Balian sighed. "We know. She keeps asking us, but she's not ready," he said with a kind of sad look crossing his face. Lyon suspected it was him who wasn't ready. He was afraid of losing her, as any father would be. On the other hand, he had to know that it was time.

"Actually, I think she is," Lyon said, pleading with the king and queen. "She gets along with Tauren and Aurelia very well. She helps us prepare food for them. She's even learning dragon tongue and is becoming rather fluent in it."

Alaria spoke up. "Balian, my love… He's right. She's not a child anymore. She's almost eighteen. She's been a very integral part of this kingdom since she was sixteen," she said. "I know you are worried about her and what this knowledge could mean for her, but she has to be told."

Balian thought about it. "You are right, as usual, my dear." He admitted reluctantly. Elia had settled a number of disputes; she had helped various villagers during the drought; she even rode off for three days to help find a missing child. She was responsible enough to handle this information. "I would appreciate it if you stay, Lyon. In case she doesn't understand. You know more about this stuff than we do."

Lyon agreed and went to get Elia. She entered the room again and sat next to her parents on their enormous bed. Alaria and Balian looked nervous, but that was to be expected when revealing a big secret like this. "Elia sweetie, we have to tell you something," started Alaria. Lyon could see that she was a little worried herself.

148

Elia nodded for them to continue. This time, Balian spoke. "So… your powers are not because of our family history. They are from something that happened when you were very young," he said.

"What happened?" asked Elia, giving them her full attention.

"Well… we went up to Lyon's house for a visit and some lunch, and you wandered off. You came across Tauren's room, and inside was another dragon. You must have touched her and accidentally bonded with her. We didn't see it happen, but we felt the rush of wind, and Lyon immediately knew what had happened," explained Alaria.

Elia looked at Lyon. "I thought the only dragons you know are Aurelia and Tauren," she said.

Lyon looked at Alaria and Balian as if asking permission to take over. They both nodded. "Well, as you know, Tauren left his home to come down and protect me when I accidentally bonded with him and my parents sent me here," Lyon spoke carefully, so as not to reveal the identity of the dragon she had bonded with. "You were only a toddler when Tauren's friend came for a visit and brought her daughter. When you touched her, you bonded with her. It is rare, but can happen if your personalities match."

Elia looked almost hurt. "Why didn't you tell me I'm bonded with a dragon? Didn't you think that was information I should know?" she said, addressing her parents now.

"We needed you focused here on Corina. She also had duties in her kingdom, so it wasn't the right time. She, of course, knew she was bonded to you, but being older, it was easy for her to see that you couldn't stay together at that time," said Alaria.

Elia wiped away the stray tear. She hugged Lyon and both of her parents. "Thank you for telling me. I only wish I could meet the dragon I'm bonded to," she said.

"She still has duties at home that take her time," said Lyon. "One day soon, though, I am sure you will meet."

"I will look forward to that day," Elia said. She really had grown up, Lyon thought. She was handling this with the maturity of a young woman, not a teenage girl.

"What do you say you walk me home and spend the evening with us?" Lyon knew that suggestion would make Elia excited.

"Well, I suppose I should make sure you get home all right," Elia smiled. "Tauren wouldn't forgive me if I let you get lost out there."

"Lost?" Lyon acted hurt at the suggestion. "My dear princess, I know every inch of this kingdom just as well as you."

"Flying over it is not the same as walking through every inch on foot," Elia said, bringing up an old argument about how you need to actually walk the land to truly know it.

Elia hugged her parents one last time before she and Lyon went back to his home. When they arrived, Aurelia and Tauren were each tearing into a deer. Jaylen saw Elia shudder and smiled. That had been her reaction the first time she saw Aurelia eating. Even though she knew Aurelia would never hurt her, she was still very intimidating. Watching her tear through a deer was kind of scary.

Noticing Elia's wide eyes, Lyon laughed. "That's not even the scariest. I've watched him *hunt* a deer. That's scary," he said.

Elia just nodded and kept walking. Jaylen was sitting by a fire cooking up three rabbits. She looked up at the sound of footsteps and smiled. "Welcome back, you two. I got an extra rabbit here. Somehow, I knew you'd be coming back with him," said Jaylen.

"I couldn't let him get lost coming back on his own," said Elia, winking at her friend. "Not sure how much of an appetite I have, though, after watching the two giant puppy dogs with fangs tear into their meal."

Jaylen and Lyon laughed at her description of their friends, and Aurelia and Tauren just shook their heads and ripped off another piece of deer flesh. They all ate together and talked about the beauty of their world. The weight of their current situation seemed to fall away when they were together. They ended up talking and laughing at Aurelia and Tauren's antics in the fields. They all knew that it would take a lot to convince the rest of the kingdoms to accept dragons again, but that was tomorrow's problem.

Elia looked at Jaylen. "By the way, I have to tell you something."

"What is it?" Jaylen asked, giving her friend her full attention.

"I am also bonded to a dragon," Elia began, then she recounted everything her parents and Lyon had told her.

"That is great, Elia!" said Jaylen. "I hope you get to meet your dragon friend soon."

"Me too," said Elia. They just sat in silence for a while, just enjoying each other's company.

Chapter 19:

The Bonding of Two Queens

It was a beautiful sunny morning in Eldoria. The sunlight was reflecting off Lyren's golden throne as she sat signing trade agreements with the neighboring kingdoms. This was usually the king's job, but as he was still feeling guilty about Jaylen leaving, Lyren thought it best if she took over some of his duties for a while. As she finished signing the last agreement, Jamore walked in, followed by a woman and her daughter.

"Your Majesty, these villagers wish to have an audience with you," he said.

"Step forward," she said in her normal business tone.

The woman stepped forward with her daughter hiding behind her. The woman was smiling as she walked toward the queen.

"Hello, Your Majesty. My name is Druelle, and this is my daughter, Giana," said the woman, bowing to Lyren.

Lyren stood and walked toward the two. She lowered herself into a crouch and smiled at Giana.

"Hello, Giana. I am Queen Lyren. I run the kingdom," she said, smiling at Giana, extending her hand for Giana to take.

Giana slowly came out from behind her mother and grabbed Lyren's hand. She slowly smiled and then hugged Lyren. Lyren enjoyed the hug. A child's love is the best. They love unconditionally. She remembered when Jaylen was younger; she would run into the throne room and hug both her and Thadis. This little girl reminded her so much of Jaylen.

When Giana let her go, she stood up and hugged Druelle, as well. After hugs were exchanged, Lyren went back to her throne.

"Your Majesty, I brought Giana here because she has been talking about meeting you forever. Every night before she sleeps, she asks when she will get to meet you. When I heard you'd be signing trade agreements today, I thought it was a good time to try to see you," explained Druelle.

"Of course, and I am so thrilled to have met a beautiful girl like Giana. You and your daughter are welcome back anytime," said Lyren, with a smile.

Giana and Druelle left, and Lyren sat on her throne looking out the window. That interaction had reminded her of the first time she met Feora in the dragon city. Her mother had taken her when she was young. She was just about ten years old.

40 years ago

It was a warm summer evening, and ten-year-old Lyren was playing in the fields of Crelonna Village where she lived. Her mother came out of the house and called for her.

"Lyren honey! I want to show you something!" she called.

Lyren's father had gone away on a mining expedition as he was a miner for Eldoria. So it was just Lyren, Kya; her mother, and Ginger; their cattle dog.

"Okay, coming, Mother!" Lyren called back. She ran back to the house and slipped her shoes on. She often played in the fields with her shoes off because she liked the feeling of the grass on her feet.

Her mother crouched to her level. "We're going somewhere special today. But you must promise not to tell anyone what you see. Do you promise, Lyren?" asked Kya.

"I promise, Mother. But why must I not tell anyone?" she asked.

"Because a lot of people would not understand, or they'd be afraid," answered her mother.

Lyren smiled, and Kya took her out to the stables. They both mounted Kya's horse and rode out to a clearing in the forest. It was beautiful. Tall trees lining the edge of the clearing, flowers peeking out of the bushes, and Eldoria's famous flower, aurelias—bright red flowers—were scattered all around the grass.

"Castiya! Please descend from your place in the clouds!" called Kya.

Within seconds, they heard the thunderous beating of dragon wings. Lyren was scared and held onto her mother. "It's all right, Lyren. She won't hurt you," said Kya.

With as much grace as any dragon, Castiya landed in front of them. She smiled at Kya and then noticed Lyren.

"Hello, Kya. It's been a while. And who's this young lady?" asked Castiya.

"This is my daughter, Lyren. I'd like to take her up to meet everyone else," she said.

Castiya's smile faded. She looked almost sad. Like there was something wrong. "What's wrong, Castiya?" asked Kya.

She watched as a tear fell from Castiya's eye. "Our king is dying. His son, Tauren, is preparing to take the throne," she said.

Kya gasped. She had known the king for many years. He had introduced her to Castiya. She wanted to see him now more than ever.

"Well, now I must see him. Please, Castiya, allow me to say goodbye," pleaded Kya.

Castiya agreed and bent forward so Kya and Lyren could climb on.

"Mother, I'm scared," said Lyren.

"It's okay, sweetheart. Castiya is a friend. She won't let anything happen to us. I promise," said Kya.

Lyren leaned closer and whispered to her mother, "She talks funny."

Kya laughed. "Sweetie, that's because you can't understand her yet."

Lyren hesitated, but climbed on. Kya held onto her and gave Castiya the signal to take off. With a downstroke of her wings, they were airborne. Lyren began to laugh, and Kya smiled at her daughter. Within moments, they were breaking through the barrier surrounding the dragon city. They touched down right outside the castle, and Lyren could see dragons everywhere.

"Mother, they're so pretty," said Lyren.

"They are, aren't they," said Kya.

Castiya instructed them to follow her, and she led them to a private chamber where a few human doctors were gathered around the king, and Tauren was seated next to him. The human doctors specialized in dragon medicine so they could help treat the sick. They were permitted to live in the dragon city and go down for herbs as long as they didn't speak of dragons.

"Your Majesty, Kya and her daughter are here to see you," said Castiya.

"Let them through," ordered the king in a raspy voice.

He was definitely sick. Kya could hear it in his voice.

"Hello, Your Highness," said Kya, bowing.

King Finnead had been king of the Dragon Kingdom for over a hundred years. He himself was approaching three hundred years old. The kingdom knew he'd be dying soon; they just didn't expect it so fast. But he had lived long enough to give his blessing for Tauren to become king.

"Hello, dear one. It has been far too long," said Finnead.

Lyren came closer and looked at Finnead. He began to speak, but Lyren didn't understand him, so Kya translated for her.

"He said 'Hello, beautiful girl'," said Kya.

Lyren laughed and waved, "Hi, Mr. Dragon, sir," she waved.

She understood the laughter of all the dragons. Soon, a bright gold dragon entered the room and observed Lyren with much curiosity. She walked toward Lyren, and Lyren walked toward the dragon. She didn't know why, but she felt drawn to this dragon. When Lyren reached this dragon, she held out her hand and touched the dragon's nose.

"No!" Kya yelled, but it was too late.

A gust of wind flew through the room, and Lyren's hand glowed a bright gold color.

"Oh, Lyren. I was afraid this might happen," said Kya.

"Well, young ones, it seems you are now bonded," said the king.

Lyren slowly turned to look at him. "I understand you now," she said.

"It's because of the bond. You can hear all of us," said Castiya.

Lyren looked amazed. She turned back toward the dragon and smiled. "What's your name?" she asked.

"I am Feora. I am forever your friend, Lyren," said Feora.

Lyren hugged Feora and thanked her mother for bringing them here. She made a new friend that day. One she'd have for years to come...

Present Day

Lyren smiled at the fond memory of her best friend. She hoped Jaylen had that friendship with Aurelia. She already knew Lyon had it with Tauren. One day, Lyren would be able to tell Jaylen about Feora. But she had to wait until Jaylen was ready.

Chapter 20:

Milvania Prepares

As the sun began to set over the mountains of Milvania, Degore rode through the castle gates after the guards gave him the signal, of course. He rode to the stables where he settled his horse in for the night after giving her lots of pets and some food. He may be evil, but he wasn't cruel; he loved animals. Then he made his way through the courtyard and into the castle. Outside of King Adrin's chamber stood two guards, as per usual.

"I have some information the king might be interested in," said Degore.

One of the guards informed the king that Degore had arrived, and the other guard stepped aside after getting the all clear from Adrin. Degore bowed to his king before speaking.

"Your Majesty, I have news on Eldoria. The king is severely unstable. He cannot even perform the simplest of duties. He is overcome with grief," said Degore.

He said the words as if it were the greatest thing he had ever discovered. He would finally get his chance to be in power. To be more than just a servant.

"Well done, Degore. You shall be rewarded for your triumphs. Now go, gather the army in the courtyard. Time for a battle plan," said King Adrin.

While Degore gathered the army, he decided to take his information to Elvaroth. He went to the stables, climbed aboard his horse, and rode off to the Howling Mountains where Elvaroth lived.

He arrived at the entrance to the cave, tied up his horse outside, and walked the rest of the way. He didn't want his horse to become lunch for a dragon. As he pulled on the latch, the door swung open, revealing the same tunnel that led to the same massive cave. And sitting on the same stone slab sat Elvaroth, busy tearing into what Adrin assumed to be a boar. Or what was left of it.

"Don't mean to interrupt your dinner, but I have some news," said the king.

An inhuman crunch followed his words as Elvaroth took another bite. King Adrin cringed and turned away.

"What is this information you have?" said Elvaroth.

"We have a battle plan and are ready to attack Eldoria," said the king.

Elvaroth snapped his head up and dropped his dinner. He slowly smiled. But it was an evil, devilish smile.

"Then let's attack," he said.

"Hold on. I think it's time you met the army you'll be fighting alongside," said King Adrin.

"You want me, a dragon, to meet your army of humans?" said Elvaroth.

Adrin knew why Elvaroth was hesitant. Humans didn't like dragons.

"Yes. They're my men. They will do as I say when I say it, so there's no danger of them hurting you," said the king.

Elvaroth thought for a moment before speaking. "Fine. I will meet your men. But if I am threatened in any way by any of them, I will not hesitate to tear their limbs from their bodies," he said, punctuating his words with a crunch of the boar's bones.

King Adrin left the cave and returned to the castle, putting his horse back in the stables before making his way to the army. Degore did as the king had asked. He gathered the army, and they all stood at attention in the courtyard.

As King Adrin came into view, the commander yelled, "All hail the king!"

The army, in unison, yelled, "All hail the king!"

This was custom whenever the king entered a room.

"I have a job for you men! Eldoria is unstable! Their princess is gone, and their king is beside himself! Now is our chance to take Eldoria!" he spoke loudly so all the men could hear him.

"But sir, we need a battle plan," said the commander.

"And I have one, Kildan. If you will let me continue," said King Adrin, already annoyed with the commander.

He explained the battle plan. They would send a few men in first to scope out the perimeter, see where guards were stationed, what weapons they carried, and where any entry points were. Then they'd send one battalion in, which usually consisted of twelve men, to take out the guards and raise the castle gates. Then they'd send the rest of the army in to take the castle. And then finally, King Adrin would rule Eldoria.

"Before we conclude this meeting, I would like you all to meet someone! A new member of the army! Elvaroth!" King Adrin threw up his hand in a fist, and at lightning speed, Elvaroth appeared from behind the castle and flew over the army, landing behind them.

All the men drew their weapons, but at the sound of Elvaroth's blood-curdling roar, they all dropped them in fear.

"This is my friend! You will address him as Lord Elvaroth and give him the same respect you give me! From this moment on, he is my second-in-command! In battle, what he says goes! Understand?" said Adrin.

All at once, the army stood back at attention and shouted, "Yes, King Adrin, sir!"

Adrin dismissed the army and went to speak to Elvaroth.

"They're afraid of me. I like it," said Elvaroth.

- - -

"Fear gives you power. They'll do anything you say," said Adrin.

Degore stood at the steps, watching Adrin and Elvaroth talk. He wondered how King Adrin could understand Elvaroth. All he heard was weird high-pitched sounds. He would figure it out one day. He also wondered why Elvaroth was black. He heard stories of dragons, and they were supposed to be creatures of color. He wondered why this dragon had no color. But that was a question for another day. Right now, he needed to prepare for battle.

Chapter 21:

The Bond

Jaylen awoke. It was still full night. She crept out of her room and went to the kitchen to get some water. Everyone was still asleep; she had no idea what time it was, but it wasn't time to wake up yet. After she had a drink of water, she decided to go back to bed.

Jaylen lay down but could not go to sleep. She was worried. A man had come yesterday to tell King Balian that her father was not well. He was grief stricken because she had left. It hurt Jaylen to think about it, but she couldn't go back yet. Not until she bonded with Aurelia and learned enough to prove dragons weren't a threat. Despite this worry, sleep eventually took her once again, and she slept the rest of the night.

The next morning, Jaylen woke to the sound of bone crunching. So, the dragons were having breakfast. She got dressed in the brown pants and blue tunic she had worn on the first day she met Aurelia. She buckled on her sword and put on the leather armor to protect her if Lyon had some new crazy training in store.

Walking to the main hall, Jaylen noticed that Elia was there. "Good morning, everyone," she said, smiling.

"Good morning, Jaylen," said Lyon. "Are you ready for the next phase of your training?" He seemed far too eager to put her through more torture.

"Well, if it gets me closer to bonding fully with Aurelia, I am ready." Jaylen kept thinking back to how Lyon and Tauren had described the bond. She hoped it was everything they said it was.

"Have some breakfast first, my friend," said Aurelia, grinning down at Jaylen. Jaylen wondered how much more she knew about the bond. She said she waited her whole life, hoping to bond with a human. She never thought it would be possible. She loved human culture and wanted to experience it through Jaylen.

Jaylen cut some of the ham from last night as well as some of the cheese and bread. She began eating her breakfast. When she had finished, she looked at Tauren. "You've been awfully quiet this morning. Are you okay?"

"I am sorry, Jaylen," he said, sounding quieter than she had ever heard him. "I am afraid. We just received reports of an army massing in Milvania. They are saying there is a black dragon with the army. I don't know what their plan is. It is most likely training. However, it feels like more."

"Oh, no!" shouted Jaylen, rising to her feet. "The reports of my father not doing well. Now King Adrin is assembling his army. He has always wanted to invade Eldoria. That is where he is heading."

Lyon put his hand on her shoulder. "Settle down, sister, we don't know that. The reports are sketchy at best. Tauren is only worried because of the dragon reports. Adrin is not stupid enough to attack Eldoria. Remember, no one knows you are gone. So even if the king is unstable, they will fear you."

It was true her father and mother would never advertise that she had left. Certainly not to Milvania. So King Adrin would assume she was commanding the army if her father was incapable. She settled down and asked, "So, can we start training? I need a distraction."

"Absolutely," Tauren said, mastering his voice. Jaylen suspected she knew this dragon that they were talking about. She was not about to upset him more by asking him right now, though. She could wait. Eventually, they would tell her.

They walked outside into the field. Elia, who had been listening in silence, followed them out. When they got outside, Elia decided to sit on a rock and watch. Aurelia stood beside Jaylen, both ready to listen intently to what their teachers had to say.

"Okay, so now that you have learned as much as you can from one another, it is time for the final step. You need to truly feel what the other is feeling. I suggest a sort of meditation," said Lyon.

"Breathe slowly and think about everything you know about each other. Put yourself in the other's shoes. What is Jaylen feeling right now, Aurelia? What is Aurelia feeling, Jaylen?" Tauren added.

Jaylen and Aurelia both immediately did as they were told. Both closed their eyes. They took slow, deep breaths and tried to recall everything they knew about each other. Aurelia thought of Jaylen growing up in the castle, training with Thadis, and enjoying her time in the woods. Jaylen thought of Aurelia coming down from the dragon city just to spend time in the human world.

They kept going through the info they knew. Both came to the realization simultaneously.

"Jaylen is sad that she had to leave her kingdom like that. She is happy that she met you, Lyon and Tauren, but she misses her home," said Aurelia.

"Exactly," said Jaylen. "Aurelia is also feeling sad that she could not go home, but also happy to be here with friends in the human world." She was starting to feel something, so she continued. "She is also scared because she is missing someone. She is not sure if she will see them again, and that scares her."

Aurelia turned to Jaylen and opened her eyes. Surprise was evident on her face. "How did you know?" she said, her voice reflecting the fear.

"I could feel it in my heart, dear friend." Suddenly, Jaylen felt it wash over her. Lyon was right. She could hear his words. 'Trust me, when the bond forms, you will know it.' The feeling was like nothing she had ever experienced in her seventeen years. It was as if Aurelia was a part of her now. Like she was inside her body. She could feel Aurelia's emotions. She loved her even more now. Aurelia was now a part of her. They were fully connected. There was no distinction; Aurelia was Jaylen and Jaylen was Aurelia. "This feels amazing," she said out loud, not meaning to. "I feel connected with you now on a deeper level than I have ever been connected with anyone."

"That is the eternal bond we now share, dear Jaylen," said Aurelia, almost purring with delight because she felt it, too.

Lyon just stared in amazement. He had no idea they were this close. He expected it would have taken a lot longer. Apparently, their thoughts had merged, and they had connected finally and for life. This was awesome. Now that Jaylen and Aurelia were finally bonded, they could finish the training easily. But first, it was time to test Jaylen with her sword.

"Well, my sister, it appears as though you have finally joined the club. It is a most amazing feeling. However, now we need to test you."

"What do you mean, test me?" asked Jaylen, not understanding what he meant.

"Since you have been here, we have worked on training with both you and Aurelia. Now it is time to see where you are individually in a few areas. First of all, is swordsmanship." Lyon was grinning now. He had been waiting for this chance. Thought Jaylen. Well, he would be sorry "Dear brother, have you not heard of my prowess with a blade? Even this far out, you should know that I am one of the best in Eldoria," Jaylen responded.

"Of course, I have. That is why I wish to test you," Lyon replied, relishing the prospect. Up until now, he had an unfair advantage, so he could not give her a fair test. Now, however, it was time to see just what she could do. He also thought it might be good to take her down a notch or two before her overconfidence got her killed. "Perhaps we should use my training swords. They are metal and have the weight of a true blade, but are blunted, so if you accidentally hit me, you won't kill me."

"As you wish," said Jaylen suspiciously. He seemed overly confident in himself. Did he really think a man raised in isolation with a dragon could know more than her about swordplay?

Lyon went inside for a moment and brought out two longswords. They looked a lot like her own longsword, except that they were blunt. It made sense; if one of them slipped past the other's defenses and didn't stop in time, the worst that would happen was a few bruises rather than deep cuts. Jaylen had used wooden practice swords when she was younger until her father believed she had enough control to graduate to real swords in practice.

Lyon tossed her one of the swords. "Catch!" Jaylen couldn't believe how quickly her arm came up to catch the hilt of the sword. What was happening? Come to think of it, all her senses were heightened. Was this a part of the bond? She had no more time to think; Lyon covered the distance between them with incredible speed, his sword whooshing through the air, swinging at her shoulder. Jaylen instinctively parried the blow. The sword felt light as a feather. What was it made from?

Lyon tried to press his attack, swinging his sword with speed and precision. Jaylen was barely able to keep up. She had never been challenged like this. She learned quickly as a child. Her first teacher had to hand her training over to her father after only a month. He told the king that she was a natural. Thadis had been so proud; his daughter was going to be the best.

Jaylen finally recovered her composure and settled into her rhythm, albeit a much faster rhythm. She began pushing back now with attacks of her own. Lyon seemed to dance out of the way or block her attacks with ease.

She couldn't understand how he could be this good. He had lived alone with Tauren his whole life practically. It is true he had some training with Thadis, but Jaylen knew it could not have been that much. He didn't start her training until she was eight. She assumed it had been the same with Lyon. That meant he only had two years. She had trained with her father for nine years.

Then it hit her just as she blocked another attack. Balian was also an accomplished swordsman. She remembered her father talking about how he had sparred with him a number of times. Now it made sense; Balian had trained Lyon. Well, that didn't make a bit of difference; she would prove her skills to Lyon.

Suddenly, Lyon switched tactics. He began a flurry of attacks, all aimed at different parts of her body. Then, when she was sure he must be tired, she countered his last attack. She put everything into that one swing right at his side, which he had left open after his last attack, but she made the mistake that so many of her opponents had made over the years. She over-committed to the attack, thinking to catch Lyon unaware.

She didn't; in fact, he was ready for it. He quickly sidestepped the attack and brought his own sword up mere inches from her throat. Jaylen gasped; she had never been beaten before. How had he managed it?

Lyon lowered his sword. "That is enough for today," he said. "You are one of the finest swordsmen I have ever seen. Once you master your new abilities, you will be even better."

"New abilities?" Jaylen said, wondering what on earth he was talking about.

"From the bond, my dear," Lyon said. She knew he was feeling as worn out as she was.

"Please, Lyon, tell me about the abilities," Jaylen said, starting to catch her breath. "Where do they come from?"

"They come from me," said Aurelia, speaking up for the first time since the match began. "Dragons knew humans were short-lived and powerless. When they created the bond all those years ago, they added a sort of physical connection."

"They granted the humans who bonded with a dragon the strength and reflexes of the dragon. This helped them to protect each other. The humans were also granted the power to heal, so that if a dragon was ever hurt, the dragoneer could heal it," continued Tauren. "Although the healing is limited. You can only heal wounds and minor injuries. To heal serious wounds would literally drain all the life out of you."

"I understand," said Jaylen. "My mother always said there is a balance in this world. If something is given first, it must be bought, made, or taken from somewhere else. I imagine it would be the same with this healing."

"Exactly!" said Lyon. "Now can we eat? Practicing takes a lot out of you."

And eat they did, content in each other's company and talking about the day's events and what it would mean to have dragons back in this world.

Chapter 22:

Invasion Begins

Denitra was sitting in his usual spot in the tower of Brancreek Village on the northern border of Eldoria. Just on the other side of the clearing was the border of Milvania. Denitra could see the tower and his counterpart on Milvania's side sitting in his tower.

Denitra sighed. It was not cold, but not warm either. He knew it was his duty to keep watch, but honestly, what was there to watch for? Ah well, he better scan the border just to make sure. His eyes stopped just to the west of the tower. In the distance, he saw smoke. Was it a forest fire? No, it was many towers of smoke. Campfires! There had to be an army out there. He couldn't alert the guard on Milvania's side that he had seen it, so he casually walked to the back of the tower and signaled one of the running men.

A small, young man came over to the tower and walked up the stairs. "Yes, sir," he said in a thick accent. "What can I be doin' fur ya?" Like most of the running men, he was fast and had great endurance but was very skinny and dirty from the hard runs from the border to the castle.

"There are campfires in Milvania, lots of them. You must alert the king as fast as your legs can take you," said Denitra. He took a small piece of parchment and melted some wax, then stamped a wax seal on the parchment. "This is my seal, so they will know you speak the truth. Now, go as fast as you can."

The running man took the parchment and wasted no time. He climbed down the tower and then bolted into a run. Within seconds, he had left the village on the road to the castle.

***

Lyren and Thadis were awoken abruptly by Minaren barging into their room. Lyren sat up straight in bed at the intrusion. She saw Minaren and was shocked she hadn't even knocked. "Minaren. What is the meaning of this?" said Lyren, rather frustrated.

"I am sorry, milady. The watchman at Brancreek Village sent word that he saw many fires in Milvania. He believes it is an army, Your Majesties," said Minaren, out of breath from running there from the city gates.

Lyren and Thadis looked at each other. They knew this day would come. King Adrin was just waiting for a chance to conquer. Why now, though? "Milvania?" Lyren asked.

"Milvania," Thadis confirmed. "You know he has been wanting our lands. But why would he attack now?"

Lyren jumped out of bed. "Someone told him Jaylen is gone," she said as she slipped on her robe. "That is the only explanation." She turned to her handmaiden. "Minaren. Gather the other handmaidens. Prepare food for the army. We have to make sure they're at full strength in case there is an attack. We can't be certain until we send out scouts to confirm it. But I fear war may be unavoidable."

"Yes, milady," said Minaren, running off to do as her queen had asked.

Thadis called for Degore but didn't get an answer. He called again, but still nothing. "He must be still asleep. Jemore!" called Thadis.

The door opened to reveal Jemore, who had been posted as morning guard for the king and queen.

"Yes, Your Majesty?" he said.

"Gather your men. Prepare for battle. We are not completely certain but campfires have been seen in Milvania; they are most likely preparing for an attack," said Thadis.

"Right away, sir," Jemore said with a salute. Thadis saluted back, and Jemore left to prepare the army.

Meanwhile, Minaren was briefing the handmaidens on the situation. Some of them looked scared. "Do not be frightened, sisters. Our king and queen will protect us," said Minaren.

"But without Princess Jaylen, we are at a disadvantage," said Aliysa, Jaylen's handmaiden. Her loyalty to the princess was unquestioned, and her belief in her could not be shaken.

"Aliysa, answer me this, who trained the princess?" asked Minaren calmly. She needed to give them all confidence so they could reassure the rest of the castle and the surrounding town.

Aliysa thought for a second before smiling. "The king," she said.

Minaren smiled. "King Thadis is just as proficient with a sword as Princess Jaylen. We will be protected. The army will also protect us. It is their sworn duty," she said.

All the handmaidens nodded and began working on the food. Aliysa was cutting fruit, but she looked sad. Of course, she missed Jaylen. She was so used to helping Jaylen in the mornings. She missed helping her pick out what to wear. She missed brushing her hair as Jaylen talked about her plans for the day. Wherever Jaylen was, Aliysa hoped she was okay.

"Aliysa, I know you miss Jaylen, but you have to have faith that she will be back. If you believe, anything is possible," said Minaren, trying to get Aliysa to cheer up a bit. She needed all of them in high spirits to show the castle that everything would be fine. The whole town took comfort when the servants in the castle were upbeat. Since they were closest to the royal family and knew if the situation was bleak or if there was hope.

Aliysa nodded and hugged Minaren. "You're right, as usual," she said. Minaren was like the oldest sister. She was always helping the other handmaidens with the work around the castle. Whenever one of the girls was having a bad day, she was the one supplying hugs and advice. They all loved her. They knew why the queen made Minaren her handmaiden. It was because they were so much alike. Kind and compassionate with top-notch leadership skills.

While the handmaidens finished up preparing the food, Jemore began gathering his men. He went to the castle gate and ordered the watchman to sound the alarm. Within minutes, the entirety of Eldoria's army was standing at attention in the courtyard. Jemore was impressed at how quickly they all responded. He began to address them, but Lyren stopped him.

"Your Majesty," said Jemore, bowing. "What would you have of us?"

"May I address your men, Captain?" asked the queen, smiling.

"I would be honored, Your Majesty," replied Jemore. Over the past few weeks, Lyren had gained the respect of the entire army. They would listen to whatever she asked of them. "All right, men, Queen Lyren wished to address you, so give her your full attention."

Lyren turned to the army and began her speech. "Good morning, everyone!" she raised her voice so the men in the back could hear her. A good leader knew how to project their voice. All the men bowed to their queen and returned her greeting. "You are Eldoria's finest! We are concerned there may be a battle coming! I won't lie to you. If it is confirmed, there will be lives lost! Milvania is the attacker! Their army is large. If there is a battle, some of you will not come home. If any of you are not ready to lay down your life for Eldoria, now is your time to step forward!"

All the men looked around; Captain Ricalda stepped forward. "Your Majesty, I believe I speak for the entire army when I say we will protect Eldoria with our last dying breath!" he shouted so all the men could hear him. Ricalda had just been promoted back to captain by Lyren herself. After the incident that first day, he had worked harder than ever and even sought her out to apologize for his deplorable behavior. He was now one of her most loyal supporters.

The courtyard erupted in shouts and cheers. Lyren smiled, knowing such an army protected her kingdom. Thadis had always spoken highly of the army and she was now seeing that it was well deserved because they are loyal soldiers of Eldoria who fight because they choose to not because they are forced to like Milvania. That was their advantage.

Lyren left the army to make preparations and headed back to her husband. She knew he would be preparing his own battle gear in the throne room. As she reached the throne room, she saw Thadis pulling his bright plate mail chest piece over his head and tying the straps at his side.

"Ah, my dear Lyren," he said, sounding more like himself. "I have sent word to bring me two hunters who are known for stealth. We will get to the bottom of this, I assure you."

Just then, the door opened, and the guard admitted two men. Both were wearing worn clothes. They wore brown pants and tunic as well as a dark green cloak with a hood about their shoulders. Each had a bow slung on their back and a short sword at their waist. They dropped to one knee before the throne. "You sent for us, Your Majesty," they said in unison.

"Klenan and Kalar. You are hunters, are you not?" asked the king. "Known for your stealth and loyalty to Eldoria?"

They both nodded. "We are also twin brothers, my lord. So we know each other well and can work much more efficiently," said Klenan.

"I have a very special job for you men. I need you to go to Brancreek Village. We have unconfirmed reports of an army attacking our kingdom. I need two men with stealth experience to confirm if there is an army attacking. Are you up for the task?" explained King Thadis.

"It will be done, Your Majesty," said Kelar. "You can count on my brother and me." Without another word, they rose and left on their errand.

"Let's hope they don't find anything," said Thadis as he slumped in his throne. So he was still not fully himself, thought Lyren. That could be dangerous for the kingdom.

**

Klenan and Kalar had been walking for about three hours when they finally reached the outskirts of Brancreek Village. Kalar heard screams and signaled Klenan to stop. They both looked closer and saw

176

smoke from fires; it was too much to be campfires. They heard the clashing of swords and the screams of villagers.

"It's true... Milvania has begun their attack. We must get back to the castle and inform the king and queen," said Kalar.

Klenan drew his sword. "You go. I'm staying to see if I can help these people," he said.

Kalar tried to stop him. "No, Klenan. It's too dangerous," he said, trying to hold his brother back.

"Kalar. We have to do our best to help the people of Eldoria. I'll be fine. They won't even see me." He pointed to the tree line. "Just have the king send in the army. They can help me when they arrive."

Kalar sighed. "Please be careful, brother," he said, feeling sad that he had to leave his brother. He knew, however, that Klenan was right. With his skills, the army would never even know where he was. He knew it was their duty to do their best at protecting the people. So Kalar hugged his brother, and they ran their separate ways. Klenan towards the village and Kalar towards the castle.

When Kalar arrived, he was panting and out of breath. Eylon, who was guarding the gate, saw him and, recognizing him instantly, opened the gate for him. Kalar made it through the gate, where he collapsed from running so far.

"Did you run all the way here from Brancreek Village?" asked Eylon.

Kalar nodded. He couldn't speak because he was so hot and tired. Eylon gave him a minute and then helped him up and into the castle. As they got closer to the door to the throne room, Kalar was able to walk. He thanked Eylon, then sent him back to his post, guarding the castle gates.

The guard at the throne room door opened it for him immediately. Thadis noticed Kalar and stood up from his throne. "Did you find anything?" he asked, hoping he'd say no, but fearing he knew the answer was much worse.

"Yes. Milvania has begun their attack. They're starting with the border villages. We saw them attacking Brancreek Village. My brother stayed behind to help the villagers," said Kalar.

Lyren could tell he was tired. He must've run all the way from the village. "Minaren!" she called.

"Yes, milady?" asked Minaren.

"Get this man some water and something to eat," she said.

She walked to the edge of the throne room and grabbed a chair for Kalar to sit in. He sat down and put his head in his hands. He was worried about his brother.

"Kalar, I am sure your brother will be fine. He is a skilled hunter, is he not?" said Lyren.

"Yes, Your Majesty, he is," replied Kalar, feeling a little better.

"Then I am sure he will use that experience to fight the army," she said. Queen Lyren was as wise as she was beautiful. She had a way of making anyone feel better. That's what Thadis loved about her. Minaren came back with a plate of fruit and cheese and a glass of water and handed it to Kalar, who accepted it with no hesitation.

"Now we need to send help. I am sorry to say this, but for the first time in many years Eldoria is at war," said Thadis, straightening and looking more like the king Lyren remembered. "Jemore!" He called in the strongest voice he had used since Jaylen had run away.

Jemore appeared almost instantly, recognizing the note in his king's voice. "Yes, Your Majesty!" he said, standing at attention and awaiting his orders.

"I need you to gather your men, and have Captain Ricalda gather the rest of the army in the courtyard," ordered Thadis. "You ride out to Brancreek Village. Milvania has invaded our kingdom. I will join you with the rest of the army as soon as we can ride out."

"Yes, sir," said Jemore with a salute to his king. He turned immediately and left to gather the elite guard.

Thadis turned to where his sword was hung on the wall. He hadn't had to use it in years, as Eldoria had been at peace. As he grabbed it off the wall, Lyren sighed. She hated it when Thadis must go off to war. This was not how she had imagined it when she arranged for Jaylen to leave. She thought they would have more time. "You know I hate when you go into battle," she said.

"I know my love, but it's necessary to protect our kingdom," said Thadis. He hugged his wife and thanked Kalar for his service and promised a reward when the battle was won. He left the castle and went to the courtyard to lead his army into battle.

***

Jamore ran straight to his barracks and found his men sitting and talking. "Attention Men." He said, and everyone turned to him and became silent. "Eldoria is under attack from Milvania. We must ride out immediately and hold them off and try to save as many of the villagers in Brancreek as we can until the king and the main army arrive. We are the elite guard. The best Eldoria has to offer. Let's show them why."

"Sir, yes, sir!" All the soldiers shouted in unison, then grabbed their gear to follow him out.

Jamore left and headed to the gate. When he arrived, he found Eylon standing by the gate. "Eylon, Eldoria is under attack. Sound the Alarm and summon the army to defend our kingdom." His voice rang in the air, and townspeople stopped and stared with worried looks on their faces. "Do not worry, good people of Eldoria. Your soldiers will protect you with our last breath."

He heard the horn that signaled the entire kingdom that Eldoria was at war.

***

Klenan stood just inside the tree line. He fired another arrow at a soldier that was about to kill a villager. The soldier dropped dead with Klenan's arrow sticking in his eye. Klenan silently moved a few feet further down so as not to shoot from the same place. He would love to do more, but this was the smartest option. He could keep the enemy off balance till the army arrived.

The entire army stopped. They all heard it, as did Klenan. Kalar had made it. The alarm was sounded. Within the next hour, the elite guard would be there. Klenan knew that they would arrive first ahead of the army. He continued to fire one arrow at a time, keeping the enemy guessing and looking for him instead of hurting more villagers.

***

Jemore met his men at the stables and started to saddle his horse when he felt a hand on his shoulder. Turning, he saw King Thadis.

"Take Jaylen's horse," said the king.

"But Your Majesty…" Jemore protested.

180

"He's the fastest in the kingdom. I'm sure she wouldn't mind. You're her second-in-command after all," said Thadis.

Jamore smiled and took the reins of Nado. Jaylen loved this horse so much. He was her most prized possession. Whenever he was hurt or sick, Jaylen would camp out in the stables just so she could be with him at all times. Jamore felt a little weird taking Nado into battle, but if it's what the king wanted, then he would do it.

"Come on, Nado. I know I'm not Jaylen, but right now, Eldoria is depending on you," said Jamore, hoping Nado would listen to him.

Nado was a very particular horse. There were only certain people he would listen to. Usually, it was only the people that Jaylen trusted. Since Jaylen trusted Jamore, Nado should listen to him. Jamore flicked the reins, and Nado was off and running. He ran fast as lightning, ahead of all the guardsmen.

They reached the village within an hour. Jamore could see the pillars of smoke and he could hear the screams of villagers and cries of children. That was the worst part of the battle. Seeing and hearing the suffering of innocent people. One thing Jaylen always told him was, "To stop the suffering, stop the thing that's causing the suffering."

And that's exactly what he did. He climbed off Nado. He and his men were not mounted warriors. He tied Nado to a tree in case he needed him. He believed Thadis had told him to take Nado in case he needed to ride for help. As his men climbed off their horses, they drew their swords and ran into battle. But, as Jaylen said, never run into a fight. So they stopped just before they reached the army.

Jemore raised his voice to be heard. "I am Jamore, Captain of the elite guard of Eldoria. Your attack on our village is an act of war. Leave immediately or feel the full wrath of Eldoria's army. You have been warned." Jamore said. He had to get their attention off the village. Too many villagers had died already.

The commander of the Milvanian army stepped forward and laughed. "You are merely a few. We will tear you apart before your army even gets here," he said.

Jamore held his sword up. "One last chance to surrender or we will have to take you by force."

The commander continued laughing and began charging at Jamore along with the rest of his men. They soon found that to be a fatal mistake as Jamore and his men fought back with much more success. The two armies continued fighting with equal force. Jamore glanced to his right and saw the king riding into battle. King Thadis agilely leaped from his horse and landed right in front of the enemy commander.

"As the king of Eldoria, I am giving you one chance to drop your weapons and surrender to me," he said.

"My king promises hefty rewards for your death. I think I'd prefer that," said the commander, lifting his sword to strike down Thadis.

Thadis was much faster. He drew his sword and sliced from the man's left side all the way up diagonally to his right shoulder. Why did people always underestimate him? Did they think he was some lazy king who sat upon his throne all day and left the fighting to his army? The enemy commander crumpled to the ground. Thadis stepped over his lifeless body and took out another of the soldiers with a quick thrust of his blade. Jamore stood side by side with his king, marveling at the speed and precision of his blows.

Soon, another battalion of Milvania's army arrived, and the balance began to shift to them. Jamore and his men fought valiantly, as did the king and his army. They were getting pushed back; however, they were holding their own.

"Jamore!" the king called as he dispatched yet another soldier.

Jamore ran to Thadis. "Yes, Your Majesty?"

"We are clearly outnumbered. I need you to ride into Corina and ask King Balian to send some of his army to help us," said Thadis. He knew they could hold the Milvanians for a little while, but not too long.

Jamore bowed and ran back to

Nado. He mounted him and flicked the reins, and Nado galloped away. Thadis watched him go. He knew Jaylen would be proud of Jamore. He was doing everything he could to protect Eldoria. That was the reason he had appointed him second-in-command, after all.

Chapter 23:

Going For Help

Degore saw Jamore breaking free from their lines and heading toward Corina. He couldn't let Jamore reach King Balian. He gathered a few men, and they rode as fast as they could to stop Jamore.

Jamore was riding fast. Degore swore under his breath. Of course, he must be riding Jaylen's horse. Why hadn't he thought to disable her horse before he left the castle? There was still a chance if they rode through the pass; they might cut him off. He would surely go around, as it was safer.

Degore led his men through the pass. He knew where to go to avoid the pitfalls and quicksand. He had gone this way many times to avoid detection when he was bringing his reports to King Adrin.

As they cleared the pass, they saw Jamore just rounding the mountain. They had him now. Jamore must have seen them because he leaned over Nado's neck, and the horse ran even faster.

Degore had one shot; he was getting close enough to fire one arrow. He had to make it count. He fitted an arrow to the string as his horse continued to run. Not many men could fire an arrow accurately from the back of a galloping horse, but he had been trained well. He let the arrow fly just as he felt his horse's gallop slow.

The arrow hit Jamore, but only in his arm. Jamore shouted above the horse's running hooves, "You'll never stop me! Tell your king that Corina will come to our aid, and he will lose." Nado never slowed his pace the whole time, but Degore and his men had to slow theirs down.

There was only one thing left to do. Degore had to get to the castle and let King Adrin and Elvaroth know. He wasn't sure why they had stayed behind, but he knew they had to join the battle now.

King Adrin paced back and forth in front of the castle walls. "We should be out there destroying Thadis and his ridiculous army right now," he complained.

"You want to destroy both the other armies and bring the kingdoms under your rule, don't you?" asked Elvaroth, smiling because he knew the answer. "If we go in now and Thadis sends for help, King Balian will not send knowing there is a dragon helping you. He would be confident of defeat and would fortify his kingdom."

"We would still defeat them," said Adrin confidently. He detested this waiting around. This was his moment. He should be there to see the look on old Thadis's face when he realizes he is defeated. At this rate, the battle would be over before he could get there.

"Of course, we would, my dear king," Elvaroth spoke as if speaking to a child. "However, it would cost us many more men, men that would be better used to keep the citizens of those kingdoms from trying something stupid. We also need to find Jaylen. She could be a big thorn in our sides if allowed to gather support."

Adrin looked up just then, hearing hooves on the cobblestone. A young man was approaching. It was Degore. "Your Majesty, Jamore has broken away and is heading to Corina. I could not stop him," he said, stopping in front of the king.

"Now can we join the battle?" asked Adrin. He hated that he still had to act like he was taking advice from this dragon. His argument was true though, so he would tolerate it for a while longer. Once his victory was assured, though, Elvaroth would no longer be of any use.

Elvaroth made the dragon equivalent to a sigh. "Give it a few more hours. It will take time to rouse the army, and we wouldn't want them to turn back now, would we?"

"What if HE is with them?" asked the king. They had heard rumors ten years ago that the king of the dragons, Tauren, had given up his throne and placed his daughter in charge. It was believed he had come to the human world to search for the three missing dragons.

"HE is a coward! He would not dare show his face. The only thing he wants is peace. There is no way he would involve himself in a human war," said Elvaroth, but he didn't seem convinced. "It doesn't matter, anyway. If he shows up, he is only one dragon, and we still have our secret weapon hiding, just waiting to be used."

Jamore was riding faster than he had ever ridden before. The arrow in his arm hurt bad, but he would not let it stop him. He had got a look at the lead rider that shot him. It was Degore. Once Jamore was able to get Balian to send men, he had to return quickly and tell King Thadis. Now he knew who had been telling Adrin everything.

He could see the castle now. Just a few more miles. Soon, help would be on its way to Eldoria, and Milvania would be pushed back. Where was King Adrin though, and why had he not joined the battle? Was he waiting to see if his army would win? That would be just like him. Sending his army in to do all the work, then coming in at the end to take all the credit.

"It is time," said Elvaroth, lowering his neck so King Adrin could mount. He did not want this human riding him like a horse, but it was necessary to instill the proper fear in the enemy. He had also figured

186

that by now the battle would be in the open plains just inside Eldoria's borders, and since there were no hills between them, they would see and hear what he was about to do.

Adrin mounted the dragon, preparing himself to be lifted into the air. Finally, he would make the other two kingdoms pay for their arrogance. They thought they were better than him. Well, he had something they didn't… A dragon!

As if sensing Adrin's feelings at that moment, Elvaroth leaped into the air. He turned upwards and released a huge jet of flame. Then he roared. It was a loud roar that shook the castle beneath him and caused everyone in the town to run to their homes in panic.

Light filtered through the windows that Lyon had made at the back of the cave where he lived. They were carefully concealed from the outside, of course, but they let light in, so that was the main thing. He needed that natural light every day to help him remember there was still a world outside this cave.

Today was a big day, Lyon thought. It was Jaylen's eighteenth birthday, and they needed to make it as special as they could. He knew she would miss home even more today. He looked up from the pan where the eggs were cooking to see Jaylen coming into the great hall. She must have just woken up because she still looked groggy. "Good morning, Jaylen," He said, "And happy birthday."

"We will see about that," said Jaylen, a note of sadness in her voice. "But thank you, Lyon," she quickly added; she didn't want to seem rude. Looking around, she couldn't see Aurelia or Tauren. "Where are our friends this morning?" She asked, guessing the answer from the feelings she was getting from Aurelia. This bond thing was still strange to her. She couldn't believe she could actually tell exactly what Aurelia was feeling.

"They went out hunting," said Lyon. "Aurelia said, and I quote, 'We need more than just a single scrawny deer once in a while.' You know how they are."

"Yeah, they are fine eating with us most of the time, but I know they have to go out hunting at least once a week to 'stock up,' as Aurelia calls it," Jalen said, sitting at the table. "What are we having for breakfast?"

"I am cooking up the eggs Elia brought yesterday, and I have some ham to go with them," Lyon removed the cooked eggs from the pan and put them on the plate, then went over to a second pan and used a long fork to remove two slices of ham. He added one to each plate, then brought the plates to the table.

They ate breakfast and just sat talking for a bit while they waited for the dragons to return. It was mid-morning when Aurelia and Tauren finally made it back. They both looked thoroughly satisfied with their meal. "Good morning," Aurelia said, going to the corner of the room and lying down. "Happy birthday, Jaylen."

"Happy birthday, young princess," said Tauren, smiling at Jaylen. "May the next year bring you more wisdom and greater happiness." He found a spot next to Aurelia to let his breakfast digest.

"Thank you both," Jaylen said, then turned to Lyon. "So, since we know those two will be out of commission for a few hours, shall we get some practice in?" She needed to keep her sword arm sharp. If she didn't, then she would be ill-prepared to defend herself should the need arise.

"Sure," said Lyon, rising from the table. "But let's take it easy today. No need to go full-on and tire ourselves completely out."

"Agreed," said Jaylen, moving to the middle of the room.

They clashed swords for a while, neither one really trying to gain an advantage. It was more about proper technique and form than about actual combat. Lunchtime came, and they ate a light lunch of bread and cheese. Afterwards, Lyon told Jaylen to open her presents.

"What presents?" Jaylen asked.

Lyon brought out two wrapped gifts. "These presents," he said and handed them to Jaylen. One was a small box, and the other was flat, like a piece of wood. Jaylen was curious, so she opened the flat one first. The tag said it was from Tauren.

As she ripped the paper off, she saw it was a piece of canvas. On it was what looked like a map, but Jaylen had never seen this kind of map before. It looked like a group of mountains with a clearing in the middle. The place names were in Draconic, so she translated them as she read. Flame Square, Orikan Castle, Market Square, and lots of street names and such. "Where is this?" she asked, awestruck by the detail.

"That is our home," Tauren said. "The dragon city Karukan, named after the first dragon to ever bond with a human." He sounded so proud, and she knew he wanted to return home sometime to see his city. She wanted to go too, and now she wouldn't get lost.

"Thank you, Tauren," she said with a bow. "I hope I get to see it one day."

She turned her attention to the box. As she unwrapped it, she saw a glass display case. Inside the case was what looked like a dragon talon, but it was forged out of silver. It was beautiful. The surface was smooth, and it shined in the light. "You didn't read the tag," said Aurelia. "That is from me. I forged it out of silver, using my breath and my claws."

189

"It is absolutely gorgeous!" said Jaylen, running to hug her friend. She couldn't believe Aurelia would do that for her. It must have taken a lot of work.

Aurelia smiled. "It was a lot of work, but worth it to see how happy you are."

"There is one more gift, but it is at the castle," said Lyon. "It wasn't finished yet, so we will have to go there to get it. I believe Elia, King Balian, and Queen Alaria wanted to see you today, anyway." She was going to be surprised when she saw his gift.

"Well, let's go then," said Jaylen. She wanted to know what this gift was. They all went today. Ever since the flying lessons, they had flown to the castle, landing behind in a clearing that was out of the way and out of sight behind the castle so the dragons could rest close by in case they were needed. Jaylen and Lyon proceeded to the front gates on foot. As they approached the gate, Jaylen noticed it was too quiet. This time of day, there should be people coming and going, but it was totally quiet. Instinctively, her hand went to the hilt of her sword. The guard opened the gate for them. Why was he smiling like that? Jaylen was ready for anything.

As soon as they entered the gates, she saw Elia, Balian, and Alaria standing there with townspeople around them. Everyone in the courtyard shouted, "Happy birthday, Princess Jaylen!!"

Jaylen almost drew her sword instinctively, but she mastered the impulse and relaxed. Jaylen smiled and hugged Lyon. "Thank you, Lyon," she said. "But you had me scared. I thought something was wrong."

"Don't thank me. Alaria and Balian are the ones who planned all this," said Lyon.

Jaylen curtsied. "Thank you both." She gave them both a hug, remembering that they had treated her like family.

"You're very welcome, Jaylen," said Balian.

Jaylen sat down next to Elia and Lyon and enjoyed the food they had prepared. Before long, Elia, Balian, and Alaria all brought out gifts. Jaylen opened the box Elia gave her, and inside was a beautiful ruby necklace that shined in the sunlight.

"Elia, this is gorgeous," said Jaylen, almost speechless.

"It reminded me of Aurelia, so I figured you'd like it," said Elia, hugging her best friend.

Next, King Balian handed her a box. "This is something I hope you never need, but I fear you will all too soon with the state of things." He said. She opened it and was absolutely stunned. Inside the box was the most beautiful armor she had ever seen. It was gray leather with red outlining it and a cloak fixed to the back, with Eldoria's crest on it. The cloak was red, and the crest golden.

She was almost speechless, but she found her voice to say, "Thank you, Balian. I Love Corina, but this shows the world I am still Jaylen, Princess of Eldoria." She missed Eldoria. But most of all, she missed her parents. Especially today.

Alaria gave her a smaller box. Jaylen opened it and gasped. She pulled out the gift. It was a crown like nothing she had ever seen. There were rubies all around it and a piece in the front and the back to hold it on better in battle. On both sides, there was a ruby carved in the shape of the Aurelia flower. "Every princess needs a crown," said Alaria.

"Thank you, Alaria. I love it," said Jaylen, and she hugged everyone. "Thank You all."

"You are most welcome," said Alaria.

Lyon came walking up just then with a long box. "You still have one more present," he said, handing her the box. She opened the box, revealing a beautiful dark gray scabbard with red outlines and rubies set in the front and back. There was a sword in it as well. The hilt was adorned with the finest cut rubies on the guard and pommel. The leather-wrapped hilt was the same color as the scabbard and was the perfect size for her hand. She drew the sword and was astonished. The metal was so shiny, and the blade was razor-sharp. Down both sides of the blade, there were words engraved. 'Crimson Warrior.'

"What does Crimson Warrior mean?" asked Jaylen, still staring at the most beautiful sword she had ever seen.

Lyon explained, "Every bonded human gets a title in the Dragon Kingdom. Mine was given to me by Tauren, and yours was given to you by Aurelia. Mine is the Azure Prince, and yours is the Crimson Warrior."

"Thank you, Lyon. Thank you all. This has been a much better birthday than I thought. I am glad to be here with you all, but I do miss my own kingdom. One day, I will return and see my parents again," said Jaylen.

The servants came walking out of the kitchen holding a huge cake. Jaylen was hoping there would be cake. Just as she was about to cut the first piece, they all heard the guard shout, "An injured man approaches!" Jaylen turned to the gate. Through the bars, she saw the familiar sight of Nado, her horse. A man was riding him with an arrow in his arm.

Without thinking, she ordered the guard to open the gate at once. This wasn't her kingdom. Why was she giving orders? To his credit, the guard hesitated, but with a nod from King Balian, he complied. As the horse came to a stop just inside the gate, Jaylen saw the man on the back of her horse and was shocked.

"Jamore? What are you doing here?" said Jaylen, running to his side.

Jamore looked at Jaylen. He was breathing heavily, partly from the riding, but mostly because of the arrow in his arm. "Your Highness? Is it really you?" Jamore said, slowly climbing off of Nado. He fell and Jaylen caught him. Leaning on her and Nado, he tried to catch his breath.

"Yes, Jamore, it is me," said Jaylen. "What happened to you?" She led him to the table so he could sit down and got him a drink of water.

"I was shot," said Jamore, by way of explanation, "by Adrin's spy."

Alaria called for one of the healers. They came down the stairs and tended to Jamore's wound. They cut the arrow and pushed it through. Jamore screamed in pain. Slathering the wound with some healing salve, they wrapped it with a bandage to avoid any dirt or dust getting into the wound.

"Adrin's spy? I don't understand." Jaylen was confused. What was happening? Why would Adrin send a spy?

"The king's servant... Degore... he's a spy for Milvania," said Jamore.

"Degore? But he's always been so nice to us," said Jaylen, getting a bad feeling about where this was going. She couldn't believe Degore would betray them like that. "How did you get shot?"

193

Jamore told Jaylen about the attack on the villages and that her father had led the army into battle, but they were outnumbered. Jaylen couldn't believe it. Eldoria had been at peace for years. No one dared to attack them. Why now? Then a sinking feeling hit her. Because she was gone. Her father must have been broken by losing both his children. For the first time in a long time, Eldoria was vulnerable.

Jaylen's whole demeanor instantly changed. "Lyon, Eldoria is under attack. We need to go. And we need backup," she said.

Lyon immediately stood by her side. He felt as she did, and he knew exactly what she meant by backup. It was time to reveal themselves and save their kingdom. They both held their hands in the air and called out, "Aurelia, Tauren, take wing!"

As soon as they finished speaking, everyone in the courtyard heard the whoosh of air as Tauren and Aurelia leaped into the air. Their beautiful scales reflected the sunlight as they burst into view above the castle walls.

"Are they..?" Jamore couldn't even finish his statement. He backed away instinctively, grabbing his sword hilt.

"Yes, Jamore. They are dragons. No, they're not dangerous. No, they won't hurt you," said Jaylen, slightly annoyed that he believed the stories. Didn't he trust her judgment? Did he think she would ever put Eldoria in danger by associating with a dangerous creature?

The courtyard cleared out fast. Everyone was scared. Only Balian, Alaria, and Elia remained with them as Aurelia and Tauren landed next to Jaylen and Lyon right in front of Jamore.

Jaylen wasted no time putting on the armor and belting on her new sword. "King Balian, it appears your gift was unfortunately needed after all. As princess of Eldoria, I now officially ask for your aid.

Milvania has attacked our sovereign kingdom. Will you help us?" she said, putting the crown on her head.

"You can count on us, Your Highness," said Balian in formal tones. "Guard, sound the alarm. Call up the men. We go to aid Eldoria." He smiled at Jaylen. "You look beautiful in that armor, Jaylen. Please be careful. Lyon, your armor is on its way as well."

"Thanks, Your Majesty," said Lyon. A small boy came running up, carrying armor similar to Jaylen's, but with blue outlines. Lyon put it on, then stood next to Tauren and looked at Jaylen. "Shall we?"

"Of course," said Jaylen, and they both leaped to their respective dragons' necks. "We will keep them at bay until you arrive, Balian. Jamore, you rest here until Balian rides out, then you can march with him back to battle." She raised her hand. "Aurelia, take wing!"

"Tauren, take wing!" said Lyon a moment after.

Both dragons leaped into the air simultaneously and turned toward Brancreek Village, and the battle that awaited them.

Chapter 24:

Help Arrives

King Thadis surveyed the battleground. There were casualties everywhere. Some were wounded; others lay dead where they had fallen. He estimated about a quarter of his men had been killed. Milvania had taken heavy losses as well and had pulled back to the big field to regroup. Thadis gathered his remaining warriors and marched to the field.

As he made it to the field, he could see over the trees into Milvania. Suddenly, against the setting sun, a black form appeared near where the castle was. It released a jet of flame and a deafening roar. Thadis's heart sank. Milvania had a dragon. It made sense that Adrin would align himself with such evil creatures.

No matter. It was almost dark. Milvania had already set up camp, and Thadis would do the same just inside the village, where they could tend to the wounded and get some rest. Not even Milvania would fight at night. It was too dangerous. By morning, the dragon would be upon them, but Thadis had a surprise waiting for them.

Jaylen turned toward Lyon. "It is too dark. We must stop for the night," she said. "We will be on our way before the sun is up and make it there by mid-morning."

"You are right, Jaylen. We must be rested," Lyon reluctantly said. "Land in that clearing; we can get something to eat and rest." He pointed at a clearing in the woods to the south.

Tauren and Aurelia touched down with their usual grace. Lyon and Jaylen dismounted, and Lyon started a fire while Jaylen opened her pack. It was a good thing she took it everywhere and always had a supply of rations, just in case. The dragons found a stream nearby and got themselves a drink.

They all sat around the fire, and Lyon and Jaylen ate their rations in silence. They were both feeling concerned for their father and their kingdom. Jaylen spoke first. "I hope Father is all right. I imagine he is not entirely himself, and it is my fault for leaving like I did."

"Stop that right now," Aurelia said more sternly than Jaylen had ever heard her speak. "Milvania has been wanting to attack for a long time. Even in the Dragon Kingdom, we knew that. Just because he happens to be attacking now, that doesn't mean it is because of you. For all you know, he might have attacked anyway. At least now you have us."

Jaylen was taken aback a little by her words. Did she know something Jaylen didn't? She could tell through the bond that something was bothering Aurelia. "Okay, spit it out Aurelia. I know something is eating at you. I can feel it," she said. "Remember, we are connected now."

Aurelia sighed, but it was Tauren who responded. "Since there is a real chance you will run into him in the battle, I guess we better tell you." Tauren's voice was sad. "Many years ago, when dragons and humans were still at peace, a few dragons decided that we should rule over all humans and make them obey us. They felt it was the only way to bring true peace."

"They started out with good intentions but shortly became obsessed with power," continued Aurelia when Tauren paused. "They knew they couldn't establish themselves while we were around, so they

197

decided to turn humans against us. They thought if the humans could weaken us, they could take power and subjugate the humans." Her voice faltered. It was clear she was deeply saddened by this.

Tauren continued, "They began attacking human villages. Their attacks looked like all dragons were to blame because the attackers were led by my brother, Elvaroth. I tried to talk sense into him, but I failed."

"Soon humans were convinced that dragons were dangerous and needed to be destroyed." Lyon picked up the narrative. "The dragoneers tried to tell the kings that it was only a small handful of dragons. But the kingdoms agreed that they needed to cut ties with dragons."

"The king of Eldoria convinced them to just banish the dragons instead of killing them all. He said they should allow the dragons time to deal with their internal conflict and that they could talk once that threat had been eliminated," Aurelia said.

"So, we retreated. I was a young dragon at the time, and my father was the king. It was hard for him to order the death of his own son," said Tauren, "but the bond with humans was too important. He ordered the elders to craft a new spell to weave into the bond fire. Any dragon who betrayed his or her oath to protect humanity would lose all color. The darker shades would become black, and the lighter shades would become gray."

Jaylen was too stunned to speak. She had never heard this tale. Now she understood how all the rumors of evil dragons got started. She found her voice and asked. "What happened to Elvaroth and the others?"

Lyon was the one who answered. "With a surefire way to find the dissidents, the other dragons could find them and arrest them. Most tried to fight back and were killed; some were sent to live in a kind of prison cave. In the end, there were only three that escaped: Elvaroth, Terikon, and Felarrin."

"Unfortunately, there have been reports of a black dragon in Milvania," said Tauren. "We believe it has to be Elvaroth as he was the only black dragon left. If he has aligned with Adrin, then Eldoria is in grave danger."

"Then we need to leave as soon as possible," Jaylen said, more worried than ever but glad she knew the truth. She had a feeling they were still keeping some things to themselves, but she trusted they would tell her when they needed to. She trusted their judgment.

"We will get a few hours of sleep, then leave. We should make the last part of the trip above the clouds so we aren't spotted," said Lyon, yawning. "Tauren and Aurelia will watch over us. They need less sleep than we do."

The sun began rising over the plains. Both armies were lined up and ready for another day of battle. The tension in the air was high, and another battalion had arrived for Milvania. King Thadis fervently hoped that Balian didn't take his time.

Thadis looked at the army before them, and his fears were realized. Standing on the ground in front of Milvania's army was a huge black dragon. Its scales were dull, and its eyes were dark. "Surrender to me now, Thadis," said Adrin confidently from the dragon's back. "I will spare you and even let you be my governor as long as you submit to my authority. You can't beat us now that we have a dragon."

Thadis laughed. "We will fight to the last man. We will never give in to you. NOW!" That last command produced an immediate response. Two large stones flew through the air. The catapults in the village had fired them.

With that, the battle began again. Elvaroth tried to get through the line to Thadis, but kept getting pushed back by waves of arrows. Degore, who had returned in the night, acted wounded and limped toward Thadis. As soon as he was in range, he would kill Thadis. Thadis still believed he was the king's loyal servant.

He was in range. He pulled his sword and was about to strike when Thadis turned and, with a flick of his wrist, removed Degore's head with one clean stroke. Thadis had received word from one of his scouts about Degore shooting Jamore. Elvaroth was getting closer now.

For a moment, there was no movement. They heard something odd that sounded like a woman screaming out her battle cry. The sound soon melded with another roar. This one was deeper and more masculine.

Without warning, Aurelia burst through the clouds, her scales glistening in the morning sun, Tauren a breath behind. "For Eldoria!" Jaylen and Lyon shouted together as they dove at Milvania's army like two falcons descending on their prey. They pulled up at the last minute, both releasing a powerful flame that burned two wide lines through the army.

For a second, there was complete panic. Milvanian soldiers were scrambling to get out of the way. The dragons had targeted the archers in the back so as not to risk any Eldorian casualties. King Adrin swore loudly, and Elvaroth turned to face these new threats. By the time things calmed down, Aurelia and Tauren had risen out of range and turned toward the main part of Eldoria's army.

King Thadis wasn't sure what to think. Then he saw the familiar form of Jaylen, and his heart jumped. This must be the dragon she rescued, but who were the other two? Aurelia and Tauren were coming his way. They pulled up at the last minute and landed right in front of him. The Milvania soldiers scrambled out of the way, and even Eldoria's men were moving back.

Jaylen slid off Aurelia. "Hello, Father, did you miss me?" she said, smiling and watching as Lyon dismounted Tauren.

"Where have you been?" said Thadis, looking over at the other man. He gasped. "Lyon, is that you?"

"Yes, Father," said Lyon, keeping his voice even. "We are here with our friends to protect Eldoria."

"We don't have time for full reunions now," said Jaylen, dispatching a Milvanian soldier that had got brave enough to charge at her with a quick thrust from her new sword. "Drive back the army first, then I will explain. Tauren and Aurelia, you know what to do." With that, both dragons leaped into the air and headed for Elvaroth and Adrin.

Jaylen fought alongside her father. Her arms were cut up with small cuts where she had just barely blocked the blades, but she continued to fight despite the pain. The two armies clashed well into the evening. Elvaroth tried to get closer but kept getting pushed back. As he saw the other two dragons approaching, he landed under the protection of the archers, who had once again gained their composure.

"Get off!" he said to Adrin. "I will deal with these two. You better send for our secret weapon, though." Adrin dismounted, and Elvaroth returned to the air, heading straight for his brother.

Aurelia peeled off and let Tauren handle Elvaroth for now. She made for the catapults that were coming out of the forest. With one huge breath, she incinerated the siege engines and anyone around them. She hated this. Taking human life was wrong. She had sworn an oath to protect humans.

She had no choice, though. Dragons could no longer sit back and let mankind resolve their own differences, or there would never be peace. They had to take sides in this war, and she knew that all the dragons would agree that Eldoria and Corina were the better choice.

Elvaroth reached Tauren and tried to end it quickly with his talons. Tauren was too fast, though, and dodged the attack with ease. "Come now, brother," he said. "I am not a little dragon anymore. You can't get me that easily."

"Maybe not, brother," Elvaroth spat the word like a curse. "But I am still older and have far more experience." He circled Tauren, trying to gain an advantage to move in. Tauren wouldn't give him one, though. They continued circling high above the battle, neither one taking their eyes off the other.

Elvaroth would move in and Tauren would dodge. The Tauren would strike at Elvaroths wing but Elvaroth would dodge. Since they knew each other so well, either one gaining an advantage was difficult.

With the departure of the dragons, the Milvanians drove in once more. Thadis and Jaylen stood side by side, fighting them off as though they were a single person. Lyon was amazed at how coordinated they were. Jaylen would move to avoid a Milvanian sword, and Thadis would take the offender down. Then Thadis would block an attack, only to have Jaylen plunge her sword into the attacker's side. It was like one person fighting with two swords.

Lyon soon had no more time for thought. He had to concentrate on fighting the men that attacked him. He could feel the tension in Tauren as he circled high above. He looked toward the back of the opposing army and saw Aurelia grab two soldiers and drop them from high over the back of the army.

Things finally seemed to be going their way. The army was pulling back. Soon, full darkness settled over them, and the armies backed away from each other. Tonight it would be Milvania that was nursing its many wounded. Tauren and Aurelia landed just outside the camp that Eldoria had set up.

Jaylen and Lyon helped treat some of the wounded with their power, but they left most to the healers. They needed their strength for tomorrow. They tended the minor wounds that the dragons had endured, then went to find King Thadis. He was sure to have many questions.

As they approached where Thadis was sitting, he got up and immediately ran to Jaylen and wrapped his arms around her. "I thought I lost you forever. I am so sorry I don't know what came over me to yell at you like that," he said. Jaylen could hear his voice breaking and realized he was crying. She couldn't remember him ever crying.

"I'm sorry too. I should have come to you sooner and explained why I chose to help Aurelia." She was full of emotion, too. "But that is the past. You always taught me to live in the present. I could not allow Adrin to attack our kingdom unchecked."

They continued to hug for a moment, then he released her and turned to Lyon. "I am sorry to you too, Lyon. I should never have sent you away. I let my fear control me. That is over. You are and always will be Prince of Eldoria." He hesitated a moment, then embraced his son for the first time in twenty years.

"Thanks, Father," said Lyon. "I never blamed you or resented you for what happened. Tauren would never allow it. He always told me that you had your reasons and that you loved me, but sometimes duty must come before love when you are the king."

"I would like to officially meet both Tauren and Aurelia if that is okay," said Thadis. "I think it is about time this king admits he was wrong." They walked together the short distance to where the dragons were laying. "Will they understand me?"

"Yes, they can understand our language but have trouble speaking it, so they only speak their language. We will translate until you choose to learn it yourself," said Lyon. Tauren was the first to raise his head as they approached.

"Hello, Tauren, and Aurelia. I am King Thadis of Eldoria. I am pleased to welcome you to my kingdom. I assure you that as long as I am king you will always be welcome here," said Thadis, bowing to them.

Tauren was the first to speak, and Lyon translated for him. "Tauren says thank you, wise king. I hope that one day dragons and humans can renew their partnership and all people everywhere can live in peace with us."

Aurelia leaned forward and touched the king's forehead with her nose. Jaylen was surprised, and so was Thadis, but he didn't move even though he was a little scared. Then she spoke. "Aurelia says hello," said Jaylen. "She also said I am glad to meet the man who raised such a kind, sweet woman. If not for her, I may have been caught by those hunters and killed. You should be proud of her. Also, know that since Jaylen is my best friend. That makes you and your whole kingdom my family. I will defend all of you with my life."

"Thank You both," said Thadis. "Please rest now; I will have meat brought to you and water. Tomorrow we must drive Milvania from our kingdom, and I would appreciate your help again. If you are willing."

"They both agree," said Lyon. "Tauren also said he will deal with Elvaroth."

Lyon, Jaylen, and Thadis walked back to the fire, where they talked for a little while about what had happened and where they had been. King Thadis was never more grateful that Balian was his friend. Balian had provided a safe place for his children even when Thadis could not. Thadis called over a messenger and told him to deliver a report to the queen about all that had happened.

They settled in and took turns sleeping so they could be rested for tomorrow. It was going to be another long day, but Balian should arrive by noon, so that would tip the scales completely in their favor.

Chapter 25:

Corina Arrives

The next morning, Lyon woke before sunrise as he had always done. He greeted the guards as he went out to see Tauren. He found Tauren sitting in the field just outside the gate, looking toward the opposing army. Lyon knew what he was thinking, but he wanted to let Tauren verbalize it. Maybe it would help him to say it out loud. "What troubles you, my friend?" he said, walking up to Tauren and resting a hand on his side.

"I wish that this battle wasn't necessary," said Tauren, his sadness clearly evident to Lyon. "Never in our history have we been to war. The closest we came were the rebel dragons, but we imprisoned most of them. We despise killing other sentient creatures, whether dragon or human. It feels like we failed."

"I know, Tauren. I feel the same way, but this battle is unfortunately necessary. Humans have always been in conflict over the smallest things. They have too much pride and are offended too easily," said Lyon, trying to comfort his friend. "We have to win this war to bring peace to the land and allow dragons and humans to once again live together in harmony."

"I understand that, and I will fight for Eldoria as if it were my home. I just don't like it. I wish there were another way," Tauren said, looking out over the field that was covered in blood and seeing his brother on the other side in front of the Milvanian camp. "He wasn't always so power-hungry. I remember we used to fly together, and he always took me to the best places around the three kingdoms."

"Hold on to those memories. That was your brother. Remember him as he was meant to be, not as circumstances and stupid decisions made him." Lyon gave his friend a gentle pat on the side. "But don't let it distract you now. He is your enemy and he must be dealt with."

"I know," Tauren turned to look at him. "When did you get so wise?" He laughed, sounding more like himself.

"I guess you are rubbing off on me, oh wise king," Lyon bowed and then smiled at his best friend.

Jaylen woke up and looked at the bed on the other side of the tent. Lyon was gone. She figured he had gone to see Tauren. Well, she had better go talk to Aurelia. She left her tent and started walking toward the edge of the camp. Thadis was standing by Captain Ricalda, talking about the battle plan. When he saw Jaylen, he sent the captain to prepare his men. "Wait for me, please," he said.

Jaylen stopped and waited for her father to reach her. "What is it, Father?" Jaylen said.

"May I come with you to see Aurelia?" said the king. "I have something I want to tell you both." He looked at Jaylen and smiled so she would know it was nothing bad.

"Sure, I am eager to hear what you have to say." Jaylen knew her father well, so she expected a very long-winded conversation. They walked together in silence until they approached where Aurelia was lounging.

Aurelia greeted them as they got close. Of course, Jaylen translated her words so Thadis could understand. "Good morning, Your Majesty," Aurelia said, dipping her head in her approximation of a bow.

"Good morning, beautiful Aurelia," said Thadis. "First of all, let me apologize for overreacting when Jaylen first told me about you."

"Apology accepted, wise king," said Aurelia, Jaylen translating for her father. "I understand how difficult it must be for you hearing all the stories of evil dragons. You wanted to protect Jaylen, and that is something we share."

"You are right there. My one goal is to protect my sweet daughter so she can one day take the throne," Thadis stood tall as he always did, but Jaylen, knowing him so well, could tell he was burdened by something. "I need to explain why I reacted the way I did."

"It is in the past," said Jaylen, not wanting her father to be worrying about it now. They needed to focus on the battle that would soon resume. "We must focus on the here and now."

"It is of the past I wish to speak, sweetheart," said Thadis in a quiet, gentle tone. "What do you know of the events that led to dragons being banished from our lands?"

"I know what Aurelia and Tauren told me. There was an uprising and the rebel dragons attacked humans to drive the two races apart. It worked, and stories have been passed down through the generations, so people fear dragons." Jaylen wondered where her father was going with this.

"What you don't know is that it was Eldoria that spoke out most about pulling away from the dragons. They even wanted to organize hunting parties and kill any dragon left in the kingdoms." He paused to let that sink in. "The king of Eldoria at the time was worse than Adrin. He wanted the dragons out of the way so he could conquer the rest. What he didn't realize is that the dragoneers already knew of his plans, so the leader of the dragoneers snuck into the castle and killed the king."

"*What?*" Jaylen was shocked. Why would he do that?

The king held up his hands to silence her protest and continued, "He knew that if the king continued to rule, the three kingdoms would go to war. Since he had no children and his wife passed the year before, the crown was put up in a contest of battling skills. Which the dragoneer won easily. As a result, he became the new king."

"Wait, was that dragoneer our ancestor?" Jaylen asked, her mind was racing. Why had her parents kept this from her? If he knew the truth about dragons, why had he reacted the way he did?

"Yes, Jaylen. We are the descendants of that dragoneer. His name was Thadis as well. He was the leader. He tried to pass down the truth about dragons, but somewhere along the line, the stories got twisted and lost. I only know the truth because of the records your mother found when we were first married."

Aurelia was listening quietly. She already knew this history. What came next, though, would be a surprise even to her because she too wondered why the king had reacted the way he had. "Dear king, if you knew all this, then why did you react so badly to Jaylen spending time with me?" she asked before Jaylen had a chance. Of course, Jaylen dutifully translated for her.

"That is the worst part. I didn't want you to know the truth." He looked directly at Jaylen. "I was afraid you would feel shame because of the way our family just took the kingdom. I was afraid you would question our right to rule. I never wanted you to have to feel like you didn't deserve to be queen."

"That explains why you didn't want me to spend time with Aurelia. Being a dragon, she probably knew the truth. But why react so violently when you found out I disobeyed you and spent time with her, anyway?" Jaylen would confront Aurelia later about why she didn't tell Jaylen any of this.

"I wish I knew. I was all set to try to reason with you and convince you that disobeying me set a bad example for the rest of the kingdom. When I saw you, though, for some reason, the anger I felt at your disobedience turned into rage, and I couldn't control myself." Thadis still couldn't understand why he had done that. "I am sorry to both of you. I should have told you the truth when you first came home that day, saying you met a dragon."

"I understand, Father," Jaylen said more formally. "However, as king, it is your responsibility to speak the truth, not cover up to spare your own feelings. What Thadis did back then may not have been completely right, but he did what he had to do to prevent a war. We are the rightful rulers of Eldoria, and now we must defend our kingdom, free of guilt from the past."

"You are right, my dear Jaylen," said the king. "You will make a much wiser and better ruler than I. So let's go rouse the army and get ready for the battle."

"My thoughts exactly," replied Jaylen, turning to do just that.

Aurelia looked toward where Lyon and Tauren were. Out of the corner of her eye, she caught sight of movement in the sky. She immediately jumped to her feet and roared. Tauren looked up, and Lyon grabbed his sword. Jaylen and Thadis turned back at her roar and followed her gaze to see Elvaroth flying in from the north. He was going to attack the camp! Aurelia leaped into the air, and Tauren followed; they had to intercept him. Jaylen shouted to the guard to sound the alarm and rouse the army.

The alarm horn sounded, and the camp came alive with men scrambling to get their gear and prepare for battle. Just then, Jaylen caught movement out of the corner of her eye. "*Ambush!*" she shouted and drew her sword, barely sidestepping a soldier who had just emerged from the woods.

Lyon had returned by then and joined her and Thadis as they ran back into camp to help repel the ambush. There were only a handful of soldiers, but they had done considerable damage. The Eldorians were organized now and drove them back. It could have been worse if Jaylen hadn't seen them moving in the trees.

She and her father moved to the front of the army to begin marching them out of camp and toward the enemy. The Milvanians were already halfway through the field. They had planned this well. They sent Elvaroth to lure out Aurelia and Tauren so they could sneak in and attack from the side. They hadn't counted on Jaylen, though.

The two armies collided once again while the dragons fought overhead. Jaylen was with her father at the front, with Lyon and Janarin. They were holding their own, but the rest of the army was flanking them. How did Milvania have this many soldiers?

"Lyon, take the left flank, I'll go right, we have to reinforce the sides and hold them back," Jaylen shouted over the loud clang of swords and the wisp of arrows.

Lyon didn't say a word; he just moved to the left and helped the soldiers push back the Milvanians. Jaylen moved to the right, leaving Janarin and Thadis to lead the men forward. She caught sight of King Adrin moving toward her and knew that he wanted her dead. He wasn't moving fast, though, which meant he was sure of victory and wanted to savor it.

A horn sounded in front of her on the road from Corina. She looked up in time to see the banner of Corina leading their army down the road. It was King Balian, and he was early. They must have ridden hard to get there so quickly. She saw Jamore bent over Nado urging him faster. When he got close to where she was, he pulled up on the reins and leaped from Nado's back, cutting his way through the Milvanians till he was at her side.

"I am here, milady," he said, smiling as he dispatched the nearest soldier with a thrust of his sword.

"It's about time, Lieu... I mean, Captain. I was beginning to think I was gonna have to kill them all myself," she said, sidestepping a soldier's sword and slicing hers across his throat.

"I am grateful you saved some for me." He bowed, then with no further conversation, they continued cutting down the enemy. He received a few scrapes, and so did she, but nothing too bad.

High above them, they could see the dragons circling each other. Jets of flame pierced the sky now and again. Aurelia avoided one such flame, then flicked her tail; it collided with Elvaroth and sent him backward. He regained control quickly. Since he was far enough away from them now, though, he dove at the Eldorian catapults before she could catch him; he had burned one down.

This distraction was enough to give the Milvanians a chance to push. It became harder to fight them off. Even with her increased strength and stamina, she was reaching the limit. Just then, she caught sight of two dull gray dragons flying in. That must be Felarrin and Terikon. She was worried about Tauren and Aurelia now with three dragons on Milvania's side.

She kept her mind on what she was doing. She couldn't be distracted now. Adrin was getting closer to her now. He had been staying back to allow his army a chance to wear her out; she realized. Well, he would get a big surprise when he finally reached her. She began to move back, allowing her men to take over most of the fighting.

Jamore saw Adrin too. He knew what the king was planning. If he took out Jaylen, then it would break their army, and victory would almost be assured. Jamore couldn't let that happen. Jaylen saw Jamore moving toward the king, but it was too late to stop him. "Jamore, don't," she said, fearing he would be no match for the king.

By now, Corina's army had reached the back side of the Milvanians and made them fight on two fronts. Eldoria continued to push back, then another wave of reinforcements arrived for Milvania. They must have called up every mercenary in the three kingdoms and every man in Milvania to fight. They had obviously been planning this for a long time.

Jamore kept pushing through the Milvanians; he had to take out the king. That should make the army demoralized, and they could finally end this once and for all. He could see the smug look on Adrin's face. One soldier came in from the left to try to stop Jamore, but he was able to dodge the attack and bury his sword in the young man's stomach.

Another soldier moved in from the right. Jamore barely blocked his blade but managed to slide to the left and pushed the man's sword aside, then swung his own sword, cutting deep into the chest of the soldier. As he got closer, he could see the king's three guards move towards him. Jamore settled in to fight them, but just then, he heard the whoosh of an arrow and saw one of the men fall to the ground. Shortly after, another arrow found its mark in the second.

By this time, the third guard had reached him. Jamore simply moved out of the way as the man swung at him. While he was off balance, Jamore dispatched him with a swing to the abdomen, and that was it. He glanced back to see where the arrows had come from. He saw Jaylen holding her bow. He smiled. She was always watching out for him.

Jamore finally reached Adrin and settled in to fight the king. Soldiers moved to attack him, but Adrin called them off. "This one is mine," he said. "I will kill you, captain, then I will kill the princess." He swung his sword at Jamore, who blocked the attack, then tried one of his own. The king blocked his attack with blinding speed and a jolt that sent shivers down Jamore's arm. How was he so strong?

The fight continued back and forth. Jaylen hoped that Jamore could do it after all. Jamore seemed to be gaining the advantage, then Adrin got the upper hand. Jaylen watched in horror as Jamore was steadily pushed back. In one last effort, he swung his sword to hit the king in the side. Adrin sidestepped and knocked his sword away, throwing Jamore off balance. Then, without hesitation, Adrin plunged his blade into Jamore's stomach. Pulling his sword free, he kicked Jamore to the side.

As Jamore fell to the ground, Jaylen screamed, "*No!*" She looked Adrin in the eye and shouted at him, "I'll kill you for that!" With newfound strength, she surged forward; no soldier could stand before her and live. Up above, she could hear Aurelia roar in response to the rage that welled up inside of her.

Aurelia and Tauren were holding their own against the three dragons. Every once in a while, one would break off and dive at either Eldoria or Corina. Aurelia tried to stop them, as did Tauren, but they couldn't keep all three busy all the time. Things were looking bleak.

Aurelia and Tauren were both exhausted. Soon, they would have to take the fight to the ground or risk not being able to move fast enough to dodge.

On the ground, Jaylen had almost reached Adrin. Aurelia could feel her anger. Jaylen had to calm down or she wouldn't be able to fight the king; she would make a mistake and get herself killed. Aurelia wanted to go down there and help, but if she did, all would be lost. Tauren couldn't fight three dragons by himself. She had to trust that Jaylen could stop Adrin.

Chapter 26:

Calling For More Help

Queen Lyren was pacing around the throne room, awaiting an update on the battle. It had been two long days, and the reports she did receive were not good. She could hear the clash of swords even from this far away. She was worried about her husband. He was still feeling guilty about what had happened to Jaylen. How could he lead his men in his state? She had to trust that he would put that to the back of his mind and defend their kingdom. Just then, a young man burst through the throne room doors.

"Milady! I brought word from the battleground!" he said as he stopped in front of her, breathing heavily from his haste.

"What is it?" asked Lyren, still worried.

"Princess Jaylen has arrived with a dragon. She has brought a young man with her, also on the back of a dragon," the young man said, finally catching his breath.

"Lyon. She found him," Lyren said, quietly, so he didn't hear her.

"Milvania has a black dragon with them. King Adrin arrived on its back," said the man. Lyren cringed at that. She wasn't surprised though; they were probably using each other.

"They have two other dragons as well. I must get back to the battlefield now to collect more information. Good day, Your Highness."

"Good day. And thank you," said Lyren. She was starting to get even more worried. Three dragons, the three that had escaped the others. She had known for a while that they would reappear and cause trouble, but not this bad.

"You are most welcome." He turned and left the room; Lyren hoped he would slow his pace going back.

Lyren stood up. How would Jaylen and Lyon fight off three dragons? I mean, yeah, Tauren had been the king of the dragon kingdom, but still, these are the dragons that tried to enslave humankind. She had to find a way to help. She knew what she had to do; she hoped they would come.

The new dragoneers were spread all over Eldoria. Could they get here in time? Would she be able to reach them as leaders had done in the past? Was the connection strong enough? "Minaren!" she called.

Minaren was never too far away from her queen. "Yes, milady?" asked Minaren, coming through the doors of the throne room, ready to do whatever was necessary.

"I need you to stay here and look after the castle. I need to take care of something," said Lyren. "It is time my friends and I fulfill our role in this war."

"As you wish, my queen," said Minaren, a little hesitantly. She was just a servant, after all. How could she run the castle?

Lyren all but ran out of the throne room. She took her horse from the stables and rode out to the clearing behind the castle. She had never done this before. She had heard of dragoneers who were able to call upon others in times of need, but she didn't know if she could do it. She needed to call Feora before she tried.

"Feora! I need your help! Please descend from your place in the clouds!" called Lyren in a loud voice. It wasn't long before she saw the familiar gold form descending from the clouds. She was always amazed at how Feora's scales shined in any kind of light. Feora landed with her usual grace and folded her wings.

"You used the traditional dragon call. You must really need me," said Feora with a smile. She was about to continue when she noticed Lyren's distraught face. "What is it, dear friend?" she asked in a softer voice.

"I know you have seen what is happening. All three dragons are now in the battle helping Adrin. Tauren and Aurelia are holding their own, but Adrin's army is too large. This battle will decide our future. We can't lose," Lyren explained. "I know it is not your fight, but we need your help and that of the other dragoneers. I just don't know how to reach them in time."

Feora laughed. "Dear Lyren, we already know what is at stake. We are ready to do what is necessary. All you need to do is lead us into battle," she said with a grin. "As for reaching the others in time, they await your call. As a leader, you have the ability to reach them. Just concentrate on who you wish to reach and focus your thoughts on your need, and they will hear your call."

Lyren did just that. Then they waited. All the dragoneers should be within an hour's ride of this clearing. That had been the agreement; they needed to be close enough to call their dragon friends whenever they needed them.

Lyren already knew who would be first. Riding up on her black stallion was Liara. Her sandy blonde hair billowed behind her as she rode into the clearing. Lyren liked Liara; she had been titled the Vermillion Princess even though she wasn't a princess; she was like a second daughter to Lyren, so it fit well. Her dragon partner was a darker red than Aurelia, but it was fitting that she and Jaylen would befriend dragons of similar color because they were so much alike.

Lyren heard rustling in the woods to the southeast. She looked over just in time to see Castien emerge from the trees. His hair was jet black and a little long; he had it up in a ponytail. His slender form and upbeat personality sometimes made him seem like a child. But he was adept in the use of his sword. He was titled the Emerald Guardian because of his protective nature.

A step behind him from the same direction was his wife, Astria. She was titled the Sapphire Huntress, and it was easy to see why. She had a bow slung on her back with a quiver full of arrows. Her brown leather armor was highlighted by dark green outlines, helping her blend into the forest. Hunting was a passion of hers, so it made perfect sense.

Finally, Myana, Lyren's second-in-command, stepped in from the south. She had come from Lyren's original home, Crelonna. Myana was one of the few women Lyren knew who refused to marry; she was far too independent. She was also the oldest among the dragoneers; she had slightly graying auburn hair with light brown eyes. Her age and the fact her dragon was bright green gave her the title Neon Empress.

That was all four dragoneers plus Lyren, making five. She was relieved they had all responded so quickly, and in full battle gear as well. It was like they knew they would be needed. Lyren wondered if Feora had something to do with that. It would be just like her friend to know what was needed before she herself did.

"Great, you're all here. Our kingdom is under attack. Milvania has brought three dragons to try to gain the upper hand. My daughter and son have brought Tauren and Aurelia to help, but I fear it will not be enough. I am asking for your help. Will you call down your friends

219

and help me defend our kingdom?" She was known as the Golden Monarch because she was the queen and they all loved her.

Four voices rang out in complete unison, 'yes.' They all turned skyward and called out the names of their dragons, each in turn then all at once, "Descend from your place in the clouds!"

Within moments, a red dragon descended from the clouds. Of course, Kiranya would be first. She was a darker color than Aurelia, but still very beautiful. She landed with absolute grace by Liara's side.

A green dragon descended from the sky shortly behind Kiranya. It was Aethelm. He was a beautiful emerald green; his scales glistened brightly in the sunlight. He landed next to Castien. Castien smiled up at his long-time friend, then patted his side.

Lyren just realized the dragons were arriving in the same order as their human friends did a moment ago. Leave it to them to be so precise. She knew who would be next then, and she was right Draylith came swooping down his dark blue scales just as beautiful as ever and his demeanor that of a regal prince. He dropped into place next to Astria.

Narema came last. She was a bright neon green. She carried herself like a queen and was always mothering the younger dragons. She landed next to Myana and folded her wings.

Feora moved to the free spot and lowered her neck so Lyren could climb aboard. "Dragoneers! Eldoria is under attack. We must protect our kingdom."

"For Eldoria!" called Myana, assuming her role as second-in-command.

"For Eldoria!" they all called out before all five dragons took off. The rush of wind from their wings almost blew over the trees at the edge of the clearing. The sky was filled with different shades of red, green, blue, and gold. It was a wonderful sight to behold. Five humans flying on the backs of five dragons. Lyren was proud of herself and her dragoneer friends. But most of all, she was proud of Jaylen. Proud that her daughter had found her brother and together they fought alongside dragons to protect their kingdom.

Hold on, Jaylen, we are coming, thought Lyren.

Chapter 27:

The Last Salvation

Not much further now. Jaylen was getting closer to Adrin and her revenge. This was the second time in her life that she had sought revenge. The first, of course, was that man who had shot Aurelia just so he could collect a bounty. She had to calm down; if she let her emotions control her, she would die by his hand. She was just so angry. Was this how her father felt that day? She looked up at Adrin and saw his smile and realized this was his doing. Somehow, he was influencing her emotions with his power. But how? He couldn't have bonded with Elvaroth; she knew enough about Elvaroth to know he couldn't bond with a human.

She reached deep inside herself and called up whatever strength she had and pushed away the overwhelming anger. She dispatched the last soldier standing between her and Adrin, stepping forward and pulling her sword up. "Your attempt to control my emotions has failed, Your Majesty. Now you will pay for all the lives you have taken. Especially Jamore."

"You are stronger than I thought, Your Highness. It doesn't matter though; you will still be defeated," said Adrin, bringing his own sword to the ready.

He wasted no time swinging his sword toward her neck. She parried the attack, then swung her sword in a quick arc in the direction of his arm, knowing he would block it. She was prepared, and as his sword came up, she quickly changed directions, intending to spin around and cut him in the stomach. He was too fast though and blocked that one too.

Jaylen glanced up and saw the dragons fighting. Tauren and Aurelia must be getting tired. She glanced around as she blocked another attack. Even with the help of King Balian, the battle was still tipping in the favor of Milvania. Terikon and Felarrin had taken turns keeping Aurelia busy and trying to give Elvaroth an edge over Tauren. King Adrin had just blocked another of her combo attacks. He was stronger than her somehow. Lyon was busy with a wave of enemies pinning him down. King Thadis was fighting off as many as he could, but with no reinforcements, they were all tired.

Milvania had gotten three or four waves of reinforcements. How did they have so many soldiers? Aurelia was busy with Elvaroth now and couldn't get to Jaylen. Terikon and Felarrin were keeping Tauren at bay so he couldn't get to Elvaroth. Was this the end? Had they failed, after all?

Jaylen blocked the king's next attack and moved to the side. A loud roar pierced the afternoon air. Everyone heard it, and everyone stopped and looked in its direction. Sitting on a hill not far away was a huge golden dragon. Its scales shone brighter than even Aurelia. The dragons recognized her instantly. It was Feora, and seated on her back in the most majestic armor Jaylen had ever seen was her mother.

Queen Lyren raised her arm, and in the loudest voice Jaylen had ever heard her use, she called out, "Dragoneers... take wing!" There was a rush of air that sent a wave of wind right through the army as four dragons—one blue, two green and one red—rose above the hill behind Feora and Lyren. All all were in perfect formation with riders on their backs.

Nobody had seen a sight like this in recent history. Feora leaped into the air at the front of the group and they all surged forward toward the battle. This made Elvaroth desperate. If he could take out Aurelia before they arrived, all the dragons loved her. They would be off balance. He could still taste victory.

Elvaroth tried to take advantage of the distraction and surged forward toward Aurelia. Jaylen caught it out of the corner of her eye and shouted, "Aurelia, look out!" It wasn't necessary, though, because Aurelia had already seen him. She moved just in time and as Elvaroth flew by, she turned on a wingtip and drove her hind leg into his wing, breaking it and sending him reeling to the ground.

Aurelia wasted no time and dove after him. As he hit the ground, she landed on top of him, pinning him to the blood-soaked grass. "Time to die for your crimes, Elvaroth," said Aurelia, holding her front leg up, ready to strike the killing blow.

"You... wouldn't kill your own uncle... would you?" Elvaroth said, his words carrying to Jaylen's ears.

Jaylen was momentarily distracted by what he said. If Elvaroth was her uncle, then that meant Tauren was her father. Jaylen felt the pain as Adrin knocked her to the ground with his shoulder.

Aurelia, overcome with many emotions, didn't realize right away that her friend was in real danger. She was focused on one thing. This was her father's brother. From what she had heard, they were close, once. But all the things he had done since, those unfortunately outweighed even blood and by dragon law, one who has committed treason in the royal family, must be put to death.

"You have never been my uncle. You abandoned your kind a long time ago, before I was born. You are just a criminal to me." She slashed her talon across his throat, slicing it wide open and leaving him to bleed out on the ground. "Goodbye, Uncle Elvaroth," Aurelia said as she leaped back into the air.

As she left the ground, she caught sight of Jaylen lying on the ground, King Adrin standing over her, sword raised. She let out a roar of anguish. Could she get to them in time?

Adrin swung his sword down and Jaylen blocked it. Their swords pushed back and forth together. Jaylen tried to push back Adrin's sword with her own, but he was just too strong. He eventually knocked her sword out of her hands and raised his sword back up, ready to end the life of Princess Jaylen. Aurelia was already making her way to them, flying as fast as she could.

"Well, Your Highness, I have you now. Any final words?" asked Adrin.

"It doesn't matter what happens to me, you are defeated," said Jaylen. "With my death, I carry the knowledge that you have failed."

Adrin laughed and gripped his sword with both hands. "You are mistaken. Today you die," he said in the most menacing tone Jaylen had heard out of any living creature.

Jaylen looked over Adrin's shoulder and planted a smile on her face as she saw the red form of Aurelia quickly closing in on them. She looked at Adrin and laughed. "You're going to regret that choice," she said.

Adrin gave her a confused look. But it didn't last long as Aurelia landed directly behind him, sliding from the speed of her descent. She was barely able to stop herself from sliding into both Adrin and Jaylen. She wasted no time and plunged her talon right through his chest. "He won't have time," said Aurelia, as she withdrew her talon. Jaylen rolled out of the way just as Adrin's sword and his lifeless corpse fell to the ground next to her.

Jaylen picked up her own sword and hugged Aurelia. "I'm sorry you had to do that, but I'm glad you did," she said.

Aurelia sighed. "I need you, Jaylen. I can't lose the only true friend I've ever had," she said.

Jaylen noticed a tear falling down Aurelia's cheek. She wiped it away and smiled. "Do not cry for me, dear friend. I'm here, and I don't plan on leaving anytime soon. We're bonded. For life," she said, smiling up at her.

Aurelia smiled, too. Jaylen was her best friend, the only human friend she had ever had. She couldn't bear the thought of losing Jaylen. Though she felt sadness for having to kill a human again, she was glad she had saved her friend. She hoped that would end the battle. She hated all this mindless killing and suffering.

Jaylen caught sight of Jamore lying in the grass, he was still moving. Adrin must have missed the vital organs. She looked at Aurelia. "Go," said Aurelia sympathetically. She knew Jamore was dying, and he needed his friend.

Jaylen ran to where her second-in-command was lying still in the grass, trying so hard to remain alive to see his friend. She knelt down next to him and lifted his head into her lap. Jamore weakly opened his eyes and looked at her.

"I am sorry, Your Highness…. I have failed you," he said, weakly.

"No, no, you have not. You did the best you could, and that's all I could ever ask for," Jaylen said through tears. The battle raged on around them, but no one disturbed their last moment, probably because there was a very large and very protective red dragon standing close by.

"Jaylen…. as much as I respect you…. as my ruler.. I have grown fond of you as a friend… I will forever be grateful… for the kindness you have shown me in all my years as… a warrior of Eldoria," said Jamore, clearly in his last breaths.

Jaylen closed her eyes and cried. As she opened them, Jamore smiled and said, "Thank you, Jaylen… thank you for your friendship." She knew the end was very near for him. She must comfort him.

"No, Jamore… thank you for your friendship. But now is the time, your battle has been fought… You can rest peacefully knowing you protected your kingdom to the best of your ability," said Jaylen through the tears.

Jamore looked to the sky, smiled, and closed his eyes one last time. Jaylen held his head and cried. After a few moments, she gently laid his head on the grass. "Rest in peace, mighty warrior of Eldoria."

Suddenly, her sadness turned to anger. Not as strong as before, but she was still angry. She grabbed her sword and turned to the enemies. She yelled out, "*For Eldoria!*" and ran straight into the battle, taking down enemies right and left. Aurelia was watching her with sadness in her eyes. She knew this part of the grieving process. The anger you feel, asking yourself why they had to die. Then comes the sadness, where you remember the moments and feel sad because you know you'll never get those moments together again.

Lyon had finally broken through the ranks of soldiers. He ran to Jaylen, grabbed her arm, and tried to calm her down. He knew if she didn't calm down, she'd burn out before the battle was over. With the king dead, the army was starting to lose cohesion; some were already running back to Milvania. However, there were still those die-hard soldiers who wanted to avenge their king, and they were focused on Jaylen.

"Jaylen, stop, listen to me!" Lyon said, as she fought him.

Jaylen tried to continue fighting; she had to keep fighting and destroy the whole army, by herself if necessary. "Let me go, Lyon!" She screamed.

"Jaylen, stop! If you keep going like this, you'll burn out too fast," he said. He had to make her come to her senses.

"No, they must pay for this." Jaylen was beyond reason. "I have to avenge him!" The Milvanians were already starting to break up and retreat. She didn't have to fight anymore. But how could he make her see that?

"His death is already avenged," said Lyon, pointing at the corpse of King Adrin. "Remember who you are. Fight for him, fight for Eldoria, but do it like a warrior, *not* a killer. We kill because we must, not because we enjoy it."

Jaylen nodded. "You're right. What was I thinking?" She took a deep breath and began crying. She fell to the ground all fight taken from her. Lyon embraced her and just let her cry. He kept watch as well, making sure no Milvanian could take advantage of her loss of emotion.

All around them, soldiers were fleeing the battle. Up above, Aurelia had rejoined the battle. She took out lines of soldiers as the other dragons got closer to where the two gray dragons were trying to take down Tauren.

They saw the others coming for them and they tried to run. That didn't work, as Jaylen saw four more dragons descend and cut them off. All four were larger than most and had a sort of symbol kind of etched

228

into their chests. Felarrin and Terikon knew they had no chance. Jaylen watched as they surrendered to these new dragons, who immediately led them up and out of sight.

With no more dragons fighting with them, even the most hardened Milvanian soldier saw their defeat coming. The commanders finally officially sounded the retreat. The fighting stopped, and quiet briefly fell over the battlefield like a moment of silence for the fallen. Then the Eldorians and the Corinians all raised their weapons in the air and began cheering.

The dragoneers, along with Tauren, who looked pretty beaten up but still in one piece, slowly descended back toward the Eldorian camp. Jaylen and Lyon made their way there as well. Thadis was already there, and Aurelia had landed next to him. Jaylen saw him reach up and pat Aurelia's side. She bent down and touched his forehead as she had done before. Jaylen almost cried. It took a war to bring her father around, but she knew dragons would be accepted now.

As the dragoneers landed, all the Corinians and Eldorians began to cheer. All the dragons seemed to take this with a regal calm. The riders, however, lifted their arms and waved and called for more cheers. Lyren put up her hand, and Feora roared, and the whole crowd became silent. "We have fulfilled our oath to defend our home, that is all. You all deserve the cheers, for you fought so much harder than we did. We salute you!"

No sooner had she finished speaking than, as one, all the dragons bowed and their human companions raised their arms in salute. Lyren turned to King Thadis, Jaylen, Lyon, and King Balian, who had just joined them. "I present to you the new dragoneers. We pledge our life and loyalty to the service of the four kingdoms and peace."

All four humans bowed, and King Thadis spoke. "We accept your pledge and make one of our own. No longer will dragons be feared or exiled. You may come and go as you please in our kingdoms, and humans will be your friends and honor the dragoneers as heroes of Lianthis."

Another cheer went up from the armies.

Chapter 28:

Aftermath

The battlefield was littered with wounded—both soldiers and villagers who had stayed to help the warriors. The dragoneers were walking the battlefield, healing those they could and honoring those they couldn't with a proper burial. It was decided that this clearing would become a graveyard, and all the dead would be buried here as a symbol of how bloody war could be. The soldiers who had survived began digging graves for the dead from all three kingdoms. They marked the ones they could, but they didn't know all the soldiers from Milvania.

Tauren sat by the body of his brother, remembering when they used to chase each other around the kingdoms. That was so long ago, but it seemed like only yesterday that Elvaroth and Tauren were inseparable. It was when Tauren had been named the rightful successor that Elvaroth began to become distant. If Tauren had known that him being chosen to follow their father as king was going to cause all of this, he would have given the title to his brother gladly.

Tauren heard heavy footsteps approaching and heard the familiar voice of his mother. "Don't do this to yourself again, dear Tauren," said Feora. "I remember when you told your father that you were willing to give up the throne for Elvaroth if it would bring him back. Do you remember what he told you?"

"Of course, Mother," said Tauren. "He said that because I would give up the throne, that was why I deserved it and Elvaroth did not. If Elvaroth had become king, we might have attacked the humans and our path would have been one of conquest instead of civilization and peace."

"Exactly, so don't question yourself now." Feora smiled. "It is so good to see you again, my son. I have missed you."

"I've missed you too, Mother," said Tauren, also smiling. He turned and looked back to see where Lyon was. He spotted Lyon talking with Lyren and decided he had better get back and say hi. Before he left, though, there was one more thing he needed to do. Elvaroth could not be buried; he was too large. He would need to be cremated. Tauren nodded to his mother, and she nodded back. "Goodbye, brother. May the wind always lift you up and your flight be easy." He opened his mouth, and both he and his mother released a jet of hot flame, burning Elvaroth to ashes, which were picked up by the wind and spread across the nearby forest.

Both Tauren and Feora turned and walked back to the camp where Lyon and Lyren were waiting.

Jaylen was helping the wounded as was her duty as princess of Eldoria. She spotted movement out of the corner of her eye. She turned and grabbed her sword, but almost immediately let go as she caught sight of a small child peeking around the corner, watching Aurelia. Jaylen knelt on the ground, holding out her hand. "It's all right, sweetie. You can come and say hi. She won't hurt you."

Just to show the child she was friendly, Aurelia laid on the ground with her head at the child's height. It took a minute, but the little girl came out and slowly approached Aurelia. She reached her hand out and touched Aurelia's head. When Aurelia purred, the girl laughed. Jaylen smiled. Aurelia was the sweetest.

She'd be a great mother, Jaylen thought.

"What's your name?" asked Jaylen.

"I'm Isa, Your Highness," said the girl with a bright smile on her face despite the horrors surrounding her. Jaylen estimated she was about five. Suddenly, Jaylen heard a woman call out for Isa.

"She's over here!" Jaylen called back, turning toward the call.

The woman ran and grabbed Isa. "Thank you, Your Highness. I thought I'd lost her."

The woman bowed and Jaylen laughed. "Don't thank me. Aurelia's the one who coaxed her out," she said, pointing to Aurelia.

The woman saw Aurelia and jumped backward. She had never seen a dragon before. Obviously, she'd be a little afraid. "It's okay, Mother. She's a nice dragon. She let me pet her," said Isa.

The woman slowly reached out and petted Aurelia's head, who purred in response. "Thank you, sweet creature, for finding my daughter," said the woman, smiling.

"I know your daughter's name, but not yours," said Jaylen, standing up again.

"I'm Kelia. I live in Brancreek Village. My husband brought us to the castle when the attacks started," she said. "We got word the fighting had stopped and I guess little Isa thought she could go home. I am sorry if she bothered you."

Jaylen laughed. "No trouble at all. Aurelia and I were glad to meet her." She had to maintain her composure, but it was hard. This woman and her family had lost their home because of a power-hungry king. Jaylen suddenly wished Aurelia hadn't killed Adrin so she could make him rot in a cell for the rest of his natural life. "I'm so sorry. We'll do everything we can to get you and your family home. For now, we're setting up a temporary camp outside the castle until we can send men to rebuild the village. You and your family will be safe there."

"Thank you, milady," said Kelia, bowing once again. Isa waved goodbye to Aurelia, and Kelia thanked them one last time. "Oh, and Kelia?" Jaylen said. Kelia turned around. "You and Isa are welcome to come see Aurelia anytime." Kelia smiled, and off they went. Jaylen turned to Aurelia, who was smiling at her. "What are you smiling at?"

"You. That's the first time I've ever seen Her Highness Princess Jaylen. You're usually just Jaylen," she said.

"Well, most of the time, I want to be just Jaylen. But sometimes I have to be Her Highness Princess Jaylen because it's required of me," Jaylen replied.

"I think it suits you," said Aurelia.

Jaylen laughed, but her face turned puzzled. "I have been meaning to ask you about 'uncle' Elvaroth. With the battle raging and everything after, I didn't get a chance. Why didn't you tell me?" Jaylen was getting a bit of anger in her voice. She had to control that. Aurelia must have had a good reason.

"I am sorry, Jaylen. I never meant to deceive you. I wanted you to know just Aurelia, *not* Her Majesty Aurelia, queen of the dragons," said Aurelia, taking from their earlier conversation. "My duty is to rule over and protect the dragon kingdom, but that is not who I am. In order for us to bond, you needed to know the real me."

"I guess I can accept that," said Jaylen. Aurelia was right. Titles can make it so much harder to know who your true friends are. "I want to learn everything for now, though. Would you go ask my mother to come see me? I am going to find my father."

"What am I, a messenger service?" asked Aurelia, smiling to show Jaylen she was kidding.

"No, but friends help each other. Right?" Jaylen grinned mischievously.

"Of course, Your Highness," said Aurelia.

"Thank you, Your Majesty," replied Jaylen. With that, Aurelia turned toward where Lyren was, and Jaylen headed to her father's tent.

Chapter 29:

The Return to Corina

As things calmed down in Eldoria, it was time to work on rebuilding and stabilizing the kingdom. King Balian had done all he could to help; it was now time for him and his army to return home. He went to find Elia, who had ridden with him to battle but stayed in the camp to tend the wounded, and Alaria, who had arrived shortly after the battle ended to help organize the temporary camp for the residents of Brancreek Village.

He found Alaria first. She was standing next to Jaylen and Lyren. They were talking, and Alaria seemed a bit nervous. As he approached, they noticed him and greeted him. He smiled. "What were the three of you talking about so intensely?" he asked.

"Jaylen and Lyren believe it is time for Elia to officially meet Sandora," said Alaria, a little reluctant.

"They are correct, sweetheart. I know how you feel, but now that dragons are welcome in the three kingdoms, then there will be no danger. We can't keep them apart forever; they are bonded and should be together," said Balian. He, too, was a little reluctant, but he had to think about what would be best for Elia.

"I know," said Alaria. "I just don't want Elia to be a dragoneer. She is supposed to learn to rule and take over for us one day."

"Not all humans who are bonded to a dragon become active dragoneers," said Lyren. "Look at Tauren and Lyon. They were never active with the dragoneers. Elia will be free to stay with you and continue as princess of Corina. Sandora can stay with her or come and go as she pleases. Even me, as leader of the dragoneers, I still rule my kingdom with Thadis and Feora, and I visit when we can."

That seemed to make Alaria feel better. "You're right, Lyren. Fine, let them meet. I do, however, ask that Sandora come to Corina for a little while so we can get to know her as well."

"I actually have an idea about that," said Aurelia. "Let Jaylen and me fly Elia up to the Dragon Kingdom to meet Sandora. Then I can convince my mother in person to allow her to come to Corina for a little while."

Jaylen smiled. "We could make it a surprise for Elia. I could offer to fly her home on Aurelia, and in reality, we would fly her to Karukan."

Balian laughed. "That is a fantastic idea!" He turned to Alaria. "We could play it up even more by making her think we are nervous for her to ride Aurelia all the way home."

Alaria was smiling now. "Well, it wouldn't really be a stretch. No offense, dear Aurelia, but it is a little scary for me to have my daughter flying. I know you would never let anything happen to her, but being so high up is not normal for us humans."

"I understand," said Aurelia. "Rest assured, though, if I can fly sleepyhead over here," she motioned to Jaylen, "all the way to Corina while she slept, I can keep Elia safe when she is wide awake."

Everyone laughed at that, even Jaylen. "All right, Elia should be here soon. She wanted to say goodbye to Aurelia, so the rest of you go busy yourselves. Balian and Alaria, we will come to you soon to ask your permission to take Elia."

Everyone dispersed, and Jaylen and Aurelia settled in and waited for Elia to arrive. They didn't have to wait long. Elia came walking up to them soon after, looking a bit sad.

She greeted them, then turned to Aurelia. "I wish I didn't have to say goodbye," she said.

"Goodbyes are never easy," said Aurelia. "I'm going to miss you, sweet Elia."

"I'll miss you too, Aurelia," replied Elia.

Jaylen smiled at her friends' interaction. She had two best friends, and those best friends were slowly becoming best friends, too. Elia hugged Aurelia, and she could sense Aurelia's sadness. She guessed it was because of her own bond.

"Don't be sad. We'll see each other again. My kingdom isn't too far. And with your speed, it won't take you too long to get there," said Elia.

They all laughed. Then Jaylen proposed her idea. "Hey, would you like to fly back home on Aurelia?" she asked.

Elia's eyes lit up like two stars on a clear night tree. She turned to Aurelia. "Is that all right with you?" she asked.

"It would be my pleasure," said Aurelia, bowing her head.

Elia all but ran out of the tent to find her parents. She spotted them by the carriages, preparing to leave. She ran to them, practically running into Thadis and Lyren.

"Woah, dear child. Where are you off to in such a hurry?" asked Thadis.

"Well... Jaylen said that I could fly home with her on Aurelia," she said.

Balian and Alaria looked a little concerned. Obviously, they knew what was going on, but they had to act like they didn't to maintain the surprise. "Are you sure that's wise, Elia?" asked Balian.

"I promise I will keep her safe," said Jaylen from behind them.

Alaria walked down the steps and held Jaylen's hands. "Please protect her with your life. She's my only child," she said.

"I promise, Your Majesty. She will be safe," said Jaylen.

"And I, too, will protect her like she was my own," said Aurelia, landing behind Jaylen.

Balian came down and joined them. He patted Aurelia's side as if thanking her for protecting his daughter. He lifted Elia up onto Aurelia's back, and Jaylen climbed aboard in front of her.

"We'll meet back at the castle in Corina. We'll probably make it back first," said Jaylen, although she knew they wouldn't.

Balian and Alaria laughed. Jaylen put her hand in the air and called out, "Aurelia, take wing!" and they were off. Elia held onto Jaylen with a death grip. She was clearly a little nervous.

"Wow. I'm surprised your father hasn't put a sword in your hand. With a grip like that, you could do some serious damage," said Jaylen.

Elia laughed and loosened her grip. She slowly opened her eyes and watched as the trees and animals below got smaller and smaller. She smiled and let go of Jaylen and spread her arms like wings. "This is amazing!" she said.

Jaylen and Aurelia laughed. "That was my exact reaction," said Jaylen.

They continued to climb until they burst through the clouds. "Why so high?" asked Elia. "I want to see the land as we fly over it."

"There is something more beautiful we want you to see first," said Jaylen, almost having to shout to be heard over the rushing wind. Aurelia stabilized them and turned toward Karukan. It was only a short distance away, but hidden from view by the spell. Only she could see it before they passed the border.

"It looks like just a bunch of clou… oh my." As Elia was talking, they passed into the border, and Karukan burst into view. Elia marveled at the island in the sky with all its marvelous mountains and the carved-out dragon caves. The sun glistened off the smooth stone walkways and the large buildings in the center. "Is this what I think it is?" She asked.

"Elia," said Aurelia, "welcome to the dragon city of Karukan."

Elia couldn't believe her eyes. This was the most beautiful place she'd ever seen. Besides her own kingdom, of course. She looked around and saw hundreds of dragons. Some flying over the mountains, some sitting in the grasslands; she even saw young dragons playing with their parents. It was like many rainbows all around, with glistening colors everywhere. They seemed to be completely at peace, not a care in the world.

"Aurelia, this is beautiful. But I thought we were going back to Corina," said Elia, a little confused.

Aurelia smiled. "And we will. But first, there is someone you must meet," she said and began her descent toward what looked like a massive castle with a mountain peak in the middle. It was the most awe-inspiring thing Elia had ever seen. The walls looked like they were carved from dark blue gemstones. There was a large courtyard, then the mountain. Just in front of the mountain was a large room with no walls, only the cave-like entrance behind it.

Aurelia landed in the courtyard. Jaylen could see into the castle. The room with no walls looked like a throne room. Sitting on the throne was a beautiful, bright green dragon. As they approached, the green dragon got up excitedly and walked toward them. She bowed to Aurelia. "Welcome home, my queen," she said in the most delightfully musical voice they had ever heard. "I have kept it warm for you, but I relinquish the throne gladly now that you are home."

241

"My dearest Sandora," said Aurelia. "I thank you for assuming the duties in my absence."

"Who have you brought with you, Aurelia?" asked Sandora curiously.

"This is my bondmate, Jaylen, Princess of Eldoria," said Aurelia.

Jaylen curtsied. "Pleased to meet you…Sandora," she said. "I am sorry to ask, but why did you assume the throne in Aurelia's absence?"

Aurelia laughed and stood next to Sandora. They both released a jet of fire into the air, and Jaylen watched in awe as the flames looked almost identical. She looked back at Aurelia and Sandora and noticed that their eyes were the exact same color. Jaylen's eyes went wide as the realization hit her.

"Is she your twin?" Jaylen asked rather loudly.

Aurelia laughed. "Yes, she is. With dragons, the only thing different about twins is the color of their scales. Everything else, like eye color, flames, and size, is pretty much identical," she explained.

"Wow. Dragons never cease to amaze me," she said.

"Excuse me. I have just one question," said Elia.

Jaylen got so distracted she almost forgot Elia was there.

"Is she my bondmate? Because I can understand her clearly, but I still have trouble understanding Aurelia sometimes," said Elia.

"Yes, dear one," said Sandora, speaking for herself. "I do apologize for not meeting you sooner, but your parents insisted we remain apart so you could learn to be queen without thinking of flying off with me. As a princess myself, I understood and kept my distance. However, I have watched you, and I must say you are truly a kind and sweet young woman."

Elia slowly walked toward Sandora and held out her hand. Sandora leaned her head down to touch Elia's hand. Elia gasped when she touched her. "I just saw the moment I bonded with you," she said.

"Because you were only a toddler, you couldn't remember it. So Sandora showed it to you. She wasn't as young, so she was old enough to remember," said Aurelia.

Just then, a beautiful red dragon landed behind them. She walked toward them and called for Sandora. "What are you doing out here? I thought you were waiting for."

She got cut off as Aurelia turned around and smiled. Of course, she recognized her voice. "Aurelia? My dear sweet Aurelia? Are you finally home?" asked the dragon.

"Yes, Mother. I am home," said Aurelia.

Jaylen's mouth dropped open. "Mother? Oh dear, I think I need to sit down," she said, nearly falling over. She sat on a rock and put her head in her hands. "Way too many surprises for one princess to handle," she said.

"Jaylen, this is my mother, Sulara," said Aurelia, almost laughing at her friend's reaction.

Jaylen looked up, and Sulara bowed. Jaylen stood up and walked toward Sulara. She pet Sulara's neck, which made her purr just like Aurelia did. Jaylen smiled. She had now met the whole family. At least she hoped so.

"You and Tauren raised a wonderful daughter, Sulara. She is my best friend. And my bondmate," said Jaylen. She looked over at Elia and Sandora and saw them talking and laughing. She was glad they finally met. It was time Elia embraced her dragoneer side. Even though she knew she probably wouldn't be an active dragoneer, she still should have the choice.

"Thank you for your kind words, Jaylen. I have known for some time that Aurelia was destined to be bonded to you," said Sulara. "As the former queen, I had a vision of you bringing dragons and humans together again. I never told your mother, though I love her dearly. She would not have wanted this for you."

Jaylen was laughing. "I am glad you didn't tell her. She would have locked me in my room and never let me out. Also, I am glad you didn't tell Aurelia; she was nervous enough telling me she was queen, let alone that we were destined to bond."

Aurelia growled low but quickly regained her composure. "I think Jaylen is right there. I might never have gone that day if I had known. The prospect of destiny still makes me uncomfortable."

"As I have told you before, my dear child. Destiny is not predetermined as most believe, but a formation of our decisions into a logical conclusion," said Sulara, obviously continuing an old conversation. "The only reason I can see the future is because the universe knows the choices we will make based on choices we have made already. It doesn't change the fact that we make our own destinies, only predicts them based on our choices."

"You are right, mother," said Aurelia, bowing. "I am glad to hear your wisdom again."

Jaylen smiled and poked Aurelia in the side. "At least one member of your family has wisdom." She teased.

"Oh, shut up, you," said Aurelia, shaking her head.

Sulara laughed. "Yes, you two are definitely bondmates."

Just then, Elia and Sandora approached. "We have made a decision," said Elia, sounding more serious than Jaylen had ever heard. "Sandora and I are going back to Corina together to spend some time together. That way, I can decide if my talents are better used as an active dragoneer or as future queen of my kingdom."

Aurelia was about to say no because Balian and Alaria were pretty much against Elia becoming a dragoneer, when Sulara cut her off. "A very wise idea, my young friend. It appears you have learned well how to conduct yourself as a princess and make choices that are right for you and your kingdom. I don't doubt you will find a solution. You have my blessing, Sandora. Go to Corina with Elia."

"You have mine as well," said Aurelia. She heard the words and what her mother was trying to say. Sandora knew that Elia must stay in Corina so she would make sure that their decision was the best solution for both dragonkind and Corina.

"Aurelia and I will stay here for a while. We have preparations to make that will bring the kingdoms together," said Jaylen. "We will see each other again soon, Elia." She walked over, and as Sandora put her head and neck down so Elia could get on, Jaylen helped her friend mount.

Elia, who had watched Jaylen's training, was already ahead of the game. She sat in the exact spot that Lyon had told Jaylen to sit. Raising her arm, she said, "I have always wanted to say this… Sandora, Take Wing!" Sandora leaped into the air, and they flew off together.

Aurelia looked at Jaylen and simply said, "I hope they make the right choice."

Jaylen grinned. "They are both smart. They will make the best decision for Corina."

Chapter 30:

Milvania Needs a King

Milvania Castle buzzed with activity. Every village was represented since every man who could fight had been called into battle. They had hoped with such superior numbers that Eldoria would fall. They had not counted on the arrival of the princess on a dragon. They also did not expect the other dragons to interfere. They had never interfered in human wars before.

Everyone was talking at once. The commanders stepped up on the raised platform usually reserved for entertainers, and quieted the crowd with a bellow. The general of the army stepped forward. He was tall, and his muscles bulged as he gripped his sword. His name was Keeval.

"Everyone listen to me," he said, and the crowd became silent. "Our king is dead. We must now determine who is to replace him and lead us to eventual victory over the entitled kingdoms."

"But they have dragons," said a man from the crowd. "We can't defeat the dragons."

"Dragons can be killed," said Keeval. "You just have to lure them in one at a time and set traps." He smiled. "We need to do this by the law of Milvania. We are not uncivilized like the other kingdoms. We need a strong king. So I propose we hold a tournament, as is the custom when no successor is available. The winner will become our unquestioned king."

Cheers went up through the crowd. One of the commanders stepped forward. "These will not be fights to the death. As the general said, we are civilized. Also, to qualify by law, you must have attained the rank of at least captain in the army or magistrate of a village. We can't let just anyone enter or we would never have a strong king," said Jimanen. "Sign-ups will be tomorrow morning."

The crowd dispersed then, some to go prepare, others setting up stands by the training grounds where the tournament would take place. Keeval along with the commanders and captains, went to the castle. Once they were away from the crowd, Keeval said, "Now we all know who is going to win this, right?"

"Yes, sir!" they all responded. Keeval had been their general for years; none dared challenge him.

Keeval laughed and went straight to the king's bedchamber to get a good night's rest for tomorrow. He knew the others would let him win, but they would have to make it look convincing. He was an expert with the bow staff, which would be the weapon of choice for the tournament because it was non-lethal, so his win would not be questioned. He was glad that idiot Adrin had been killed. This time tomorrow he would be king and nobody could stop him. That meant he could finally fulfill his destiny to rule over all of Lianthis once he eliminated the dragons. His father was a dragon hunter. So was his brother, but that crazy princess had killed him just because he smuggled a few plants. He was going to make her pay for that one day soon.

Lyon and Tauren flew high to avoid being noticed. As they passed the castle, Tauren could see the activity. "You were right, Lyon, they are preparing for a tournament." Tauren was glad he had encouraged Lyon to learn all the laws of the land so that he would never break one by ignorance.

"That is good. So they probably have no idea of the provision that will allow me to participate. Boy, are they going to be surprised," said Lyon, pointing to a clearing not far behind the castle. "Land there and we can get some rest for tomorrow."

Tauren descended and landed in the middle of the indicated clearing. Lyon dismounted and set up camp while Tauren went to get them something to cook for dinner. Lyon got a fire going just in time. Tauren landed again with a whole big buck in his mouth. Lyon peeled the skin off the side and sliced some meat for himself. Then he left Tauren to eat the rest.

While Tauren ate the rest of the deer, Lyon cooked his portion and added some seasonings that he always brought with him. After their meal, Lyon set up his bedding, which consisted of a wool blanket that Balian had given him and his bag for a pillow.

The next morning, Keeval woke and went to the dining hall to get some breakfast. The tournament would start as soon as signups were complete. He estimated there would be about fifteen people participating. In the event of an odd number, then, as the ranking officer, he would get a free pass in the first round. He knew the four magistrates that would enter wouldn't let him win like the captains and the commanders, but he was confident he could easily defeat them.

As he made his way to the signup table, he thought about what he would do first when he became king. Rebuild the army and invest in more catapults, most likely. As he approached the table to sign up, he saw, as he had predicted, fourteen other names. All ten of the current commanders and captains plus the four magistrates he predicted would enter. He put his name down on the list, and Jimanen stood up. "Is there anyone else who wishes to sign up?" He held up the list. "I will ask once more if anyone else wishes to sign up. You must do so now or you will be disqualified." He was about to open his mouth to declare time's up when all went quiet as they heard the now familiar beating of a dragon's wings.

The courtyard emptied quickly as Tauren gently touched down, and Lyon jumped from his back. "I would like to enter," he said as he walked to the table and wrote his name under Keeval's.

"You are not a captain, commander, or magistrate," said Keeval. "You aren't even Milvanian. You do not qualify." He stood in defiance of Lyon's presence there.

"I am afraid you are mistaken, my dear general. Milvanian law clearly states that any person of royal blood in all of Lianthis may participate," Lyon straightened up and declared. "I am Prince Lyon of Eldoria. Please check with King Thadis or King Balian, and that will be easily verified."

"He is right, sir," said a smaller brown-haired man, whom Lyon recognized as Tamil, a farmer who frequently visited Corina. "He is the prince."

"Unfortunately, he is also right about the law. I just looked this morning," said Jimanen.

"Fine, it doesn't matter, anyway. I will defeat you all," said Keeval, storming off.

"Well, it appears he is confident," said Lyon, smiling. "This is going to be fun."

"Listen up, Your Highness." Jimanen spat the title like an insult. "Keeval has led us for many years and is more than capable of destroying some spoiled prince in battle. I held up your claim only because it is the law of Milvania and I am sworn to obey that law. If it were up to me, we would all attack and kill you where you stand for all your kingdom has done to us."

"That would be a costly mistake, my dear commander," said Lyon, pointing up at Tauren. "When I win this tournament, your oath will require you to obey me as your new king. I will expect nothing less from all of you. Milvania has potential, but only if it stops worrying about conquest and focuses on more important things like cooperation and patience." With that, Lyon took his place with the other participants.

A tall man in fine clothes stood before them as the crowd gathered in the newly constructed stands. Lyon recognized him as well. It was Karigen, Milvania's ambassador. He was the most impartial person in Milvania, so it made sense for him to preside over the tournament to assure fairness and an untainted victor. "All participants listen up," said Karigen in a loud voice so all could hear. "The rules of this competition are simple. You gain one point for hitting your opponent and five points for knocking him down. The first to ten points is declared the winner. The head and the fork of the legs are not allowed. Fight clean and fight well."

Lyon looked at the board where all the participants were listed on the ladder. Of course, they would put him on the exact opposite side as Keeval. Obviously, they were hoping to tire him out, so Keeval had a better chance of defeating him.

Lyon was in the very first battle. They paired him with one of the captains. Karigen introduced him as Jemanor. Lyon settled in with his staff in hand, ready to follow his plan and let each opponent, except maybe the magistrates, get a few points. He wanted Keeval overconfident when he faced him. Lyon knew Keeval was a real threat unlike the others. His whole plan was to get the general overconfident and make him make a mistake.

Karigen gave the signal to begin, and Lyon moved forward, watching his opponent carefully. Jemanor swung for Lyon's head. He blocked it easily and twisted away. So they were trying to take him out. He wasn't surprised. Milvanians were almost fanatical about duty and following the law. It is how Adrin kept them in line for so long and wasn't overthrown when he continuously made his own people suffer so he could have the best stuff. They would rather sacrifice their own personal honor by cheating rather than have to take orders from Lyon. They knew if he won, they would have to accept him as king. However, if they took him out, even if against the rules, Keeval would pardon them.

Lyon decided his original strategy wouldn't work. If they were going headhunting in order to injure him so badly, he would have to forfeit then he was going to have to end the matches quickly. He continued his twist motion, coming back around and sweeping the back of Jemanor's knee, sending him falling hard to the ground. Lyon only needed five more points, but he wanted to show a little more of his speed just to make them nervous.

Jemanor got to his feet and charged in with a flurry of attacks, which Lyon promptly blocked with his own staff. He decided to make Keeval cringe in anticipation. Using all the speed he had, he began twirling the staff. Jemanor stepped back, confused, which is all Lyon needed; he moved in with lightning speed, smacking the younger man five times in rapid succession. Jemanor couldn't even bring his staff up in time. Karigen declared Lyon the winner and thus ended round one. Three more to go, and Lyon knew it was going to get worse.

The other seven first-round matches went by fairly quickly. The four magistrates were already out, which Lyon predicted. They had no chance against hardened soldiers. And that, of course, was the reason that a king was determined by this tournament. Milvanians wanted a strong leader. Which was commendable in theory, but strong in a fight didn't make one a strong leader. There were other types of strength that were way more important.

His next match was against Jimanen. Lyon could almost see the malice in his eyes. When Karigen called for them to begin, Lyon didn't hesitate. He swung his staff then as Jimanen moved his staff to block, Lyon quickly changed directions, giving him a good smack in his left side. He pressed the attack with his shoulder, knocking the wind out of Jimanen and sending him flying to the ground, and receiving five points.

Jimanen recovered quickly, using his staff like a long club he hoped to catch Lyon off balance. Of course, it didn't work and Lyon punished him with a low sweep and knocked him down, gaining another five points and becoming the winner again. Jimanen stormed off the battlefield, but he could not contest it because the match had been won within the rules.

The round two matches were more highly contested since everyone was tasting victory. Keeval was the only other one who won his match with ease. Lyon suspected he was getting really frustrated by now. Their plan to take him out early had failed, and Keeval was realizing he would have to fight Lyon.

Karigen called a break for lunch. Lyon went to the corner of the courtyard and sat beside Tauren as he ate some bread and cheese that he had in his pack.

Chapter 31:

The Tournament Continues

Lyon saw a young man walking his way, and he got up. As the man drew closer, he recognized Yanin, a blacksmith who traveled between all three kingdoms. He owed allegiance to nobody, and all wanted his services because he was one of the best.

As Yanin approached, Lyon waved. "Good day, Master Yanin," he said. There were very few craftsmen in Lianthis who ever attained the title of master, so when one did, everyone used it, including the kings and queens of the kingdoms.

Yanin waved back. "Good day, Your Highness," he said, a little somber. "I must tell you that you are in grave danger if you continue in the tournament. I have heard word from several of my colleagues here that your next match will be against Commander Tylan and that he is under orders from the general to take you out. This is getting out of hand. Keeval's desire to rule is making him ignore the rules, and that is dangerous."

"Are you saying he won't abide by the decision if I do win?" asked Lyon.

"No, I think he will have to because the majority of the army would not follow him if he broke the law in attaining power," Yanin said, shaking his head for emphasis. "You know how fanatical Milvanians are about the law. They were even on the fence when Adrin invaded Eldoria, even though technically he followed the law; they were unsure if his reasoning held up."

"Good," said Lyon. "If he won't go completely against the law, then I have nothing to worry about."

Yanin shook his head and kicked at the ground. "I really hope you know what you are doing, Lyon," he said, dropping the formalities. "Don't be too overconfident. Keeval is a battle-hardened warrior who knows how to win. He didn't achieve the rank of general on politics alone."

Lyon laughed. Yanin didn't understand that being bonded with Tauren gave Lyon a tremendous advantage over other men in a fight. Plus, all the time he trained, knowing one day he would have to fight. "My dear Yanin, I am quite the accomplished warrior myself. I actually beat my sister once." That caught Yanin off guard. "This time tomorrow I will be king, and I will make Milvania a strong and independent kingdom and earn their respect while making them a better people."

Yanin couldn't argue anymore because at that moment, they both heard the horn that signaled break time was over. Lyon knew he would be first up in the semifinals, so he gripped Yanin's shoulder to reassure him, then hurried to the battlefield.

Upon arriving, he saw his opponent was Tylan, as Yanin had said. This he had already figured from the second-round matches and the way the ladder was set up. He also knew how dangerous Tylan was. Lyon settled into his fighting stance and waited for Karigen to call for the match to begin.

As soon as the word was given, Tylan jumped forward, hoping to knock Lyon off balance. Lyon stood his ground and allowed Tylan's first attack to connect. They needed to see that he could take anything. This was the time to prove to the Milvanians that he could take it as well as he dished it out.

Tylan's staff landed square on the side of Lyon's head, but not completely; he turned his head partially away so none of the blow hit his temple. Lyon stumbled a little but remained standing with great effort. Tylan stepped back, pleading with Kerigan that he was aiming for the shoulder and that it was a mistake. Lyon knew it wasn't, but he gave the OK for the match to continue. Tylan received a warning for attacking the head, and no points were awarded. Right on cue, Tauren roared from his place in the courtyard, and every eye showed fear. Tauren, of course, knew what Lyon was doing, but he had to make it look good.

The match resumed, and this time, Tylan came in more slowly. He was looking for an opportunity. So Lyon gave him one. He stumbled a bit to make Tylan think he was off balance, then just as Tylan swung his staff with all his force, Lyon brought his staff up to block. The two staves connected with a loud crack. Lyon looked up and smiled at Tylan.

This was Lyon's chance; he had Tylan right where he wanted him. Lyon kicked Tylan in the gut, sending him back, then unleashed a flurry of attacks one right after the other. Tylan blocked most, but still gave up five points. This made him angry. He saw his chance slipping away, so he needed to do something, or Keeval would have him sent to the furthest northern village for guard duty.

Tylan let out a scream of rage and jumped on Lyon, knocking him down. He raised his staff like a sword, hoping to jab it into Lyon's face, either killing him or wounding him enough to take him out of the tournament. This was the opportunity Lyon was waiting for. As the staff came down just a few inches from connecting, Lyon grabbed it, and all of Tylan's strength could not make the staff move.

"My dear Commander Tylan," said Lyon, smiling. "That was a grave mistake." With that, he used his legs with the staff as leverage and flipped Tylan over his head and onto the ground behind. He kicked up to his feet and put his own staff against Tylan's chest. Two soldiers came onto the field and grabbed Tylan, escorting him to the dungeon.

"You have our sincerest apologies, Your Highness. Tylan will be punished severely for his actions. That was a most disgraceful display. Are you alright? Will you be able to continue to the finals?" Karigen said, bowing respectfully.

"I am perfectly fine, Karigen," said Lyon, judging by the crowd reaction the majority of Milvania was against what Tylan did. Good, they were ready to accept the outcome, whatever it may be. "Please proceed with the last semifinal match so that we can proceed to the finals."

"As you wish," Karigen said and called the two participants to take their places. Keeval had a telling face. He was livid. All his plans to keep Lyon out of the finals had failed. Once he defeated Captain Olin, which was his opponent for this match, he would have to face Lyon.

As he figured, the match didn't last long. Keeval made short work of Olin. Also, as predicted, Keeval didn't want to wait; he wanted Lyon immediately. Lyon calmly agreed, then stepped onto the battleground one last time.

Karigen made sure both were ready, then signaled for them to begin. Lyon knew Keeval would not risk being disqualified himself, so all he had to do was weather the early storm from Keeval's anger, and he would be good.

Keeval advanced, barely controlling his anger. That was smart. Keeval knew he had to stay in control. Lyon, of course, was ready, and the initial engagement lasted for almost a minute as their staves clashed back and forth, neither gaining a clear advantage. Then Lyon saw his opening. He twisted to the right side and swung his staff at Keeval's side. Keeval tried to block, but wasn't fast enough.

The point was good, and Lyon danced back, preparing for the next attack.

Keeval grinned. "Very good, Your Highness." He twirled his staff. "But you will never rule Milvania."

Keeval charged forward, initiating a flurry of attacks at blinding speed. Lyon blocked all of them. Then he swept Keeval's legs, knocking him down. "That is six for me and none for you, General," said Lyon, also grinning.

Keeval got up and settled back into his fighting stance. This time, he just circled Lyon. Lyon pressed the attack, knowing that Keeval would be ready for him. He went for one side, then the other. When Keeval blocked the last attack, he twisted his staff, hoping to disarm Lyon, but he failed. Lyon held onto his staff but was thrown off balance.

Keeval took advantage, jabbing Lyon in the gut, then shoulder tackling him to the ground. Lyon had underestimated Keeval a little. He expected the tackle, but he had been ready for it, so he thought he could stay on his feet. Keeval really was as good as they said. "Well, Your Highness, now I have six too," said Keeval, his grin broadening.

Lyon got to his feet and smiled. Time to get serious. If he got knocked down again, then they would have to sit back and wait for Milvania to try another takeover of the world. Keeval moved in and tried a sweep. Lyon jumped and swung his own staff at Keeval's arm.

Keeval blocked the attack, then tried one of his own, but Lyon noticed something. Keeval was a little off balance. It looked like he was limping. That must be from the earlier fight when he got hit in the knee. This was what Lyon needed. He summoned his remaining speed and strength and initiated a flurry of attacks, all aimed at the arm and side of his opponent. Then suddenly he shifted the staff and ducked, swinging it like a long club, and it connected with Keeval's knee. Keeval couldn't stop himself, and he fell to the ground, ending the match.

The crowd cheered. Lyon hoped he had earned some respect from his perseverance. He attempted to help Keeval up, but his hand was batted away. "I'll never accept your help!" spat Keeval. "I will wait for you to make the smallest mistake as king, then I will take your throne from you." He got up and left the battleground.

Karigen raised his hand, silencing the crowd, then declared, "Our winner, and the new king of Milvania, is Lyon. Long live the king."

"Long live the king!" chanted the crowd.

Lyon stepped up on the raised platform and raised his own hand. "Listen to me, Milvania! Too long has this kingdom been deprived of proper leadership. King Adrin thought only of conquest. Now that I am king, we will become more self-sufficient. I swear to rule according to the ancient traditions. I will always put my people first. I know that many of those in the army may not wish to follow me, and so I give you all the opportunity to retire from the army and go home. Those who stay must follow me without question."

Karigen smiled. "I will be here to take anyone's letter of resignation until tomorrow morning. After which time, you will not get another chance." He bowed apologetically for interrupting the king.

"Thank you, Karigen," said Lyon, now absolutely sure that Karigen would become his chief advisor. "I think we can safely assume Keeval will be retiring. Any of the commanders who choose to stay will be tested in a competition to rise to become the new general. I must rest now. So I bid you all a good evening." With that, he walked to the castle, ready to collapse and enjoy his new bed.

Keeval stopped at the stables. There were about a hundred men waiting for him there. All of them had decided to retire and go with him. They would set up a village near the mountains and bide their time.

"Sir, we are with you," said one of the men.

"Good, we will not let this Eldorian sit on our throne for long. We will kill him, somehow," said Keeval, making that his only goal from now on.

They left town and headed north. Keeval knew of someone that would help. He had to be careful, though. If the dragons learned of Keeval's 'friends,' they would destroy them before they could organize. He hoped they were in the same location.

Chapter 32:

Forever Living in Harmony

King Thadis stood in the clearing, surveying the scene before him. It had been decided that today was the day for all kingdoms to reaffirm their commitment to the treaty with the dragons. They would all go to the bond flame in Karukan and pledge their kingdom's support.

Of course, King Thadis would represent Eldoria. Lyon had brought Karigen with him. Karigen had become his advisor and friend, so he would represent the unbonded humans of Milvania. Of course, King Balian and Queen Alaria were there as well. Balian came aboard Aurelia. Jaylen had returned to Corina a week ago in order to help teach Elia a little more and to bring Balian to Karukan. Alaria was in Sandora with Elia.

Thadis approached Feora and bowed. "May I have the honor of flying with you, dear Feora?" he said.

"Of course, Your Majesty," replied Feora. Ever since the battle ended last month, Thadis had spent many hours learning the dragon language, so he no longer needed translation assistance from Lyren.

"Thank you, mighty dragon," said Thadis, and he pulled himself up behind Lyren as she had taught him. They had become closer than ever now that the whole truth was out. Their marriage was stronger, and he loved her even more, knowing how much she had done to help her kingdom.

"I have waited for this day for so long. Today, we can finally reaffirm the bond between humankind and dragonkind. Elia, since you are new to all of this, when we enter Karukan, break away from us and head to the back of the castle. Sulara will explain how it all works. Lyon and I will find Jaylen and Aurelia. May the wind always lift you up and your flight be easy," said Lyren once Thadis had settled himself.

At Elia's confused expression, Lyon clarified, "It's the traditional dragon farewell. Lyren is all about tradition." Lyon playfully rolled his eyes.

Lyren raised an eyebrow at her son. "You're not too old for me to chastise you," she said, smiling.

"Well, I am best friends with a dragon, so chastising me might be tough." Lyon laughed and prepared for flight. All of them raised their hand and called out their dragon's name.

Then, as one, they all shouted, "Take wing!"

All three dragons leaped into the air with a powerful downstroke of their wings. They flew high above Eldoria. Lyren could see the castle slowly getting smaller as they got higher and higher into the sky. Before long, they emerged from the clouds into the beautiful city of Karukan. Elia was still awestruck by the beauty. And to be honest, even Lyren was still captivated, even though she had been there frequently.

Thadis, Karigen, Balian, and Alaria were all staring with their mouths open at the sheer beauty of it all. None could find their words.

"Wow… it's been so long since I've been up here," said Lyon.

"Me too. But it's just as beautiful as I remember," said Lyren.

Lyon silently agreed. He and Lyren continued flying until they noticed Aurelia standing by the castle. She was pretty hard to miss, being the brightest dragon in the city. They landed in the courtyard, and Lyon barely had a chance to dismount before Jaylen practically crushed him with a hug.

"I haven't even been gone that long," said Lyon, returning his sister's hug.

"I didn't even know you for seventeen years of my life, so I think I'm allowed to miss you," said Jaylen.

Lyren laughed and watched her children. She was so happy they were all together again. Those twenty years were the hardest of her life. She had moments where she'd cried alone in her room because she could see that Jaylen was lonely. Of course, Lyren and Thadis had told Jaylen about Lyon when she was old enough. She had always been curious about what it was like to have a brother. Now she knew.

"Greetings, Queen Lyren and King Thadis," said Aurelia.

Lyren bowed. "Greetings, Queen Aurelia." They usually didn't care about formalities, but as this was a special occasion, Lyren thought it was only right to use formal titles.

Thadis bowed as well, adding his greetings. "Greetings, Your Majesty. Your Kingdom is beautiful. I am honored that you would allow me to see it."

"Of course, King Thadis," said Aurelia, "you are always welcome. As are you, King Balian and Queen Alaria."

"Thank you, great queen," both said in unison.

Aurelia turned to Lyon and smiled at the man hiding behind him. "Greetings to you as well, Karigen. I understand you have been a great help to my friend Lyon, as he is trying to rebuild Milvania."

"Yes, Your Majesty," Karigen managed to get out in a hurry.

263

"Do not be afraid; dragons are proud and noble. They would do no harm to anyone who did not first do them harm," said Aurelia, inwardly laughing at his reaction.

Jaylen looked at her mother. "You're not going to call me Princess Jaylen, are you?" she said.

Lyren laughed. "Of course not, sweetheart," she said, hugging her daughter.

Aurelia made her way to Tauren, pressing their foreheads together. She smiled when she heard Tauren purr. Jaylen heard it too.

"I guess it runs in the family," she said, laughing.

Elia finally made it behind the castle after dropping her mother off with the others. She saw Sulara waiting for her. She landed and dismounted, still a little wobbly, but getting better.

"Looks like you need a little training," said Sulara.

Elia laughed. "Jaylen's been teaching me, but it's hard to climb on and off such a large creature," she said. Sandora nudged her. "Large, but very beautiful," said Elia, smiling. She and Sandora had been getting along really well since going to Corina. They understood each other completely and always had lots of fun.

Sulara smiled, then got serious. "Today's ceremonies are going to reshape the world of Lianthis for the better. The first ceremony will be to reaffirm the promise of the dragoneers to protect Lianthis. When your name is called, you will need a lock of your hair. There are flat rocks laid all around the fire. You'll place the hair on the rock, and Sandora will burn it. That solidifies that you're bonded for life." Sulara looked at Sandora. "Do you have a title for her, Sandora?" she asked.

"The Caledon Hero," Sandora said. "She may not have fought in the battle, but she tirelessly healed and comforted the wounded. That makes her a hero in my book."

Elia smiled. "Awe, thank you, sweet Sandora. I was only doing my part. Nothing special."

Sulara smiled as well. "All right. So once the hair is burned, you'll call out your name and title. Then Sandora will call out her name. Then you'll both say 'as bonded dragon and human, we swear to protect Lianthis with all our strength,' then we move on to the next person," explained Sulara.

Elia nodded. "I understand." She hesitated. "However, I have decided not to be an active dragoneer. Sandora and I have decided that my place is with my kingdom, and she would like to stay with me."

Sulara laughed. "I knew you would make the right decision. It doesn't matter though; you will still be protecting Lianthis as a princess and one day a queen. So you will still participate."

"Okay, but what about the second ceremony I heard about?" Elia asked.

"That one will be presided over by Aurelia and King Thadis. You only need to be present for that one," said Sulara.

That said, Elia remounted Sandora, and she and Sulara took off and glided to where the bond flame was burning in the center of the city.

"Okay. Everyone's here. Let's do this," said Lyon.

Everyone walked to the flame and sat around it. Aurelia, being queen, started the ceremony with a roar. Elia flinched, still not used to dragon roars yet. She had heard plenty during the battle of Eldoria, but she was still new to all of this.

"Today is a great day," began Aurelia. "Today we finally get to solidify our vows to protect Lianthis with our bond mates for life. The bond can never be broken except by betrayal or death. Today we solidify that bond. Father, would you be so kind as to begin?" asked Aurelia.

"It would be my pleasure, dear child," said Tauren.

Lyon pulled out his dagger and cut a lock of his hair and placed it on the rock in front of him. Tauren gently burned it. "I, Tauren, king of the dragons," he said.

"And I, Lyon, Azure Prince," said Lyon.

"As a bonded dragon and human, we swear to protect Lianthis with all our strength," they both said together.

Jaylen and Aurelia were next. Just as Lyon had done, Jaylen cut a lock of her blonde hair and placed it on the rock. Aurelia burned it and said, "I, Aurelia, queen of the dragons."

"And I, Jaylen, Crimson Warrior," said Jaylen.

"As a bonded dragon and human, we swear to protect Lianthis with all our strength," they said in unison.

The rest of the dragoneers all, in turn, solidified their vow. Finally, it was Lyren and Feora's turn as the leaders of the dragoneers; she went last with a very special vow.

Lyren cut a lock of her hair and then put it on the center slab. A small human woman went through and gathered up the small ashes left of the others' hair and placed it on Lyren's lock. Then Feora gently burned the lock and scooped up the ashes with her tongue.

"I, Lyren, the Golden Monarch," said Lyren loudly.

"And I, Feora, former queen of the dragons," said Feora.

"As a bonded dragon and human, we swear to protect Lianthis with all our strength. Further, as leaders, we have taken a piece of each of those we command and are now sworn to lead and protect them from harm."

Every dragon gathered for the ceremony roared all at once. It shook the entire city. Elia grabbed onto Sandora's leg before she fell over. Jaylen laughed.

Aurelia Roared louder than all and the whole city went silent. Jaylen looked at her. This must be Her Majesty Queen Aurelia. Jaylen had seen Aurelia slowly taking back the duties as queen of the dragons. She was so proud of her. Her kindness and gentleness with her subjects amazed Jaylen.

Now, though, Aurelia was all business. "King Thadis of Eldoria, King Balian and Queen Alaria of Corina, and Lord Karigen of Milvania, please step forward." She said in the most commanding voice Jaylen had ever heard.

All four of them stepped forward. "We are here, Your Majesty," They said and bowed.

"Rise, all of you. We are equals now and forever. This flame signifies the bond of dragons and humans that forms the dragoneers. But it is also a symbol of the friendship that all humans and dragons should have bonded or not. As such, I have had our scholars craft an addition to the spell." She smiled.

She is obviously going to enjoy dropping this surprise, Jaylen thought.

"From this day forward, *all* humans will understand dragons. No longer will a language put a barrier between us."

A cheer went up through the crowd, both dragons and humans. No one knew about this except for Jaylen and Aurelia. Jaylen could see the absolute joy on the dragons' faces. They hated having to wait for translation to talk to humans.

"To solidify this new bond of friendship, we need a lock of hair from each of the unbonded humans here." Each one, in turn, cut a lock of hair and placed it before Aurelia. She burned it with her flame then, as Feora had done, she licked up the ashes. Then she turned to the bond flame and released a powerful jet of flame. The bond flame grew in intensity for just a moment, then returned to its normal gentle flame.

One of the other dragons present his name was Geonkin the oldest among the scholars stepped forward. "Humans of Lianthis, do you swear to be friends with all dragons? To protect them as your own subjects and give them freedom to come and go as they please in your kingdoms?"

"Yes, Master Geonkin!" they said.

"Then the spell is complete, and the promise is made. Humans and dragons are reunited at last," said Geonkin.

Another cheer went up, and all dragons roared. It was a happy day. With the ceremony complete, everyone went back to their own kingdoms. Elia returned home to be a princess. Jaylen spent her time between Eldoria and Karukan so Aurelia could handle her duties as queen. Lyon focused on rebuilding and reshaping Milvania. Everyone was happy, and life was good.

Over the next few weeks, Eldoria was rebuilt. Brancreek Village looked brand new and not a single sign of battle. Lyon frequently visited his family. As did Aurelia and Tauren. Elia came over once in a while to see Jaylen and Aurelia. All was right with Lianthis. Dragons and humans once again lived in harmony.

Epilogue

Dikron looked down at Eldoria from the mountaintop he was perched on. "They think they have won," he said out loud, though there was no one there but him. His pure white scales caught the sunlight and made him almost look like an extension of the sun. He was the oldest of Elvaroth's children. His brothers and sisters looked to him for leadership.

Now that his father got himself killed by his own niece and his mother and that idiot Terikon had got caught by the other dragons, that left him and his eight other siblings to finally do this their way. Let the kingdoms rest thinking they eliminated the threat. There would be no more cooperating with humans. Elvaroth had been a fool to trust Adrin. Dragons were meant to rule over humans and not cooperate with them.

Elvaroth had insisted that they would need humans to overthrow the other kingdoms, then they could swoop in and take over, giving them an army to keep the other dragons at bay. He had been a fool. The other dragons would not sit by and let that happen. So now it was up to him.

Dikron knew the only way to truly win was to take the dragons out first. If they could take out the bond flame, then their precious city would come crashing down and then Dikron and his siblings could lay waste to what was left.

They needed a plan, though. They had plenty of time. No one was looking for them since no one knew about them. He looked toward Milvania. He knew that Lyon and that blasted Tauren would have their hands full with Keeval. That was one man who was easily predictable.

270

He would raise an army and try to take back the kingdom. Of course, he had already asked for their help and Dikron had refused.

It was time to start his plan. He knew he couldn't sow mistrust like his father had. So, instead, he planned on weakening the outer villages with what seemed like natural disasters. Forest fires and rockslides that caused floods. Just a little chaos to bring the dragoneers to the rescue.

One by one, they would kill all the dragoneers, then sneak into Karukan and destroy the flame. Once that was accomplished, they could finally defeat the other dragons and then humans would fall easily.

Pleased with his plan, he leaped into the air and headed back to the others in the mountains on the north side of Milvania. Let them get comfortable for a little while. He would wait until the time was right and when he was done he would be high king over everything.